THE CHOSEN ONE

The Chosen One

CAROLINE SIBSON

ST. MARTIN'S PRESS
NEW YORK

Library of Congress Cataloging-in-Publication Data

Sibson, Caroline.
    The chosen one / Caroline Sibson.
        p.   cm.
    ISBN 0-312-02885-7
    I. Title.
PR6069.I27S54   1989
823'.914—dc19   88-35162
                                                         CIP

First published in Great Britain by Robert Hale Limited.

First U.S. Edition

10 9 8 7 6 5 4 3 2 1

For Erica Jong

Be good, sweet maid, and let who will be clever;
Do noble things, not dream them all day long;
And so make life, death, and that vast forever
One grand, sweet song.

Charles Kingsley, 'A Farewell to C.E.G.'

One

Within the room there was silence. In the corridor beyond
footsteps went past, voices murmured. Outside the
window figures moved along the crucifix-shaped pathways, drifting or hurrying according to their obligations
and commitments.

Elizabeth reissued her invitation.

The six young people facing her, four women and two
men, were displaying an unswerving interest either in
their shoes or in the books and papers balanced on their
knees. They were bored, faintly embarrassed and possibly
tired as a result of too much drinking and sexual activity
the night before.

It was not yet ten o'clock. They had done well to make a
nine-fifteen tutorial at all. Being expected to make the
kind of contribution which required the formulation of
some original opinions was really too much.

On the whole Elizabeth was sympathetic. Year Two,
Semester Two course in Developmental Child Psychology
was hardly the stuff to stir the vitals of the average
twenty-year-old. Her students were still little more than
children themselves; throbbing with life, self-centred, fully
engrossed in their own needs, charmed with their own
vigour and seeming immortality.

'Miss Baxter,' Elizabeth said – she invariably addressed
her students in a formal manner, it preserved dignity and
distance for both student and tutor – 'perhaps you would
like to make some comment on Mr Weston's somewhat
provocative statement regarding Freud's theory of the
development of sexual instincts?'

Mr Weston fidgeted with the essay from which he had
just read extracts. The merest trace of unease momentarily disturbed his features.

7

Ah, thought Elizabeth, now I have the attention of one of them at least.

Miss Baxter flushed. Her eyes were wide and helpless. She had been put on the spot and was clearly out of her depth. Elizabeth chided herself for causing the girl discomfort. She kept forgetting that her students were not very bright – not in the strictly academic sense at any rate. Intellectual brightness was, of course, relative. When Elizabeth had worked as an advisor on school failure and mental handicap, even the most stolid and unimaginative neighbours' children had appeared like geniuses. She attempted to help Miss Baxter out. 'I think perhaps Mr Weston was trying to shock us – goad us into some sparky conflict of discussion. We are a rather quiet bunch on the whole – don't you think?'

Miss Baxter stared ahead, a trapped and anxious expression on her face. Elizabeth directed her glance to Mr Weston who shifted his position on his chair. He had long well-fleshed thighs and solid workman-like hands. 'You invite us to dismiss the notion of the Oedipus conflict. A brave and interesting proposition?' She smiled and raised her eyebrows.

'Yeah,' he replied, just a trifle defiant.

Elizabeth was well aware that Colin Weston had no axe whatsoever to grind with either Freud or the Oedipus conflict. He would have lobbed his proposition into the essay with all the unthinking impulsiveness of a schoolboy taking a shy at a cat with a windfall apple. 'Are you all familiar with the story of Oedipus?' she enquired generally.

Six heads drooped wearily.

No, of course they were not. The great Theban legend could not be said to stiffen the backbone of the curriculum in a modern comprehensive school – nor should it, when the syllabus now had to include computer studies and economics, technology and design: areas of relevance to modern life. There was not room for everything.

Elizabeth proceeded to tell them the story – right from the beginning. The tale had always attracted her with its central theme of child abandonment; the searchings of the young adult for his origins and the subsequent destruction and tragedy brought about by discovery.

She found herself warming to the telling of the story, for it was undoubtedly a ripping yarn: a baby left on a hillside with a stake through its feet, rescued by a kindly shepherd, reared by royal ˙and loving adoptive parents, then as a young man going out into the world fighting battles and winning himself a beautiful queen – the only snag being that the said queen happened to be his mother and the traveller he waylaid and killed, his father. And for years the poor man did not know. It was hardly a tale of happy families, Elizabeth thought, in fact the story-line was not unlike the dramatic and unlikely formulae used in the current rash of TV soap operas.

Miss Baxter looked gratifyingly spellbound. Perhaps no one had told her a story before. Elizabeth's educational colleagues frequently deplored the fact that the young of today were deprived of stories at their mother's knee. Mothers' knees had been replaced by radios and cassettes and glamorous television mums forever available on playback at the touch of a button.

The rest of the audience was not so easily impressed; not very much entertained at all until the question of incest arose. Now there was something to sit up and take notice of. A young guy making it with his mother …

Colin Weston opened his thighs a little. Elizabeth looked up. He was watching her, amused and relaxed, an expression of uncomplicated well-being on his face. Elizabeth's eyes were drawn to his crotch. She noted the tubular bulge pushing against the faded blue denim. She raised her eyes and met his directly. He smiled; unabashed, at ease, unequivocally pleased with himself.

'Cocky', her mother would have said, in all innocence.

There was an air about him, something strong and definite, something which told Elizabeth of his unconflicted belief in his right to be part of things, of his unshakable conviction concerning the significance of his own existence. Elizabeth suddenly saw the unremarkable, pedestrian Colin Weston – a student of hers for more than a year – in a new light; saw him as a serene young adult swallowing life down with quiet calm relish, saw the easy digestion and the relentless thriving, whereas she, at the same age, had been like some furious red-faced toddler: picking and spitting and choking, forever frustrated, unsatisfied and undernourished. That picture of herself she saw now, for the first time, quite clearly.

Colin Weston continued to smile, not really cocky, simply permitting himself a little mild amusement. His state of carefree tumescence seemed to be filling the room.

Elizabeth's breathing quickened. She got up from her chair, walked across the room and struck him sharply on the cheek. The blow cracked out like a gunshot. Without hesitation he reached up and slapped her back hard.

The room lurched into stillness. Everyone froze.

She looked directly into his eyes and saw no apology there. No challenge or ill feeling either.

She had overstepped the mark. He had responded. They were quits. So be it.

She returned to sit behind her desk. 'I think it's time we moved on to a new topic,' she said evenly, despite the insistent and painful explosions in her chest. 'Miss Critchley, would you read us the opening paragraph of your essay please?'

For a few minutes the students regarded her with covert and suspicious glances. She had shown herself to be unpredictable – who knew what she might do next?

But very soon things returned to normal. A polite and tolerant boredom re-invaded the room. Eyes looked out of the windows tracing the movement of the figures on those decisive, bisecting paths. Beyond the confines of the tutorial room there was life to be lived; beer to be drunk, phone calls to be made, hair to be washed, shopping to be done. Beyond the tutorial room was the mundane, raw, real stuff of life.

Elizabeth did not blame her students for not wanting to live vicariously. Only a tiny minority do. The main body of her students would never pick up a classical novel, a literary essay or a volume of poems once they had gained their qualification and left the college.

Colin Weston was the last to vacate his seat at the end of the session.

Elizabeth wondered if that was deliberate on his part. Maybe, maybe not.

He hesitated by the door.

Elizabeth occupied herself fully squaring the essays into a neat pile on her desk, thus sparing him any further embarrassment and permitting him to leave without further delay. She was aware of a long-forgotten flutter in the depths of her as he closed the door behind him.

On the floor beneath, in the Senior Common Room, the business of taking coffee was in progress. The ripe discreet murmur of academic voices drifted among the tweed-covered settees and the low pine tables. Greetings were being made and pleasantries exchanged. The front pages of newspapers were receiving passing glances before more serious proceedings commenced on the crosswords.

In the centre of the room Herbert Bailey, the College Principal, was holding court. He rarely sat down in the staff common room, not wishing to indicate allegiance with any particular group. Staff ebbed and flowed around him, sharing problems, requesting advice, seeking to impress, getting themselves noticed. He dealt with them all with the smooth precision of a well-oiled engine. His glance strayed briefly towards Elizabeth as he stood in patient submission under the heavy verbal assault of a member of the mathematics department. He smiled – the College Head acknowledging the newly appointed Department Head in Human Development Studies. He had backed Elizabeth strongly for the post, dismissing and demolishing some quite formidable competition from external candidates because he had such an admiration for the knowledge, competence and integrity of the quiet controlled woman who had joined the staff just two years before as a novice to academic life. He had told her so quite openly.

'Elizabeth,' he had said, claiming her full attention at the end-of-term garden party the previous summer, 'in this department we need fresh ideas, a vigorous and original approach. But we need stability also. Firm, reliable leadership. Too much of the mercurial does little to enhance the reputation of higher education. I want you to consider applying for the headship of the department. I want you to consider it very seriously ...' He had taken her arm, in the way that her father used to do with her mother, and strolled with her over the college's great lawns to the shade under the beech trees, where the light meandered down through the leaves, dappling the ground with gold.

His smile now transmitted a definite, though fleeting, reminder of that June sunshine; the smile of an attractive man for an admirable woman. A smile which indicated the existence of a special rapport between them – an unspoken frisson of sexual interest maybe. But there was no hint of flirtation. Herbert was a committed married man – and colleagues did not flirt with Elizabeth. Even plumbers and gas engineers had been known to retire defeated in the face of her coolly quizzical gaze.

She finished her coffee and then went through to the administrative office and requested the key for the T – Z section of the cabinets which housed the students' personal files. Mrs Parker, Chief Administrative Clerk, was juggling with the demands of the switchboard, a cup of coffee, and the queries of her new assistant. On her desk was a white paper bag, its top pulled into an arch for the protection of a frothy cream-cake.

'Mid-morning comfort,' she remarked, smoothing her skirt over solid and significant hips. She unlocked her desk drawer, taking out a key which in turn unlocked the top section of one of the four steel cabinets which flanked the wall. Dipping her hand inside she pulled out yet another key with a tag attached on which was written T – Z. Security regarding personal documents was taken seriously at the college. Access to files was theoretically open and free to staff and students alike, but the small practical obstacles involved were an effective safeguard against casual abuse.

'If you want to look at the medical records you'll need another set of keys,' Mrs Parker said.

Elizabeth made a negative gesture with her hand. 'No, no. That won't be necessary.' She smiled at Mrs Parker, calm, unhurried, outwardly serene. 'How is Craig getting along these days?' she enquired, as she knew Mrs Parker wanted her to. They had discussed her son on many previous occasions.

Mrs Parker leaned forward and lowered her voice. 'Dyslexia,' she said with an evangelical gleam in her eye. 'We're going to take him for some special lessons to help him catch up. It'll cost a fortune, but what can you do? He's almost ten and he still can't read.'

Elizabeth, listening politely as Mrs Parker expanded on

her theme, was sympathetic, but non-committal. These real-life education problems had been very much her province before she retreated to the sedate dispassion of the college. She had talked with hundreds of parents, comforted them in the face of real or manufactured anxieties. Now she switched herself on to automatic professional pilot in order to respond to Mrs Parker's need to unburden herself. Occasionally Elizabeth would reflect back a negative statement in a positive light, suggesting that perhaps a seemingly unsympathetic class teacher was in fact demonstrating dismay at his or her own failure to help the child, pointing out that although Craig was not on a level with his peers, he seemed to have made tremendous strides since their last discussion. Through her relaxed stance and her patient demeanour she gave Mrs Parker permission to continue with her theme for as long as she wished. But in her head was an image of that jaunty, unrepentantly bulging crotch and its equally unrepentant owner. In due course a winking light on the switchboard claimed Mrs Parker's attention and the dialogue was terminated.

Elizabeth took Colin Weston's file from the cabinet and sat down with it at a table in the far corner of the office. His identification photograph, taped firmly to the front cover, elicited an involuntary smile from her as she recalled the exchange that had taken place between them in the normally placid and sober confines of her tutorial room. How little in awe of her he had been, how swift and sure in offering an eye for an eye, a tooth for a tooth. She had trespassed across the boundaries of social convention – for a few months emotion had been allowed to transcend reason, the shifting sea of consciousness had parted to afford a public glimpse of the still blackness beneath. Such transgressions in the past, rare enough, had invariably brought about a temporary state of catastrophe, as Elizabeth had always felt the need to pay heavily for impulsive or shameful actions. But today, with Colin Weston, there had been emotional free-trading. He had been neither passive, sympathetic, nor forgiving. He had left her untouched by condemnation. She had acted. He had responded – simply, instantly, appropriately. She had put a foot wrong and he had kept in step. He could perfectly well have left her presence with the triumphant superiority of the wronged on his face. That he had not done so filled her with a keen delight.

She opened the file and read carefully through the initial details: full name, address, names of parents, date of birth. Her eyes looked in fascination at those six typed figures. She had already worked out the year in which Colin would have been born – a year that had been so significant for her and Michael. She had not bargained for the fact that the month would be the same, the actual day of his birth within four days of Edward's. She reflected on Mrs Weston's production of the whole and healthy Colin, whilst she had laboured and brought forth something resembling a rubber dolly with stick limbs and the brain of an eternal infant. They had not known about that at the time – the brain, that is. It took some time for it to become apparent that the thing they had set in motion was a sham, a sub-grade egg, futile and faulty. A poor hapless thing who would never achieve independence.

Poor, pitiful, pointless Edward.

She resumed her inspection of the file. Colin Weston lived in Barnet. He had gained two 'C' grade A-levels at the local comprehensive. His reference from the school suggested that he might have achieved rather better results with a little more application. His father was a stores manager and his mother a part-time secretary for a firm of estate agents. Colin also had two older siblings – a sister and a brother in their late twenties and mid-thirties respectively. He was obviously the baby of the family – a late afterthought maybe.

Elizabeth wrote down Colin Weston's term-time address in her diary. As a second-year student he was required to live out of college in lodgings. She noted that he had either selected, or been obliged, to take digs some distance from the college. That meant that unless he drove a battered Mini or Ford Fiesta passed on from his mother – as did many of the students – he was reliant on the rather fitful local bus service for transport.

She worked late in her room. Outside the window the number of figures moving along the pathways swelled as

lectures finished, then gradually decreased, the remaining
stragglers in due course fusing with the dusk. Elizabeth
progressed steadily through the pile of articles, books and
essays which would enable her to approach the next
academic day fully prepared. Her interest in her work was
keen and her concentration-span for any task she set
herself both lengthy and undivided. It was not until
eight-thirty that she got up from her desk and went
through into the private washroom adjoining her office.

She surveyed her appearance in the mirror. The thin
white light overhead had a curiously flattening effect,
making the night-time face blandly unlined, in contrast to
the daytime image which was illuminated by a small
east-facing window producing exactly the opposite effect.
She noted that the momentous intentions proceeding
inside her head had made no impression whatsoever on
her face; it looked just the same as usual. She re-arranged
her hair a little and stroked some perfume on her neck
and wrists.

Her face was very pale. She was always pale; it was
natural and right for her and always had been so even
before her chestnut hair had modified itself to silver-
streaked sable. Her mother had been concerned by the
whiteness bestowed by nature. 'You need colour in your
cheeks,' she would say, approaching purposefully with a
bottle of liquid rouge. 'Colour to make you pretty.' The
bottle of rouge would inevitably appear as Elizabeth
prepared herself for a classmate's party, as would the steel
curling-tongs heated up in the glow of the fire, with which
her mother would frizz and singe her shining hair until it
was all dull and bushy like steel wool. In the car with her
cheerful, oblivious father Elizabeth would rub at her
cheeks with a wet finger and bite back the tears as she
tentatively explored the charred and spiky mass surrounding her head. She would arrive at the party smelling like
an autumn bonfire.

And all that had gone on until she was fifteen. Her
mother had always maintained that she alone knew how to
make Elizabeth look her best. And Elizabeth, wishing
above all things not to upset her mother, had diminished
and denied her own needs and walled them up in a dark
hole.

Elizabeth locked her room and went across the college's inner courtyard to the newly-constructed leisure-block. The staff-student section of the college bar was only sparsely populated: two rather serious groups who looked as though they were drinking for reasons of college politics rather than pleasure. Beyond in the students' bar there was noise and movement, smoke and laughter. She walked through into the hazy gloom, hearing the soles of her shining court shoes lisp and squeak on the beer-spattered lino.

She spotted Colin Weston straight away, lounging and at his ease with a group of second-years, listening with scant attention to Ken Powers, the head of the Community Studies Department, who propped up the student bar regularly and held forth with voluble indiscretion.

Elizabeth sat down, positioning herself in a manner which clearly indicated a wish to be included in the group. She crossed her legs and relaxed into the back of the chair. Colin Weston smiled. He pointed to his glass and raised his eyebrows questioningly. 'White wine – dry,' she mouthed over the din and Ken Powers' monologue.

Colin got up. He wore horrendously shabby jeans and a home-knitted sweater with a big pink pig on it designed to look as though it had been fashioned on a computer from matrix dots.

'Elizabeth!' Ken exclaimed, noticing her and breaking off abruptly. 'We don't often see you in these lowly places.'

'Indeed no,' she agreed, smiling.

Ken aroused both her irritation and her pity – in roughly equal amounts. She also felt a gentle affection for him. The college hierarchy, having plucked him from a research project on inner city deprivation and promoted him way beyond his competence, were now making him pay for their heinous mistake. It was becoming fashionable to include on the staff those deemed to have 'relevant life experience' and on paper Ken fitted the bill extremely well. But he was a fish out of water in the deceptively tranquil but treacherous shoals of an academic institution. Subtly despised and ostracised by the clever and sophisticated academics in the senior common room, Ken fought back by braying raucously in departmental meetings – for which behaviour he was courteously ignored – and then seeking refuge in the students' bar. He was currently cradling solace in the form of a pint of best bitter between his smooth red tubular fingers, at the same time inhaling deeply from a king-size cigarette. He sucked hungrily at the smoke and turned his pale blue eyes on Elizabeth, eyes like marbles; slightly bulbous and veined. 'It's time we put some life back into this place,' he remarked, presumably continuing with the theme he had started on before her arrival. 'We need to get some trades union blokes in – men who've seen life, know what it's all about out there.' He waved an arm in the air without any clear purpose.

'Ah,' said Elizabeth who had heard all this once or twice before. She wondered if the students would be offended to draw the inference that they were ignorant of what it was all about out there.

The students, predictably, looked bored and un-involved.

'Let's face it, Elizabeth, there's only you and me who've really been in the shit, rubbing our noses in poverty and deprivation and – *real life*. This academic bunch are just living in cloud-cuckoo-land; waited on hand and foot like lords.' His hands gestured vaguely in the direction of the college's main building and, presumably, the hallowed precincts of the senior common room.

Colin Weston returned to his seat. He sat with his thick strong thighs widely spaced and leaned across to place the glass of wine in front of Elizabeth. A brief glance passed between them – a glance of bonding and conspiracy because they were the only ones in the party who knew what had taken place in her room earlier on. Elizabeth experienced a strong sense of relief. She smiled again. 'I rather enjoy living like a lord; the fresh coffee and the waitress service and the smell of polished floors that I don't have to polish.'

Colin Weston released an appreciative laugh.

'I'm from Liverpool,' Ken announced to the disinteres-ted audience in the manner of proclaiming a qualification. 'You don't see much of the rosy side of life there.'

'I once worked with a psychologist colleague from Weybridge who regarded coming from anywhere north or west of Manchester to be both a diagnosis and a disability,'

Elizabeth said mischievously. She recollected with amusement that on more than one occasion, when wishing to impress top management in the senior common room, Ken ignored Liverpool and made heavy reference to his Scottish origins – Glasgow of course, nothing to do with the élite in Edinburgh.

Ken was now proceeding to elaborate on the thorny nature of life on Merseyside. It was clear that the audience was not going to be let off lightly with one or two throw-away remarks. It was Ken's practice to discourse at considerable and tedious length about his 'inner city experience', and his knowing what it was to be one of the 'mucky hands brigade', these being his main claims to fame and his only defence when confronted with his formidably intellectual and informed colleagues.

On first meeting Elizabeth, Ken had marked her down as one who had had a privileged childhood, most likely attended public school and then gone on to Oxbridge. One, in other words, who had had it easy. Elizabeth, being scrupulous and fair, had not been offended. She knew that she projected a certain 'out of the top drawer' image. Ken was not the only one who had assumed that she had proceeded sedately from the élitism of the choicest education on offer to a succession of refined professional posts and from there to the elegant and protected confines of the college. His long nose had been put out of joint to discover that the posh and gauntly glamorous Elizabeth had, in fact, not only been born and bred in a Yorkshire wool-producing city, but had taught for a number of years in its most disadvantaged schools at a time when class numbers exceeded forty and a high proportion of the children suffered from impetigo and head infestation and wore soiled underwear.

She looked around at the group of courteously bored students and had a sudden wish to entertain them. There was something of the kindly aunt in Elizabeth, the aunt who is sensitive to the needs of the young and skilled in the ways of meeting those needs through her own inventiveness. It was so easy for her to slip into that mode of behaviour learned early in childhood – *find out what others want and provide it for them*. Such behaviour had become mainly automatic by the time she got to school and proved to be a wholly satisfactory and effective way of dealing with the demands of others. It was a form of behaviour she had violently rejected in later years. But now she judged that she knew how to use it for her own ends rather than as a means to make people like her.

Taking up Ken's theme of bygone real life experience she let loose on the company one or two anecdotes from her own working past with the education service. She told them about the head teacher who summoned a parent to school to harangue him on the wayward habits of his son, how he had yanked the man out of the corridor into his office and lectured him soundly on parental responsibility for half an hour. 'But,' said the bewildered listener when the tirade ceased, 'I'm only here to check the central heating boiler.' She told them of the matron of a special school who had a problem with words, confusing the children by consecrating their cigarettes, putting their soiled clothes in the atomic washing machine and informing them that she was not inflammable and could not be expected to know everything. They were silly stories, but true, and the students enjoyed them, giving her their flatteringly full attention. They laughed a lot and allowed their own store of reminiscences to be unlocked. More beer was drunk. More opportunities were afforded to make eye-contact with Colin Weston and check that what she had read in his face previously was in fact valid.

Time moved on and the last buses would have gone.

The little group began to disintegrate.

Elizabeth thought longingly of her quiet, well-ordered house, of a late-night malt whisky by the fire, of a little violin and piano music – Debussy or César Franck perhaps. She had attained a stage in life when things were temperate and methodical; when things were, more often than not, under her control. She had served a long apprenticeship in a situation where another had held the true reins of control and now she guarded her solitary and independent state fiercely. There was a structure to her life, the freedom to live by a careful code – a code which might appear to others unduly restrictive, but as the rules were those she had made herself, there was a deep satisfaction in abiding by them. She liked the unflurried and serious nature of her work and actively relished the freedom to devote herself to it. To be able to get up occasionally at dawn and be at her desk by seven a.m., or to work on at the college until nine or ten in the evening, was a new and wholly delicious luxury.

Yet this thing that she was contemplating, this absurd and presumptuous plan – as clear in her mind as a midsummer snapshot – would inevitably stir the quiet pond of her regulated existence. For a while at least. She was perfectly aware of that. She was not in the habit of taking things lightly; even the business of acting on impulse was afforded due gravity.

She drove her car out through the massive wrought-iron college gates and took the road which led to the north side of the town. It was well after eleven and the streets were mainly empty of traffic and pedestrians.

Colin Weston was a fast walker. He had made good time since leaving the college, having progressed about half a mile in no more than seven or eight minutes. It was a raw cloudy night with rain falling thinly in just sufficient amounts to moisten the windscreen in between the intermittent sweep of the wipers. Elizabeth slowed to a halt and pushed the passenger door open. 'Would you care for a lift?' she asked, leaning over so that he could identify her.

'Thanks.' The hesitation was minimal, really only sufficient to account for the time required for recognition. 'Kerb-crawling,' he commented with an effort at humour as he clipped himself into the seatbelt.

Oh, the confidence of him, the cheerful lack of respectful distance, the ease with which he turned to her and smiled. 'No,' she said, after consideration, 'a kerb-crawler is looking out for a likely quarry. It could be anyone, tall, short, fat, thin, dull, bright – young or not so young. The kerb-crawler's only concern is that the quarry should share in the driver's preconceived plan of the forthcoming activities.'

'Hmm,' he said after a pause.

She might have unnerved him – just a little. Students were frequently disconcerted by her style of speech, quite aside from its content. 'I knew exactly for whom I was looking,' she explained.

He was silent for the rest of the journey.

They pulled up outside a row of small Edwardian villas, their sadly decaying splendour apparent even in the pale light of the streetlamps; sagging gutters, crumbling pointing, rotting or absent woodwork on eaves and windows. She recalled the dreariness of it all from her own student days. Colin Weston freed himself from his seat-belt. She freed herself from hers. He noticed and turned to her. She thought that he released a small sigh. 'Would you like to come up for a coffee, then?' he suggested politely.

'Yes, indeed. I would like that very much.' She was amazed to discover how easy it was to behave with dignity even in preposterous circumstances. She was pleased about that. There had been a time when the smallest deviation from what she considered to be proper and approved-of behaviour would pitch her into a state of unbearable confusion and uncertainty.

She recalled the doom-laden teachings of the psychology textbooks – 'What one is in childhood will be carried into adulthood. Conflicted and troubled children do not grow into serene and happy adults'.

So be it. But perhaps troubled, uncertain, uneasy children could turn into decisive and steadfast adults. One might not be in command of one's emotions but one could be in command of one's behaviour.

She followed Colin Weston's trainer-clad feet up the uncarpeted stairs and found that her heart was beating with perfect steadiness.

Two

What happened that evening was not what Elizabeth had expected. For, on the whole, she was used to reality running a poor second to expectation. She was, of course, aware of being in no way fully committed at this point. She need do no more than release some gentle but meaningful phrases and allow him to draw the appropriate inferences. This could then, as she would be quite free to choose, lead in a week or two to a courteous little note being dropped in his pigeon-hole. 'Dear Colin, I would be very pleased if you would like to join me for dinner at my house one evening soon. Do please let me know which day might be convenient, etc., etc.' That invitation she might or might not care to issue in the future. She was also still free, even in the present circumstances, simply to do nothing; nothing more than conduct the interview with propriety and impartiality and then return to her house and César Franck.

'I'm afraid this place is a bit chilly,' he said, reaching up to flick a switch beside the door and throwing the room into the dreary illumination of three sixty-watt bulbs hanging from a central light fitting which resembled outstretched claws.

The room was in an appalling mess. Clothes, both outer and undergarments, were strewn on the floor and over chairs. The bed in the corner, which looked totally inadequate to support Colin's height and weight, was rumpled and unmade, giving every appearance of having recently been the scene of a rugby scrum.

Was there a girl then? A live-in lover? Elizabeth looked in vain for female shoes, bottles of nail enamel, telltale photographs. There was a tiny camp-cooker in the far corner, with a pile of greasy pans heaped on it. On the big cheap post-war table was a jumble of textbooks, pads of lined A4 paper, disorganised files and copies of *Cars of the Year* and *Playboy*. Four or five empty coffee-mugs were scattered about, their insides encircled with rusty black bands.

It was a college boy's room; squalid and hideous. And all of this horror was overlain by the smell of stale smoke, and lit with a sour yellow light that made Elizabeth's eyes ache. She should have been prepared – but her thoughts had been on other things; things more abstract and spiritual, like Colin Weston's firm and open air of having the right to be who, how, and as he liked, without any doubts or apologies.

'Sit down,' he said, bending to light a gas-fire which flared up dramatically in a roar of cold orange flames. He poured water in the kettle and cursorily rinsed out two stained mugs.

Elizabeth perched on her chair, automatically reverting to behaviour she had learned when visiting parents of children she had worked with in depressed areas. School failure, which had become her specialist area after she had given up teaching, was irretrievably linked with squalor, and she had learned to become suspicious of all covered and upholstered surfaces. Quite frequently, as one sat discussing the remedies for reading-retardation, a cold dampness would spread along buttocks and thighs – old spilt drinks, baby vomit, baby urine, animal excrement; one could never be quite sure of the nature of the wetness. It was always vile-smelling and stubbornly resistant to subsequent efforts to erase it.

Reminding herself that healthy student squalor was more in the line of untidiness than serious filth, she allowed her hips to nestle into the back of the chair.

'Cheers,' he said, sitting down and taking a drink from his steaming mug. He sat back and emitted a sound that was a mixture between a cough and a snort, then he smiled hopefully, clearly embarrassed and at a loss what to say next.

'Colin, I do hope you will forgive my inexcusable behaviour this morning,' she said to him gravely.

'Yes. No. Well really I …' His cheerful features had become suffused with colour.

'It was quite unwarranted and I do apologise most
sincerely. Senior staff are normally considered able to
exercise the kind of self-control that precludes their
making unprovoked attacks on their students.'

He was baffled. Was she sending him up or was she
genuine? Whichever was the case he was not inspired with
confidence. 'Yeh, well it wasn't entirely unprovoked, was
it? I was asking for it I suppose.'

His discomfiture was deepening by the minute.
Elizabeth felt a great tenderness for him, for his
uncomplicated ordinariness, his simple niceness.

'My dear Colin,' she said with soft decisiveness. 'You
have no need to ask for anything from me. It is all there
for the giving.'

He stared at her amazed – and she herself was surprised
at the ease of it all. She suddenly saw the scene from the
viewpoint of the onlooker; the onlooker who judges, as the
majority do, by observable behaviour, by the manifest-
ations rather than the motivating factors of human
actions. The onlooker would see a serious-minded,
restrained, deliberate woman falling soft for a pair of
rakish blue eyes and assertively muscular thighs. It would
have been clear to such an onlooker that on the woman's
side there was loneliness and desperation – probably a
long-term state of sexual deprivation which had led to
such unaccountably foolish and inappropriate behaviour.
The word 'menopausal' might well have been murmured
sorrowfully. She imagined the disapproving faces of her
colleagues, and for one terrible moment, the saddened
face of her mother, looking back from the grave. Aah! –
how they would all shake their heads. We are, in the main,
she thought, empiricists, we favour the view that what is
real and what is of significance is that which can be
observed. We are not, most of us, analysers – searchers
into that area of conjecture and hypothesis which lies
below consciousness. That is both problematic and
disturbing territory, much better left alone.

Colin Weston cleared his throat. 'Would you like some
more coffee?'

She looked into his eyes and saw that the embarrassment
had cleared. He reached out a hand and placed it over
hers. They smiled at each other. It was a scene of sweetly

trivial seduction – to the onlooker at any rate. What the onlooker could not know was that in Elizabeth's tutorial room that morning, in that astonishing interchange between a clever and fastidious senior tutor and one of her rather less able and insouciant students, a spring had been activated, something of remorseless, insistent significance had been set in motion.

In Colin Weston was something which Elizabeth needed to explore. By linking herself to him she made it possible for such a journey of exploration to take place. As yet she was not sure what was being sought, she was simply aware that his unconstricted appetite for life was something she found wholly reassuring and totally delightful.

She set her coffee-mug carefully on the floor and took his hand in both of hers. 'That was a proposition, Colin, not a command performance. You're entitled to say no. I should be disappointed but not at all offended.'

After a pause, he slid his hand obligingly under her skirt.

'Stockings!' he said appreciatively.

She smiled. 'Is that unusual?'

'Mmm,' His hand began to burrow about with growing insistence.

'No, not here.' She needed to divorce him from his squalor as soon as possible.

'Where then?'

'At my house. I'll take you there now.' She rose to her feet, tall and narrow and dignified.

As they drove across to the other side of town he apparently felt it necessary to make small-talk. 'Nice car,' he said. 'Buy British!' That kind of thing; something to fill the silence.

'I'm very traditional,' she said drily.

She sensed his growing and deep unease and knew that he was reflecting on the task ahead. She was alerted to the fact that he was most probably a deeply conventional young man, who would see their respective roles in the act of love as clear and simple – his to perform, hers to judge. In all probability such uncomplicated conceptualising regarding the roles of the sexes would extend to other areas besides sexual coupling. He would have certain expectations regarding the servicing of his needs – expectations more implicit than understood. There would be washing to be done, bath rings to be cleaned, jeans to be ironed, meals to be planned for and prepared. So be it. At least with a very young man she was likely to be spared the subtle control of contrived courtesies. She did not see herself incurring many debts to Colin through his holding open of doors and carrying of bags.

Approaching a stretch of deserted dual carriageway she thought it would be kind to offer him some distraction. She pressed her foot down hard on the accelerator.

'Christ!' he said. 'Do you always drive like this?'

'Only in de-restricted areas,' she told him calmly. She was reflecting on his automatic use of a profanity and was rather touched that he had not pussyfooted around with some other milder expression in deference to the supposed delicacy of female sensibilities. She realised that with Colin there would be much mention of Jesus and blood and fucking.

Especially fucking – ah yes. 'Swearing,' her mother used to say, 'I don't ever want to hear it. There is absolutely no need for it. Why say 'D' (cough) 'M' when 'dash' will do just as well?'

'Christ,' she repeated to herself inaudibly and smiled. She thought she would rather enjoy it all – for a while at least.

Colin walked into the entrance-hall of her house, was impressed and uncharacteristically subdued. The place was totally immaculate, and luxuriously, almost tropically warm. Elizabeth knew better than to start fussing around with alcohol or further coffee, producing in him a state of latent anxiety that would preclude any activity until the next day. She threw her coat onto the big carved oak chair that had belonged to her grandmother, then put her arms around him, pressed him against the wall and declared love on him with a vengeance.

'Jesus!' he muttered, struggling to gain some control. He wondered what on earth she would do next. He was astonished, and inordinately flattered. Mrs Lashley was generally regarded amongst the students as unapproachable, an ice-maiden, a total no-go area. She was, of course, intriguing with her frail, wand-like body and her sad, stern eyes – unfathomable and mysterious like a fantasised Russian spy, but hopefully not quite as dangerous.

Her bedroom was pristine and regal. His anxiety reasserted itself as he waited for her to return from the bathroom. She looked untouchable and troubled, her slender feet protruding below the white pedestal of a simple nightgown. 'Colin, my dear,' she said, moving her hands over him slowly, 'I'm a novice. Two-score years and more, and I am hardly less innocent than the majority of today's sixteen-year-olds.' She looked up at him as though for forgiveness and he experienced a sharp bolt of reassuring lust, some unexpected tenderness also. The tumescence of the morning was swiftly re-established, and now fully desirous and securely throbbing, he was able to comfort her.

'Don't talk so much,' he told her, feeling rather splendid as this great lady tugged persistently at his zip and then fell on her knees in front of him, worshipping him between soft parted lips, her small, still firm, breasts pressed against his thighs.

It was hard to say who made love to whom. On the whole the two protagonists in this particular fray were pretty much a match for each other.

Elizabeth had not made love with a man for fifteen years, and was surprised to find that her body could rise up from its chaste and private tomb of neglect and respond with such genial and joyful delinquency. And Colin, the partner she had chosen to awaken her slumbering body with such industrious, diligent, imaginative kisses, was revealed as a true craftsman. He delved and carved and burrowed and sculpted with rigour and sensitivity. He roamed over her flesh with a precision and an expertise that spoke of committed and conscientious apprenticeship.

So this, then, was where Colin's creative propensities were channelled. Who could expect him to have the energy, or the inclination, to expend effort on the construction of critical essays when so much life-force was required for the perfecting of the skill of love-making? Choices had to be made, priorities determined. Such physical proficiency as he possessed could hardly have been developed and nurtured with the attendant distractions of learning the rules of grammar or the discipline of slotting sentences together in order to communicate a simple logical idea.

Moreover – and most delightfully – once Colin got into the swing of things he showed no signs whatsoever of a respect for Elizabeth's status. He was neither a circumspect visitor nor a triumphant trespasser. He simply hewed ecstasy out of every hollow and crevice of her skin and left her gasping, sore and aching with pleasure.

At the end they stared at each other, astounded by how well it had all gone. 'Mmm,' said Colin, sated and content, 'Mmm,' then rolled over and went straight to sleep.

In the morning he was awake early, rearing over her. Elizabeth pulled him down against her. She was thinking with voluptuous envy of his parents, of those two fortunate people who had started off this creature of youth and energy and perfection.

'Ah my dear, dear darling,' she murmured.

'Why me?' he said later, looking straight into her eyes.

She stroked the fashionable, boyish stubble above his ears. 'Because, my dearest Colin, you give the impression of one who has a glorious, unabashed, gluttonous and uncomplicated appetite for life – and I would very much like to share it!'

A short silence followed.

'Christ Almighty!' he said. 'You talk *far* too much.'

Three

Hers had been a happy childhood. Despite the trauma of separation and death, it had been secure and happy. She had been so much wanted, so much loved. It was true that she had very early on become impaled on the pin of guilt, destined to continue forever pierced and spinning, but this was normal, surely? Guilt is the price the sensitive child pays in return for the mother's love.

'My children are everything,' her mother used to say. 'For some women the marriage is everything, but for me, it is my children who come first. They are my life.'

Elizabeth could remember the shiver of excitement she would feel on hearing these words. She pitied and faintly despised those girls at school whose mothers were distracted by the pursuit of glamour or a career or colourful relationships with their husbands. It was not until later, as she approached adulthood, that she began to understand the terrifying responsibility of being loved so much.

Her father, an elegant, remote and often absent figure, spent long hours building up the business he had launched soon after his marriage, and in perfecting his considerable sporting skills in the fields of golf and billiards. It became clear to the young Elizabeth that it was her duty and her privilege to entertain her lonely mother. Early photographs showed her well up to the task; a truly engaging child with huge round eyes, a thick trellissing of black lashes and an adorable rosebud mouth. She sat on her mother's knee, her childish glance firmly fixed on her parent, the expression in her eyes worshipful and just a touch coquettish. Her mother's face, on the surface registering the complacent, possessive maternalism that professional photographers strive to capture, had an unmistakable quality of uncertainty and wistfulness about it. It was as though she were projecting into the harsh cold future and already experiencing the yearning of grief and loss, seeing how the passage of life would strip her of so much that she held precious.

Elizabeth's sister, four years her senior, sat gravely on the arm of the chair, her thick blonde hair severely waved in accordance with the fashion of the time for any female over the age of about seven. Margaretha was not expected to be entertaining, for she was a deeply serious and delicate child who suffered from frequent bouts of asthma and painful episodes of bronchitis. Elizabeth loved her in a stark and total manner and would creep into her bedroom at nights and stand guard until the heaving and wheezing eventually subsided. Margaretha was gentle and generous, her capacity for sharing was well in advance of her age and Elizabeth could never remember her raising her voice in anger or snatching away a possession. Elizabeth, in fact, could never remember her in any other way than as a serene, good and beautiful angel.

The two sisters shared the emotional care of their mother to everyone's satisfaction. Elizabeth diverted with her flashing eyes and her excessively bright, precocious chatter, whilst Margaretha, in the background, was a bedrock of tranquil devotion who provided her mother from time to time with the added fulfilment that springs from caring for a fragile and grateful invalid.

The happy trio, linked lovingly together, pursued a life of pleasurable domesticity, leaving their father free to spend his time shining in the outside world where he was most effective and at ease.

As Elizabeth progressed through the early years of her private preparatory school it soon became clear that, academically, she was a very able child. Her parents were on one or two occasions summoned by the headmistress to be alerted to this fact almost as though it were something to be alarmed about.

This cleverness, this ability to swallow, digest and regurgitate all that was put before her in that intense little school, produced a degree of troubled ambivalence in Elizabeth who was painfully aware of the fact that Margaretha was struggling simply to maintain a place in the middle of her own class group, whilst she, with quite minimal effort, was unfailingly top in hers. Kind, lovable, loving Margaretha appeared to be a trifle on the dull side. Elizabeth began to see in her own success an element of evil which could, despite her strenuous wish to avoid it, cause Margaretha unhappiness. Not that her parents ever made Margaretha feel inadequate or miserable. Her father rather feared academic achievement, having been, in his own words, only 'fair to middling' at school and leaving as soon as was legally permitted. Her mother had gained her School Certificate but not gone to college – her one act of defiance against her own parents who wanted her to be a teacher, whilst she wanted to be an actress. In the final event she did neither and after a succession of disliked jobs was only too willing to abandon the world of work when she married. She would comfort Margaretha with quotations such as 'Be good, sweet maid, and let who will be clever', and reassurances that it was not always a good thing to do too well at school as it put off prospective husbands.

Elizabeth was alerted to the fact that cleverness was an attribute to be wary of and so, at the age of six, she had rather clumsily experimented with the possibility of becoming an educational also-ran.

This had taken the form of her contriving to get all her multiplication sums wrong on two separate occasions, and concocting some bizarre letter-sequences to produce in the weekly spelling-test.

Her form-teacher had been very severe about it. 'Elizabeth,' said Miss Grisdale, who wore her hair in a Cumberland sausage around her head and had two stern and hairy warts on her upper lip, 'this will not do.' She tore the offending pieces of paper vertically into neat halves. The form watched, the sound of the tear striking terror into their childish hearts as they sat in frozen stillness. 'You are my cleverest little girl and I expect the best from you. Always. Rubbish I will not tolerate – from you – or anyone!' Her fierce gaze ricocheted up and down the row of desks, pausing momentarily on Joyce who was her dullest little girl.

Joyce could not read aloud from *The Wind in the Willows* and she often spelled words backwards or wrote

things as they would look in a mirror. In those days
children did not have 'specific learning difficulties', and
dyslexia was not yet fashionable; children were just stupid
or lazy. Joyce was pitied and despised and a lesson to all to
be grateful for the mental attributes they possessed.

Elizabeth's face turned fiery and then pale under Miss
Grisdale's gaze. She returned to her place and from then
on – as far as cleverness was concerned – lived a double
life.

Four

It was not turning out to be a good day. She had got up
early, showered, dressed and put on her make-up as usual.
She had listened to the News on Radio 3 and then the
morning concert – also as usual. Breakfast was the juice of
half a lemon in hot water followed by toast and butter and
marmalade, and Jacksons' Breakfast Tea. All as usual.
Except that Colin Weston was in her bed, sleeping like a
baby. She had been in twice to look at him and on each
occasion her heart had contracted. He was obviously not
going to wake up for some time and she had a nine o'clock
meeting. There was much she wanted to say to him –
although perhaps it would be best to say little. In any event
it looked as though she would not have the chance of
saying anything at all.

She finally left the house, placing on the table beside
Colin a cup of tea and a gentle note hoping he was well
and requesting that he dropped the latch on the front
door. She hoped that was neutral enough.

At lunchtime she sat in her tutorial room unable to
contemplate food. The morning had not gone at all well.

In the Heads of Department Meeting she had found it a
struggle to maintain her concentration on the points at
issue, and had declined to make her usual vigorous
contribution, owing to fatigue and a vague sense of
unreality, which warned her that her facility for clear and
sequestered argument might be temporarily impaired.

The Principal raised quizzical and concerned eyebrows
at coffee-time.

'Not enough sleep,' she murmured. 'I'll be fine
tomorrow.'

He was a man of tolerance and expansive mind. She
knew that he would not condemn her behaviour out of

hand, should he ever come to hear of it. He would, however, be mindful of the social and political risks involved should a professional tutor and her student become emotionally entangled. There were things to be considered, such as a clear mind when evaluating work assignments, and impartiality in the preparation of references. And, of course, there were the parents. Parents were still quite protective about their twenty-year-olds. If they chose to make a fuss the college could suffer considerable embarrassment. In the normal run of things it was the parents of young girls who protested at the lechery of male tutors old enough to be their fathers. Elizabeth was not sure of the moral niceties that would apply in this case.

But it was not the moral niceties of the case that were troubling her. It was not in consideration of them that she was irritable and incompetent, that the hours were crawling by interminably and her stomach was in a state of revolt. It was not the 'should' and the 'ought' that were concerning her but the 'can' and the 'might'. She had passed way beyond the point of debating whether or not to continue what she had started, and was now faced with the terrifying likelihood that she might not have the opportunity for doing so.

Her approach to Colin the previous evening had been flamboyant and splendid. Taking the initiative had been tricky and heady and dangerous. And it had come off. But that could happen only once. The initiative was now entirely out of her hands. He had performed and she had judged. But now the choice was his. A woman can command only once. After that, requests in any form are interpreted as pleading. That is the lot of a woman. Still. And Elizabeth would on no account plead.

Shaken and powerless she remained in her tutorial room, marking essays with grinding determination, rationing herself severely in the number of times she was permitted to look out of the window and search for Colin's cheerful bulk amongst the scattered and moving throng who hurried laughing along the paths, their heads held in a butting position against the freezing slash of February rain. Every knock on her door caused a painful acceleration of her heart rate. Her ears strained for the sound of his footsteps down the corridor. The scenes that were rehearsing in her head were gloomy and disturbing. Colin penitent; 'Look, Elizabeth, let's forget about last night. We were both a bit over the top ...' Colin flippant; 'Cheers! Great stuff. Must try it again sometime.' Colin embarrassed; his eyes sliding away from hers and no words spoken. In every case he was in retreat, and she was deserted.

Four o'clock. Five o'clock. She had, for two years now, luxuriated in the anticipation of returning to a quiet, empty, orderly house. This evening she dreaded it.

She drove to the local supermarket, and reflected as she walked up and down the aisles, how comforting it would be to embrace the philosophy of the Stoics. To finally accept that life was inherently painful and that the prime cause of pain was desire. Eliminate wanting and you eliminate the pain of not getting. All one had to do was see the absence of pain as the major good in life. But did she want to opt for such a small existence? Had not years of it been enough?

She paused at the meat counter and allowed herself to fall back on fantasy – an old and trusted form of comfort. She saw herself and Colin at her Georgian dining-table, eating meals she had prepared with meticulous consideration for his preferences. She picked out two plump fillet steaks then went on to load up the trolley with a whole week's feasting for two; avocados, kiwifruits, pâté, farmhouse cheeses, a joint of lamb, steak and kidney, fresh pasta, frozen strawberries, freshly-baked pizza. She progressed on to the wine section. She did not know what he liked. She took two bottles each of Italian Chardonnay and Portuguese burgundy from the shelves, for at least she knew what *she* liked, and a dozen cans of beer and lager just in case.

The loaded bags banged against her legs as she walked towards the house. She slipped her key in the lock and manoeuvred herself around the door, heaving the bags through the gap.

Colin appeared at the door of the sitting-room, dressed as though it were summer in a short-sleeved T-shirt and jeans.

'Hi!' he said, coming down the hall and taking her enthusiastically in his arms, clearly delighted at her return.

'Hello.' She felt rather faint. The bags dropped onto the

floor. 'Have you had anything to eat all day, my dear?'

His appetite was enormous. Elizabeth delighted in watching him eat. Over the weeks her own appetite began to revive. She found that she was beginning to eat again for sheer pleasure rather than as a sensible precaution.

After her mother died she had become greyhound-thin with pointed bones which poked against her white flesh. She saw colleagues looking at her and wondering about anorexia. But in fact she was eating very sensibly. It was just that there was no enjoyment, the exercise was merely one of fuelling a system to keep it ticking over.

'You're just skin and bone,' Colin told her. He would lift her in his arms, run effortlessly up the stairs and drop her on the bed. His mouth and hands and loins devoured her as hungrily as the food she placed before him on the table.

She noticed how his body unprotestingly dealt with and processed everything he put into it, rich food in quantity, beer, wine when he felt like it, any amount of cream and butter and full-fat cheese. She marvelled at the robustness of his digestive system. She remembered her mother in the later years, a slave to the dictates of a tyrannical stomach and the caprices of a faulty gall-bladder. The mere sight of a wedge of yellow butter, the faintest smell of dark plain chocolate could set her back for days. 'This constant sickliness,' she used to say. 'I hope you never get it.' She made herself bowls of Slippery Elm Food which she ate in the sitting-room with a tea-towel spread over her knees.

Colin's amazing body also responded to every demand made of it in terms of exertion. This was currently almost exclusively of a sexual nature, in other respects he was quite astonishingly static.

She found his presence entirely soothing, even though the extra work incurred in looking after him was quite considerable. Colin was no stranger to being waited on and cherished. The care of his mother had clearly been of the most devoted and subtle kind. He had no idea of the energy and discipline required to keep a house and its occupants running smoothly. Little treats like breakfast in bed every morning (delivered to him on a tray with china crockery, silver cutlery and a linen napkin before she set

off for work) he accepted with cheerful casualness. 'You
spoil me,' he said, his eyes lighting up with greedy anticipation of the feast before him. He accepted without comment
the fact that the jeans and pants and socks he dropped in
complicated puddles of fabric on the floor reappeared on
the chair by his side of the bed washed, ironed and folded.
He grumbled good-naturedly if she spent time washing the
dishes when he wanted her spread-eagled on the rug by the
fire, or if she stayed up to prepare the vegetables for the
next day when he wanted her in bed.

She discovered that living with easy-going selfishness
(especially when one was getting so many other benefits)
was surprisingly relaxing. It never occurred to Colin to
wonder why she had allowed her house to be taken over by a
great untidy, lazy boy. He was enjoying living with her and
simply assumed that she, too, must be having a good time.
And she was to discover that caring for the committedly,
unflinchingly selfish – as long as they are cheerful and
charming – causes very little trouble at all. She had frequently to pick up his underwear and his coffee-cups, but she did
not have to expend energy reassuring him that he was not a
burden to her. Nor did she ever feel obliged to raise his
spirits. They were in splendid form already.

Colin adored good food; she bought it and cooked it for
him. He liked fine white wine; she filled the cellar with it.
He loved comfort; she set herself out to discover exactly
what luxuries pleased him best. *Find out what others want and
provide it for them.* Ah yes – her earliest maxim was surfacing
again. But this time it felt different. This time she did it
because it gave her intrinsic pleasure to do it, not because
she was seeking approval. And this time she was joining in
the fun. There was no element of 'Please like me, please
think that I am obliging, obedient, clever, submissive, the
best girl in the world'. For she had no need to worry on that
score. She had his absolute approval. He was hers. He had
never had a woman like her, one who accepted all of him.
His eyes told her that. And he, for all that he was superficial
and sybaritic and solipsistic, entranced her. For in his eyes
she existed as the person she had always wanted to be; vital,
decisive, in control and unrestrainedly passionate.

Not that Colin was unappreciative, 'Jesus,' he would say,
'the service here is second to none.' He liked to be cared for.

But he felt no unease. To be cared for was as natural for him as noting that the sun had risen yet again each morning.

Five

From an early age Elizabeth had been fascinated by her father's business. It had started, some years before she was born, as a very small concern with a handful of employees engaged in the design and production of high-quality gowns for middle-aged ladies with ample figures. The firm specialised in large hip-sizes, anything from forty inches to the infinity of 'extra outsize'. Elizabeth's father supervised all the production personally and was also primarily responsible for the sales side of the business, although by the time Elizabeth was able to grasp something of the nature of the enterprise he had three or four agents selling for him also. He called them 'commercial travellers'. Elizabeth knew all their names and locations and was also able to list each shop and department store, up and down the country, with which her father opened up a new account.

She learned that customers were only of value if they honoured their debts. 'Anyone can open an account,' her father would inform her. 'The knack is to find the customer who is a good payer.' He personally had no difficulty in finding them – and he was hugely popular with the female buyers, being elegant, eloquent, witty and just a shade flirtatious.

Her father knew all there was to know about large female hips. He could size up a 'forty-two-inch' or 'forty-four-inch' lady at a glance. He had a number of customers who came up to the factory to order 'specials' – individual garments taken from the stock designs but made to their own measurements. Her father, with his design-cutter standing courteously by, would run a tape-measure around the lady's vital aspects. On occasions a reserve tape had to be employed in order to complete the

39

journey around especially monumental haunches. This
her father would do with the utmost gravity and tact.
Recounting the tale to his family later, however, the tears
of mirth would run down his cheeks.

Elizabeth soaked up all the information he volunteered
and clamoured for more. She amused him well, this
vivacious quick little daughter, and flattered him also with
her unswerving wide-eyed attention. But he could not
help feeling that it was a pity she would not grow up to
play cricket or fill in the pools coupons or drink whisky
with him. He would rather have liked a boy – but his wife
preferred girls, and she was in charge in the children
department. His time was taken up with other things.

He would take Elizabeth with him to the factory on a
Sunday afternoon when the boiler needed re-lighting in
preparation for the week ahead. The caretaker who
looked after all the manufacturing units in the big old
building was a little unreliable in winter, being prone to
bouts of bronchitis – 'chesty', her father called it, coughing
in sympathy as he inhaled on the twentieth cigarette of the
day before peering into the grey ashes underneath the
small furnace to determine whether or not he should rake
out the clinkers before ignition took place.

Elizabeth would wander around the silent electric
sewing-machines, observing the complex route taken by
the cotton thread between the spool and the needle,
examining the wads of old fabric, wrapped around the
machines' iron frames and stuck with hundreds of pins.
More interesting than that were the postcards taped to the
sides of the machines, nearly all of them colourful and
rude, depicting ladies with red melon-sized bottoms
disporting themselves on striped deckchairs, wearing very
little besides the indignant and amazed expressions on
their faces. There were cryptic accompanying captions
which Elizabeth did not always understand, although she
read each one carefully. The cards seemed to tell of some
other life of which she had no knowledge. It was certainly
not at all like the life of her parents' friends and relatives
judging by the serious and uplifting views of Brixham
harbour and Bridlington promenade which they posted to
her parents in the summer.

Elizabeth opened up the boxes of buttons and buried

her fingers in them. She picked out some that especially attracted her and arranged them in columns and towers on the vast expanse of the cutting-table, where the bales of cloth were chalked and then cut out with huge, sharp shears. Replacing the buttons carefully in their appropriate boxes, according to their design, size and colour, she lifted down the enthralling boxes of brooches from their high shelves. Many of her father's gowns were sold complete with an adornment of costume jewellery. Elizabeth was entranced by these gaudy assemblages of coloured glass which nestled in luxurious beds of tissue-paper. She examined each item individually and with much reverence, turning it so the light spurted from its facets in glinting rapiers. An hour could easily slip by whilst she was occupied in this way. Another hour could be spent looking through the boxes of trimming, ropes of sequins, motifs made from minute glass beads. There were huge heavy boxes of loose beads also. These were spooned out into individual bags and taken out to local women who painstakingly sewed them onto lapels and cuffs in the shape of leaves and flowers. Beading was a highly skilled and shamefully lowly paid job. Her father lamented this fact but could only be competitive in pricing his garments if he paid the lowest going rate. He presumed the beaders got a certain satisfaction just from doing the job.

Margaretha did not come on these Sunday afternoon excursions to the world of work. The factory was too cold without the heating and she would begin to shiver and an attack of asthma was likely to come on. It was Elizabeth's one chance of being sure of having her father to herself — even though he was fully occupied with all his various jobs.

She had never seen the factory in operation. She longed to come when all the machines were running. She longed to see the mysterious women who sat behind them all day operating the ornate iron treadles with their feet, pushing the material under the jabbing needles. 'My girls', her father called them — an unseen army with names like Evelyn and Mavis. Some of the 'girls' were grandmothers apparently. They were clearly fond of her father, and bought beautiful presents at Christmas for him and her mother. They bought presents for Margaretha and Elizabeth also; things that remained constantly at the level of middle childhood, so that at fourteen Elizabeth still received copies of the *Famous Five*.

'Come on – home, James!' her father said, emerging from his office and standing in the doorway looking across the factory floor – master of all he surveyed. Elizabeth had an image of him on a working day, dressed in one of his beautiful hand-tailored suits, the monarch of his realm, distinguished and authoritative, kindly yet remote. There was an air of the aristocrat about her father, as though he were accustomed to wealth and privilege. Elizabeth in her daughterly way thought that he was the most wonderful man in the world and in her magical childlike way of thinking she felt sure that she would marry him when she grew up.

'Daddy?' she asked. 'When I'm big can I come and work here with you?'

He was absorbed in selecting the keys on his ring which would lock the premises. 'Being in business is a hard life,' he said in a casual, distracted way. He spoke as though that were all there was to say in answer to her query.

Elizabeth did not treat the matter so lightly. Children are used to picking up the messages underneath words. It seemed to her that in some way she had been dismissed as being lightweight, of little consequence in this serious world of commerce. The sensation of wounding was quite considerable. What was wrong with her? Was it to do with that thing her mother had once mentioned to her? She had not really thought about that; it had not seemed important at the time.

Elizabeth went to an all-girls private school. She had no brothers or boy cousins, and was thus, as yet, completely innocent of the fact that her gender might be a disabling factor in the consideration of future employment. She took the burden of inadequacy upon herself personally and searched for offending flaws which could be rooted out and eliminated.

The business flourished. Her father was vital and cheery. Sales were accelerating, new accounts being opened-up weekly, annual turnover increasing steadily. At each financial year end her father would bring home the balance-sheet. 'Two thousand up on last year,' he would say, and then 'three thousand up,' the year following. It was a perpetual upward spiral.

Elizabeth examined the rows of figures on the accountant's sheets and began to discern a pattern in them. Her father swept them up off the table laughing. 'Daddy makes the money,' he said, 'and you girls spend it!'

There was nothing in his manner to suggest that this was not an entirely satisfactory state of affairs. Moreover, what he said was faithfully borne out in reality. Her mother had accounts at the local department stores, the butchers and the grocers. Each month the bills would arrive and her father responded by writing out appropriate cheques. He never ever did any domestic shopping himself.

This was Elizabeth's happiest time. She felt that no child was as lucky as she – not even Margaretha; for Margaretha was having a rough time at school, she had her asthma and bronchitis to contend with, and she did not have the special rapport with their father that Elizabeth had. Margaretha, however, was showing signs of growing up to be beautiful. She was more feminine and rounded than her beanstalky younger sister, and her thick blonde hair was more able to withstand their mother's determination to impose waves and curls on it.

Both girls were regularly taken to the hairdressers to be plugged in to a hot permanent-wave machine, a process Elizabeth found actually painful more than merely unpleasant, and one that left her hair as regimentally crimped as a middle-aged matron's – until it was washed, when it would assume the texture of candy floss around her head. Margaretha's hair on the other hand looked like Rita Hayworth's, all tumbling glossy waves with not a hint of frizz in sight.

Elizabeth came to understand that Margaretha's asthma attacks were linked with especially problematic times at school. Elizabeth, still in the infants department, would hang around until four o'clock when the junior section finished school so she could walk home with her sister. She would question Margaretha on her day, and attempt to absorb and diffuse the anxiety the older girl expressed about her school performance. It was agreed between the two of them that their parents need not be worried on this score, and Elizabeth was certain that her mother knew nothing of the real depth of Margaretha's unhappiness.

She herself was doing very nicely, being clever for Miss Grisdale, whilst at the same time diverting and helping her mother and reassuring her father with her girlish admiration. *Find out what others want and provide it for them.* She congratulated herself on having discovered this invaluable formula for the satisfactory management of personal relationships.

Six

Colin was at an age when existence is directed towards the physical rather than the cerebral, the active rather than the reflective. He was either firing on all cylinders, pulsing and vigorous (mainly in the sexual area), or in a semi-comatose state in Elizabeth's bed, or sometimes sprawled dozing on her sofa.

Elizabeth envied him his unselfconscious delight in his own body. She at the same age had been comparatively ignorant about her body and its pleasure zones, she had been afraid of its potential for capricious misbehaviour (at her first period she had haemorrhaged so badly she had been rushed into hospital for a transfusion) – especially that of becoming pregnant, and she had been ashamed of what she had been taught to regard as shortcomings – legs too long and thin, breasts too small, pubic hair too abundant, vaginal secretions too ripely odorous. Because her body was not like those of the film stars and beauty queens her mother so admired she judged herself to be deficient and hid herself in panty-girdles, dark stockings and high-necks.

As a girl of the fifties she had not owned her own body. Her body had been something to trade-in for the serious things of life – namely position and money to be acquired through marriage. She understood that she must be virginal, fully deodorised and asexual in order to win such a man. She must make herself attractive to men but must always be a pure little princess, never a mate. She learned also that the same code did not apply to boys. They were permitted to be sexual whilst still retaining that respectability – possibly even enhancing their social desirability. All of this seemed perfectly reasonable. She accepted it as part of the natural order and never considered it in any way unjust until much later.

For Colin, a boy of the seventies, sexual activity was not only permissible but more or less compulsory if one was to maintain any self-respect. Notwithstanding these social pressures, Colin seemed genuinely to enjoy sex just for its own sake.

Their sex was fleshy and warm and messy. It was entirely unrestrained and thus rather undignified and absurd. But in no way was it shameful. It was entirely fulfilling. Like childbirth.

Colin had no dainty reservations about odour and secretions and menstrual blood. He was hungrily, healthily, youthfully animal.

He was loud and loutish and lustful. It seemed to Elizabeth that he was at a stage in his life when he existed solely to be sexual and she felt that it was both desirable and right for him to be allowed to fulfil this function. Making love with Colin, being under his eyes, his lips, his trunk, his thighs, brought a focus to her existence. She had learned to live in the safely narrow confines of intellectual excellence and rigorous physical self-discipline. He put her in touch with the earthy stuff of raw living. He burrowed deep inside her and awoke an exquisite pain in the red darkness of her.

This is real, she thought, as she looked down at his body spread-eagled on the bed, almost instantly asleep after his huge expenditure of energy. This is real and good although it is often humiliating and absurd. He probably describes me to his friends as a 'goer'. He probably tells them that there are things you can ask an older woman to do that you wouldn't care to mention to a girl. He might well let it be known that the forty-five-year-old body is holding-up pretty well, all things considered. He probably says all of those things to his friends, my students, and I am degraded and made foolish in their eyes. It is possible that my career will be damaged. So be it. For the moment that is of small importance.

Colin had now been with her for three weeks and the fishy fragrance of human sex was constantly in her nostrils, giving her a sense of having at last found a true purpose in existing. In some strange way she was reminded of the sweet-sour autumn rotting in the atmosphere as she stood over those open graves, terrified of the time when her turn would come to be lowered into the earth. But now, now that at last her flesh had had its turn to be active, she felt both worthy and unafraid to be a member of the primitive, inexorable procession towards death.

Colin enjoyed his body. It was big and fleshy and young with thick tufty outcrops of hair. Elizabeth turned up the central heating so he could wander about naked, appreciating his own physique.

'What would your friends think,' he asked cheerily, grabbing her from behind, 'if they called in unexpectedly?'

'They won't,' she said.

'Why not?'

'I haven't got the sort of friends who drop in ... I haven't really got many friends at all,' she confessed.

'Christ! What a lonely existence. Good thing I came along.'

Ah, the presumptuousness of youth, she smiled, watching as his fingers skilfully unbuttoned her blouse.

Colin made massive claims on her time, as an active toddler demands the attention of his mother. He caused the sort of untidiness and mess that a big muddy dog does. He needed frequent feeding and nurturing. He lay around watching TV chat shows. And he smoked. And he said 'Okie, dokie.'

But none of that mattered very much. She delighted in his company, in the fresh newness of him and his clear unjaundiced view of life.

Moreover, he bathed her in approval. He liked the way she cooked. He liked her looks, and her style, he thought her greying temples delicious and her clothes elegant. He admired her taste in furnishing and cars and was awe-inspired by her taste in books and music. He envied her knowledge and her capacity for earning money, and all in all he felt that he had struck lucky.

Here was an exceptional, highly intelligent woman who was quite obviously infatuated with him, who seemed prepared to put herself out in every way possible to please him – and who never had a headache. True she spoke in formal convoluted sentences – and was generally rather weird – but so what?

Elizabeth sensed all of this and felt herself luxuriously floating in a warm pool of pleasure. It was a state of existence quite new to her. She was well aware of its transient nature, knowing that nothing in life remained static and she resolved to appreciate it to the full.

She was mildly perturbed by Colin's laziness, in a somewhat maternal fashion, but was not inclined to take any action for the moment. I have adopted him, she thought. I have adopted a great big hairy lusty boy with meaty muscles and little on his mind beyond food, drink and mating. The three basic animal drives – hunger, thirst and sex. How enchanting to be able to gratify them. How delicious to have the power to make another person happy. Elizabeth recalled once again her mother's words concerning her own personal notion of motherhood. 'My children are everything to me, I live only to make them happy.' Elizabeth began to remember, not just one, but a number of occasions on which these words had been spoken – some of the recollections having been quite firmly locked up in her unconscious mind for years.

She could not, however, clearly remember the first occasion on which her mother had told her that she was adopted. By the time she could think rationally the notion had become incorporated into that network of thoughts, impressions and yearnings that make up the essential self.

She understood that she was somehow 'different' and marked out from others, yet at the same time, felt that it was quite odd that everyone was not 'chosen' like her, but emerged instead from between their mother's legs.

She felt rather sorry for the children who were 'ordinary' because she was 'special'.

'Ordinary' was the word her mother had used. 'You are luckier than ordinary children,' she had said reassuringly. 'You are special because we chose you.' Elizabeth had gazed at her wide-eyed and known that much was owed.

Seven

Ken was in jovial mood. He was a man of few main moods – the other ones being gloom and quarrelsome irritability. He swung through this repertoire quite easily and most appreciated those people sensitive and obliging enough to swing with him. He had mixed feelings when Elizabeth sat down opposite him, daintily balancing her coffee-cup and wodge of lecture notes. One could stimulate Elizabeth into a certain raciness but nothing approaching the sort of boisterous vulgarity he was currently craving. With Elizabeth one had to turn the volume down in deference to her delicate serenity. There would never be any question of her kicking her legs in the air and being raucous. She was on the whole a sip of very dry sherry. But unlike the rest of the academic staff she did not seem to despise him and so he felt generally at ease with her.

'Have you found a house?' she asked accommodatingly, noting the photographs of a desirable-looking property spread on the table in front of him.

He nodded. 'What a relief to get out of those digs. Sheila's been nearly going crackers living on her own. We're signing-up next week.'

'You've sold your house in Liverpool then?' Elizabeth queried politely.

'Well, not quite.' He gave a series of gruff smoker's coughs and reached for a cigarette. Elizabeth wondered if he truly believed that she had not guessed how very nicely set up he was financially. His mother had died just before he joined the college staff and it was perfectly obvious that she had left him a good deal of money. His rusting CV6 had been changed for a new Renault 20 and the prices of the houses on the brochures he flourished around the common room were far in excess of what could be

49

afforded even on a Head of Department salary.

Ken was as clumsily conflicted about his wealth as a left-wing adolescent whose father keeps him in sports cars, beer and skiing-holidays. In the lecture theatre and the students' bar he extolled the virtues of the working man and shared urban living, but the house he was about to buy was named 'Long Paddocks', and he had recently had a number of varicose veins removed from his legs in a smart and luxurious private clinic.

'Like it?' he crooned, passing one of the photographs over for closer inspection. Elizabeth looked at the vast garden flanking the house. She imagined Ken sauntering in it wearing designer cords, and a hairy sweater with suede patches on the shoulders. He would draft in unemployed lads from the local village to do the heavy work, would pay them not ungenerously and patronise them with beer and cigarettes.

'I think it will suit you very well,' she said drily.

'I'll have to get it triple-glazed and new heating installed. Sheila's a delicate plant. Can't survive in a cold house. These Nordic types …'

Elizabeth smiled inwardly. She had met Sheila at a departmental party. She had bleached blonde hair, a kindly plainish face and a stumpy little figure.

From a psychologist's point of view Ken was interesting in providing an example of a man whose proficiency in self-deception was awesome. His ego defence mechanisms appeared to be functioning faultlessly, allowing him to cling to the idealistic notion of a working community bound together by common toil, poverty and ale-swilling camaraderie (females were shady to the point of absence in his fantasising), whilst at the same time manoeuvring himself into a position where he and his family could enjoy all the benefits of wealth, privilege and exclusiveness.

He came up to her tutorial room later. She had drawn the curtains and switched on her reading-lamp and the room was filled with a welcoming peachy light, creating an atmosphere of comfort and luxury similar to that in her house. He threw himself into the soft, low chair at the side of her desk and shook a cigarette from a crumpled packet. Elizabeth disliked smoke in her room but smiled at Ken nevertheless and passed him the ash-tray she kept for emergencies.

'Nice,' he said, looking around. 'Woman's room. All the little touches.' He flicked at his lighter. His hands were shaking slightly. 'These your own books?' he said, reaching over and taking a few soft-cover volumes from the box Elizabeth's publisher had sent her that morning. He flicked over the pages, noting the simple story lines, the skilful repetition of words in order to aid learning and retention, the bright and modern illustrations designed to capture a child's attention.

'I'm surprised you're interested in writing this sort of thing,' he commented. 'You always strike me as a true academic. Articles in the psychology journals and so on.'

She smiled and handed him a recent journal containing an article of hers. He gave it a cursory glance. ' "The relationship between reading interest and comprehension skills in eight-year-old primary school children" – Mmm. Psychology's dry stuff, Elizabeth. You want to try something spicier. How about a survey of sexual deviancy in the mature and educated female?' He gave her a raw and naked look.

Elizabeth's heart lurched. 'How about something on the subject of sexual harassment in the higher academic institutions?' she countered coolly.

He shrugged, quickly losing interest in the topic. 'I've been closeted with the Principal all afternoon. He doesn't like the new courses we've got on offer. Thinks they won't attract students.'

Spending cuts loomed over the college. Each year the threat became more serious; cutbacks in equipment, cutbacks in student quotas, and now the finger of redundancy rotated remorselessly amongst the staff. Tutors eyed each other over coffee with hostile suspicion. Early retirement was in the air, the golden handshake, or just plain getting the push.

'It's a market-place situation, Elizabeth. Get students or go to the wall.' He fixed her with a suspicious eye. 'How many students have you enrolled for next semester?'

She got out the list of proposed courses and let him see the information for himself. As usual, Child Psychology and Human Development had attracted far more student support than Sociological Theory and Community Studies. The really able students were at the university studying pure sociology. The less able students here in the college tended to steer clear of Ken and his department. He was known as an unpredictable and sometimes savage marker. Returning the list without comment, he then took a pile of essays from her desk and began to look through them half-heartedly. Ken was a compulsive fiddler – always touching; picking things up, squirming about, smoking, unwrapping and sucking sweets – just like a hyperactive child. 'Bit of a dull bunch this year two lot,' he commented. 'Can't spell properly, appalling grammar! What on earth are you educationalists playing at in schools these days?'

Elizabeth never argued with Ken in this truculent mood. He displayed all the bigotry and prejudice of ignorance, except that being highly educated also, he was potentially quite dangerous.

'I see you've got an essay in from Weston. He'll be lucky to scrape a degree together,' Ken commented sourly. 'Lazy sod!'

Elizabeth felt a rush of panic.

'He hasn't handed in the last two assignments for me,' Ken noted. 'In fact I haven't see him for quite a while. He is one of yours, isn't he? Have you seen him recently?'

'Yes.' Her heart was thundering now.

Ken glanced at her. 'Takes a good pair of legs to pull 'em in,' he said with a vulgar grin. He lit a new cigarette from the old one. Elizabeth was enormously relieved to realise that Ken's remarks were merely routine, his interest in Colin casual, and already lost.

'It's time we tightened up on these kids,' Ken told her. 'Jumped-up middle-class thickies, who come to college so their parents can impress the neighbours. They think they can lie around taking it easy. If it was up me they'd all have a spell on the assembly line. Compulsory!' He rattled on some more in similar vein.

Elizabeth could sense the frustration and disappointment, the anxiety and bitterness of a middle-aged man who has been promoted beyond his capabilities and now has to live under the constant fear of exposure and humiliation. Displaced anger, she thought, still finding it a relief on occasions to place a label on the behaviour of others, caused her a certain amount of stress. Her psychologist's background was full of labels, 'neurotic', 'dyslexic', 'autistic', 'maladjusted'. One could sweep all the distressing signs and symptoms into the confines of a label, write it on the case-sheet and file it away in the cabinet. It took a lot of the discomfort and responsibility away.

Her mother too had been fond of labels but of a less specific type than those Elizabeth learned in her professional training. They were mostly concerned with the gentle and compassionate snobbery that formed the basis of Elizabeth and Margaretha's early sociological perceptions; concerned with the notion of certain people being 'not quite like us', or 'not quite our type' or possibly 'a little common'. Elizabeth and Margaretha listened respectfully and then disappeared into their room to giggle together.

Elizabeth did not like Margaretha to laugh too much as it made her cough, and sometimes the coughing developed into unstoppable wheezing and gasping, and brought on the asthma. Margaretha hawked green globules of phlegm into the basin during her asthma attacks. The two sisters stared at this bodily produce, and giggled with delighted repulsion.

Then one night the coughing stopped. The house was silent. Elizabeth woke with alarm, unable to hear all the normal morning-time noises. Her grandmother, her lovely rosy little fat grandmother, came to stand by the bed. 'I'm making your breakfast this morning, love,' she said.

Elizabeth stared at her over her plate of bacon and egg. She forced the food down, swallowing hard and almost choking on the fried bread. She sensed terrible tragedy and knew with childlike premonition that her former happy life was slipping away.

'Mummy and Daddy are at the hospital with Margaretha,' her grandmother explained. Elizabeth scanned her grandmother's habitually merry features, and saw that her eyes were full of gravity and fear – she herself was terrified in case her grandmother might cry.

The rest of the day was a blank. Elizabeth was never able to recall it, although in later years her grandmother told her that she had gone to school as normal, come home, had her tea, done her homework, listened to the radio and gone to bed.

*

The following night she recalled vividly; lying alone in the empty darkness hearing a low muted howling of grief. She knew then that Margaretha was dead, although it was not until the end of the next day that her grandmother told her.

The house seemed abandoned. She had not seen her father at all. He had sought solace at work and at the nineteenth hole. Elizabeth, when much older, had understood that the powerfulness of her mother's ripe misery had been too much for him to bear. Her grandmother cared for her and told her stories about her own girlhood. Elizabeth clung to her. Her mother was still in bed. She had had tablets from the doctor. Elizabeth was not allowed to see her.

Elizabeth had not until now believed in death; she was only seven. She did not know how she could live without Margaretha, and she planned a number of elaborate and magical strategies to bring her back. She would take off and put on her clothes in a certain order and place a variety of objects in her pockets which would charm Margaretha back at a specified time. There was a smooth pebble Margaretha had liked and a pearl bead and a lavender-scented cube of bath salts. These things were taken to a certain place at a certain time and Elizabeth would count up to one thousand and close her eyes – and when she opened them Margaretha would hopefully be there. She hoped to succeed in her plan before Margaretha was buried as she thought the operation might be more difficult after that.

She wept tears of hot futile anger because they would not let her go to the funeral. The sensations of being excluded and dismissed bit deep into the bone and soul of her. She raged and screamed and made her grandmother cross and flustered. 'A funeral is not the place for children, love,' she said helplessly.

'But Margaretha is only a child,' Elizabeth protested, hot tears plumping her eyelids.

'It'll upset you, love,' her grandmother soothed, her eyes worried. Elizabeth was sent to tea with her friend, Julia. She was polite and quiet and still at the table and swallowed the little triangles of bread and the cubes of cake obediently. She felt isolated. Happiness is catching, but grief alienates. The people around the table monitored her progress through discreetly lowered eyelids, and no one was permitted to tease or make a joke.

A bleak despair lodged painfully inside her as though a stiff wing of blackness had opened in her chest. It was there every moment of the day. She could not shake free of it. In the night-time she was wakeful, constructing fresh strategies to bring Margaretha back, but as the rituals grew more elaborate and the failure became a thing of reality she began to lose even that frail thread of hope.

Each morning she got dressed and contemplated the day ahead with misery. The effort of simply maintaining life, of walking about and talking and appearing normal was so great that she felt tired all the time.

At school she did not always hear what Miss Grisdale said. She put up her hand to answer questions and forgot what she had been going to say when her turn came. When she did her essays she lost track of things in mid-sentence. Her achievements did not actually decline but remained static so that as all the other children developed and pulled ahead, she slipped from her place as top performer to a level only just up to average.

Three days after the funeral she heard her grandmother's voice in her mother's room talking with urgent severity. 'You've got to get up, you can't lie here wanting to die. Your life isn't over, you have another daughter to care for!'

There were some weak protests, then a shrill cry, 'My Margaretha, my first child!'

These were the first words Elizabeth had heard her mother speak for some days. They roared in her ears. I should have died, she thought. Me, the younger one. It is wrong for me to be alive when she is dead. I should not still be here in this world from which Margaretha has gone. She determined to make up to her mother for the injustice, for the error that had been made by the moving hatchet of death.

Life no longer seemed to make sense, but death was an

ever-silent presence. Its empty aching finality was clamped on her. Moreover, she now understood that no one was safe from its threat. The noiseless blade could fall at any time, not mistakenly but randomly, whimsically, without any clear motive. No creature, human or animal, was safe. The punishment descended wherever it chose, with the caprice of a fickle tyrant. Good behaviour offered no protection. The deathly despot had no regard for the merits of the gentle and the good.

Elizabeth became accustomed to sitting on the floor at her mother's knee and absorbing her anguish. Sometimes it was quiet melancholy, sometimes it was uncontrolled weeping, the tears gushing forth from her mother in an unquenchable flood as though all the veins and arteries and pipes within her had burst. 'I'm sorry, I'm sorry,' her mother would say afterwards, 'it isn't fair to burden you with this when you're so young.'

Elizabeth pressed herself against her mother's thigh in sympathy.

Her father was not there to share in the family sorrow. He had become ever more absent, more remote. He became increasingly unattainable and, therefore, increasingly desirable. Most of his nights were spent working late and many others drinking whisky and developing his skill in billiards. His golf handicap was down to four.

Elizabeth longed for his presence. She began to experience happiness again on those days when she knew he would be home for supper. She knew that he was sad too, but he still told jokes (usually waiting until her mother was out of the room) and his eyes still sparkled with life. She needed this kind of reassurance. With childish premonition she apprehended that the family had been marked out for tragedy. She felt as though she were shrinking down into the root of herself. She and her father conspired together to make merry – but quietly and in perfect secrecy. 'Your mother will get over it,' he told Elizabeth, 'but it'll take time; she's always been a bit emotional – on the nervous side.' They nodded sagely at each other in understanding. 'You're good for her,' he said, 'she relies on you. She's always been one for the children.'

'But she loves you too!' Elizabeth said in alarm, some
new fear stirring inside her.

'Yes – of course. But men have to get on with making a
living. Men must work and women must weep,' he
concluded in a quoting voice.

Elizabeth pondered a good deal on this strange little
maxim. Its message certainly seemed to have some validity
regarding her own family circumstances.

Her father she desired – but it was her mother that she
clung to, for her mother was the one who was so terribly
needy – and the one who was always there.

Gradually the loss of the older child became as much a
factor in their lives as any living reality. Predictably,
Margaretha soon assumed the status of a saint. The
recollections of her actually spun away into the distance
and became coiled around in wispy mythology. 'She was so
quiet and uncomplaining,' her mother would say, 'even
when she was ill. I never remember her answering back or
being disobedient or rude or mean or selfish. And she was
so beautiful – what a lovely woman she would have been.'

Elizabeth and her mother sat together reflecting
uncomprehendingly on the nature of calamity and waste.
Feelings of miserable unworthiness swept through
Elizabeth as she clung to her grieving mother. The two
females drew ever closer to each other. The mother drew
comfort from the child and the child drew comfort from
being needed and able to supply the wants required. The
father withdrew more and more into the outside world.

These were perhaps the most terrible days; when all
there was to occupy the depleted family was their
experience of loss. Later, when harassment and stress and
another child invaded the void – at least there was
something to fight against.

Eight

Colin lay back in bed spent and exultant. It pleased him greatly to be able to make such a stern lady throb so wantonly. He watched Elizabeth dress. The way she rolled on her stockings gave him a fresh erection. 'Hey,' he said, 'come here!'

She put on her suit and her shoes and then sat on the bed stroking his chin thoughtfully. She shook her head in gentle admonishment observing the bluish-grey fuzz.

'Three-day designer stubble,' he said grinning.

She touched the bristles with her lips. 'Sheer unadulterated laziness!'

'Oh come on, Elizabeth!' He gave a cheery, heart-melting smile.

'I'm going to put my make-up on,' she said.

'You don't have to do that. You're great without it. You're obsessional about the way you look.'

Ah, so he had remembered something from her lectures. 'I've told you before, I'm very orderly, very methodical, very practical, very thorough – no doubt very dull. That's my style.'

There had been a time when orderliness had been denied to her, a time when her underwear had hung on the rack in the kitchen beside old ladies' knickers; when her beautiful blouses had been tumbled in the washing-machine alongside fluffy moulting bed-jackets and tubular elastic leg-supports. Her mother was so helpful. 'I'll do the washing, leave it to me.' Elizabeth started to hide things, but her mother ferreted them out and bundled them into the machine and sometimes mistakenly turned the switch to 'whites' instead of 'delicates'.

His eyes twinkled. 'You're certainly thorough,' he said, taking one of her hands and placing it on him under the duvet.

'Colin – are you really content to spend the whole of your life in my bed?'

'Yeah, where better? Especially when you're in it. Come on, Elizabeth. Come on!'

She stood up. 'I have a living to earn,' she said, tender yet severe.

'Oh Christ.' His lower lip jutted forward, clearly a winner in the past.

Elizabeth stood looking down at him, reflecting that a boy of twenty exists to be a sexual creature. She had become increasingly convinced of the rightness in acknowledging this during her weeks with Colin. He was at a stage in life to be passed and enjoyed for what it was. She could find no reason to quarrel with that. 'My dear,' she said, 'I think you should know that your spasmodic attendance at lectures and tutorials has been noted.'

'Hell!'

'You're going to fail your end of semester exams.'

'I'll be OK.'

She hesitated. Should she leave it at that? People were entitled to their own disasters, after all.

'Work is good for the soul? Is that what you're telling me?' he asked. 'Spiritual beauty in honest toil, and all that crap?'

'Certainly not. I abandoned the notion of the protestant work ethic long ago. It's a simple question of money, finance, wherewithal – the stuff that'll get you a house and a car and your beer and cigarettes.'

He stared at her, then laughed out loud. 'Why go into college when you can get a boring lecture here?' he queried provocatively. He smiled a smile to melt glaciers. His hand was already past her stocking tops.

'You leave this college without a degree, and you're nothing, Colin. You probably won't be able to get even the most punishing, draining type of manual job. You'll be on Social Security and you'll be utterly and totally miserable. It's as simple as that. Passing exams is a ticket for getting money – unless you have substantial private means, in which case you can study for aesthetic satisfaction.'

He was silent. She had amazed him.

She smiled, clipped on her earrings, returned to kiss his forehead and left. Later on she decided to make a concession for once, cut short a tutorial and came home early.

He was sitting on the sofa amidst a pile of cake crumbs and empty lager cans. He looked like a detail from a still-life painting. Bright chatter emanated from the television; an intelligent pretty woman was having no difficulty in coaxing life confessions from a grey-suited politician.

'Hello there!' he said, with a smile of welcome that made her heart turn over. He sprang up, switching off the TV and divesting himself of his T-shirt in a series of rapid energetic movements. His arms closed around her and the smell of his skin filled her nostrils.

'Mmm,' he said, burrowing. 'Mmm.' The discussion of the morning had left no trace of rancour, and if he felt any bitterness it was now entirely dissipated.

Colin was a master at purging himself of anything psychologically unpleasant. He protested, he sighed, he sulked, he brightened – he forgot.

Ah, how she loved that quality in him. And whilst he offered little in the way of intellectual stimulation, being in that respect simply not her equal, he was so restful to be with. She might not get the good conversation but neither did she get the sermons. He demanded much of her body but he left her soul alone.

The next day he put in an appearance at Ken's tutorial and spent a dutiful and disconsolate afternoon in the library.

She made a steak and kidney pie for supper, the tiny sauté potatoes he liked and a variety of fresh vegetables gently steamed to buttery tenderness.

'Can you manage some raspberry sorbet?' she asked as he swooped around his plate with a hunk of bread to mop up all the gravy.

He puffed and grinned. 'What do you think? Have I refused one of your offers yet?'

She gave a laugh from which she hoped indulgence had been purged.

'I'm a greedy pig!' he said.

'You know what you want and you get on with enjoying it, my darling, I find that totally delightful.' She reached over for a kiss but he had started to speak again.

'I'll get fat. Mustn't get fat!' He paused. He seemed serious for once. 'I'll have to take up swimming again; best all-round exercise there is!'

'Is that so?'

'Yes, actually it is, stimulates muscle, respiratory and heart activity, without imposing dangerous, artificial stress.'

She smiled. 'I'm impressed. You sound like a medical textbook.'

'Oh – I have my little areas of knowledge. Humble beside yours, of course.' His remark was entirely good-natured. They smiled at each other. She put out her hand and stroked him.

'I'll get some practice in at the pool when I'm at home,' he said.

Her heart leapt in panic. 'Home?' she said stupidly.

'Easter hols ... End of term next week.' He smiled in his cheery way. She stared at him uncomprehendingly. She had not linked up the approaching term end with Colin's leaving her.

'Have to go back and see the parents,' he went on.

'Yes – yes, of course.'

'I'll drop you a postcard,' he said teasingly.

Her hands shook as she cleared the table. She poured herself an extra glass of wine. 'Colin,' she started uncertainly. 'Colin, you needn't feel, you mustn't think ....'

'I'll be back,' he said, wrapping her in reassuring arms.

'No. No – I don't want there to be any sense of ...'.

He placed a hand over the lower part of her face. 'You're always talking, Elizabeth. Just be quiet.' His tongue filled her mouth and she offered no resistance. In bed later this big child of hers rolled her over and rubbed her back with the tender authority of a father. Ah, how she would miss him.

It began the hour that he left. Her house was filled with his absence. She had not been prepared for the pain of wanting; she had hoped never again to expose herself to abandonment. A soft murmuring of longing rippled through her, a gentle yearning throb beat insistently in her breasts and flanks. He was in her head and in her ears and the sweet touch of him was on her skin so that his absence seemed like a tender wound within her.

Mentally she followed him back to Barnet. Barnet – what was there in Barnet? It was territory entirely unknown to her. She got out the map and let her finger travel down the M1. Barnet – it would mean something special to Londoners like Barnsley and Cleckheaton and Pudsey meant something special to her. 'From Hull, Hell and Halifax may the good Lord defend us' her father used to quip. The family all laughed and knew exactly what was meant. So what was said of Barnet? What special character did it have, what tender, derogatory jibes were made about it which indicated the comradeship of emotional sharing?

She followed him up the path to his house – a suburban semi, 1930s most likely, with a small round stained-glass window in the front door and behind that, clean, comfortable and unremarkable furnishings. What sort of people were his parents? What did his mother look like? (Ah – his mother, his lucky, lucky mother.) Did they have a dog? Were his brother and sister still at home? He had never mentioned them. He had in fact mentioned little about his family at all. They had seemed merely an ever smiling, unconflicting, non anxiety-provoking backdrop to the unfolding of his normal undisturbed childhood. She could, of course, be wrong on some or all counts. But at least she knew that there had been no deaths. She had asked specially about that. The early experience of death was significantly linked to a higher than average level of neuroticism in the young adult. She knew that both from her readings of research findings and her searchings of self. If she had discovered that the child Colin had been in contact with death then her whole hypothetical construction of his persona would have crumbled.

Would there be girlfriends; lovers to keep him 'topped-up' whilst he was absent from her? Ah, what torment. Maybe he would not return. It was quite on the cards that he might not return. Time – even a few weeks – is highly effective in altering emotional states – especially that of specific sexual hunger. She and Colin had, after all, satisfied each other most adequately. The whole episode could be regarded as a job well done, a completed assignment. There was none of the wistfulness of unfinished business in what she and Colin had been up to.

She sat on the bronze-leather sofa with a glass of Californian Chardonnay in front of her. In her mind was Colin – and a firm nubilé girl whose head nestled between his thighs. Dear God!

She had thought to find the sole occupancy of her bed inviting and restful. She had imagined it would be a luxury to search out and find cool places on smooth sheets, that it would be delightful to stretch herself across the diagonal and have no need to curl up her long legs. But instead, the bed's undented orderliness was shroud-like and void and she longed for Colin's big sticky warm body and the firm beat of life in her ear as she laid her head against his heart.

She reminded herself of the benefits of renewed freedom. She could come and go as she pleased. She could eat whatever she liked. She could use the time she had spent in picking up soiled underwear, smoothing jeans, emptying ash-trays and vacuuming crumbs from the carpet in order to ... To do what? When one sinks one's will and one's time into someone else's, one's own will shrivels and shrinks. She of all people should know that; she who had spent much of her life hinged on the conditional: if only I did not have a family to support I could build a library of records and hardbook books; I could buy wine and pure wool suits and an interesting car. If only I did not have to be responsible for my mother's happiness, I could have a light heart and laugh without guilt.

If only ... She had been informed later by professional colleagues that to bow to the dictates of 'if only' was an indication of a feeble cringing character and little to do with personal circumstances. 'If only' was nothing more than mawkish self-pity.

Elizabeth found herself spending a lot of time in college. She seemed to need a lot of time to get things done. Administrative work that usually took her the first hour of the morning now dragged on until lunchtime. And she had begun to make mistakes.

'Are you all right, Mrs Lashley?' the clerical assistant

enquired, handing over some typing, whilst mentally adding up the value of the clothes on the Head of Department's back and coming up with a figure around double her own monthly salary. 'Aren't you going to have a break, or go away for Easter?'

'Where do you suggest?' Elizabeth asked, smiling.

The girl thought of the Canaries or Tahiti. 'Paris or Spain?' she said, playing safe and pitching things on the modest side. She observed that Mrs Lashley's large, grave eyes twinkled so that she looked almost human.

'I might do that! Yes – I might do just that.' But in the end she stayed at home. A woman abroad alone – unless she is an adventurer, an athlete or in pursuit of some recognised form of sport – tends to be an object of interest, of speculation – of gentle pitying contempt.

She had lifted Colin's home number from the file on that first occasion. By now it was firmly programmed into the numerical filing circuits within her cerebral cortex – as indestructible as early childhood jingles. She picked up the phone and dialled it, then replaced the receiver before a connection was made. On Easter Saturday she telephoned her sister in Redhill. 'Can I come and stay for Easter?'

'Yes, yes, yes. We never see you! You never want to come! Stay for the week.' Helena seemed genuinely pleased.

'Oh – just over the bank holiday. I've a lot of work on …'

'Liza – no one's that busy. Wait and see how you feel once you're here.'

Elizabeth went out and bought Easter eggs for her nephews – dark old-fashioned eggs that were not boxed, and were weighed on sale. They had tiny violets and primroses on them made out of icing sugar. She hoped the children would not prefer milk chocolate ones filled with miniature Bounty bars or hideously mis-shapen chocolate rabbits. They would be sure to get those anyway. For Colin she bought a similar but larger egg, half a dozen chocolate hearts wrapped in blue and silver striped foil, some hand-made rum truffles and five packets of his preferred brand of cigarettes. She also bought him an Italian wool-and-silk sweater from a hushed and discreet men's outfitters, together with some very daring briefs which emerged incongruously from extremely sedate and old-fashioned wood and glass drawers.

In her head she rehearsed the pain of finally abandoning hope of ever being able to give them to him. She saw herself sorrowfully handing over the chocolates to the local school for children with severe learning difficulties, storing the cigarettes in her desk to offer to Ken when he sought solace in her room, folding the clothes away tenderly amongst her own things so that at least the fabrics could mingle. Rehearsing pain was both superstitious and self-protecting behaviour.

Nine

She drove down to Surrey flagrantly breaking the speed limits. Her brother-in-law came to greet her in the drive, making a polite lunge at her cheek with hygienically dry lips.

'Good journey?' he asked. 'How long is it taking, door to door, these days?'

Her reply, together with his swift appraisal of her new two-litre fuel-injection car, caused him a twinge of envy and annoyance. Always the perfect gentleman, however, he picked up her bags and led her into the house, through to the kitchen where her sister Helena was preparing a soufflé with asparagus. A French cookery book propped up on the work unit showed a picture of *filet de boeuf en croute* which was presumably to be consumed after the soufflé.

Helena was a trained *cordon bleu* cook, and although she did not work at present, having two school-age boys to care for, she kept her hand in by catering for neighbours' and friends' parties in return for gifts of malt whisky and claret which she consigned to her husband's drinks store, as she liked neither. She hugged Elizabeth with genuine warmth and a hearty dash of respect. As a child, Elizabeth had seemed to her like a goddess – one who could do no wrong. In fact, as far as Helena was aware, she never *had* done any wrong. Their mother would point Elizabeth out as an example and model. Helena had recognised the goodness and obedience in her elder sister but declined to follow it. She had hell-raised right the way through childhood and adolescence, she had defied all the family rules, had made contact with her natural mother in her early teens (an event which had been so bitterly devastating as to cause her to decree that the existence of her natural mother should never be referred to again), had flirted with the neighbours' sons and fornicated with assorted car dealers and sales directors when she started working. She had got all her wayward naughtiness out of her system, and at twenty-three had married Philip and settled down to contented, conventional motherhood.

The boys were eight and six years old, sound in brain and body, and everything the good offspring of aspiring middle-class parents should be. Helena was a very pretty blonde, now thickening into early middle-age, but delightfully presented in ever more expensive clothes as Philip's income increased. 'You'll stay for the week, won't you?' she asked warmly.

'No – no dear, I don't think so.'

'I'll be hurt.'

'Oh, Helena, don't say that.'

'Reminds you of Mum?'

'Yes.'

'Sorry. It wasn't deliberate. Habit. What was it Dad used to say – when you live with folks you get like them?'

'I think it went something like that. But it's a very long time since you lived with them. I would have thought all the habits would have been extinguished by now.' Elizabeth did not really think that – but she felt it would be more acceptable to both of them than the truth.

'You know,' Helena said thoughtfully, 'it's amazing how these things die hard. I'm always coming out with one of Mum or Dad's little phrases – usually just the ones I used to think were rubbish. Frightening, isn't it?' she concluded cheerily.

'Give me a child until he is seven, and I will give you the man,' Elizabeth murmured, looking around her and noting that Helena and Philip were on the up and up. The kitchen throbbed with life: a new fan oven, huge freezer chugging, tumble-drier, dishwasher, microwave ... 'Where are the children?'

'At a party. Don't worry, they'll be back soon. Justin's booked a bedtime story from his Aunty Liza. He thinks there's no one like you. Did I tell you that we're taking him away from his school? He's not doing a thing there, hates it. There are forty in the class.'

Elizabeth murmured non-committally. She loved her

sister, but already she was wishing that she was back in her
own house, able to choose her own occupation, to move
silently down the corridor of her own thoughts, free from
obligation to absorb chatter, free to open a bottle of wine
even though it was only five o'clock.

'We're sending him to this school in Godalming. It's a bit
of a drive – and colossally expensive. Only six in the class. I
really wanted your advice. What do you think?'

As Elizabeth struggled to frame a diplomatic, kindly
answer, Helena mercifully moved straight on to her next
point. Elizabeth hoped she would have the resources to
cope good-naturedly until the regulation single glass of
Philip's amontillado sherry at seven-fifteen.

They sat eating dinner at the large oak table – just the
three adults. The boys had been tidied into bed and given
half an hour for quiet reading before they turned their
lights out. Elizabeth had brought two of her newest books
to read to them. The audience appreciation had been
gratifying and heart-warming. Elizabeth thought Helena's
boys were intensely lovable – and so relaxed and carefree
despite all the bribing and pressurising they had to endure
from their pushy parents who were totally taken up with
the notions of competition and achievement.

Philip poured the wine. He did it properly – having a
napkin wrapped around the neck of the bottle. Elizabeth
shivered in the chilly atmosphere. Philip monitored the
temperature of the house carefully and kept it at a steady
sixty-seven degrees. Even with a thin wool sweater under
her blouse Elizabeth was still cold.

But Philip was a careful and courteous host and kept her
wine-glass topped up, which was a relief. By the time they
had progressed to the *filet en croute* Elizabeth began to feel
more optimistic about the chance of some actual pleasure
being gained from the visit; warmth came back into her
frozen feet and her brother-in-law's face seemed a little
less pinched than she usually found it.

'Ah,' she said, appreciating the excellent fruitiness of his
claret, 'a day without wine is dull indeed.'

'Then I'm afraid you will think us very dull here,' Philip
said with appalling pomposity, 'we can't afford to brighten
every day with the fruit of the vine.'

'Oh don't be boring, Phil,' his wife said affectionately.

Thereafter ensued a number of predictable and safe topics, led out into the field by Philip and safe because neither Elizabeth nor Helena chose to challenge him. After all, what could Elizabeth, a trained and experienced psychologist, say in reply to Philip's statements that when he was young, schools had standards, whereas nowadays he heard a lot about 'learning through play', and 'considering the needs of the individual'?

'When I was in primary school,' he assured them, 'we had to learn our tables and how to punctuate a sentence. There was no time for psychology – with all due respect to you, Elizabeth, of course.'

'Of course,' she murmured, not really listening and occupying herself by watching Helena. She judged that Helena was happy, and was glad it was so. She remembered her younger sister's early life well, and had she not now been contented and full of psychological well-being, she, Elizabeth, would have been inclined to accept some of the responsibility: not because she felt herself to have been the cause of any early unhappiness, but simply because she had witnessed it and *been* there. Proximity in itself incurs responsibility.

Helena had yelled and screamed and raged for three years non-stop (or so it had seemed) from the day she arrived in the family – red-faced, protesting, frail and skeletal, resembling a skinned rabbit because she had been three weeks premature.

The run-up to her arrival in the family had been a time of wrenching pain, disbelief and grotesque nightmarish imaginings – most of which had been brought about by the very kind intentions of Elizabeth's very kind parents. Anxious to appear duly grateful for the efforts being made on her behalf, Elizabeth had kept her feelings of despair well hidden and had shown to her parents only those emotions which she felt would best serve their needs.

It was her mother's grief particularly that terrified her. She dared not stare into the face of it, and skirted around it as best she could as though she were on the dark edge of a tall cliff from which she could slip and fall, clutching only at emptiness. She sensed the dangerously fragile quality of her mother's brittleness and felt that the slightest disturbance of her precariously balanced state could cause her to shatter. In order to avoid such a tragedy Elizabeth adopted a demeanour of quiet watchfulness. At eight years old she was as carefully vigilant as if she were the parent and her mother the child.

Her parents had been the recipients of much unsought advice regarding the nature of childish grief and the loneliness suffered by an only child. It was not natural to be an only child: such a child became solitary and spoiled and selfish. It became clear to her parents that they must take appropriate action.

'You're going to have a sister,' Elizabeth's mother told her some months after Margaretha's death. 'We're going to go and meet some little girls and perhaps choose one.' She instructed Elizabeth to put on her Sunday school coat and her new red patent shoes.

Her father drove them across the city to a children's home where fifteen children between the ages of three and thirteen were eating high tea. A woman with a scrubbed face and a firm stride asked them to sit in the lounge. They sat together in a line on chairs arranged against the wall. In the middle of the room was a dull, scratched table on which were piled well-thumbed books and comics. Elizabeth looked around in horror, taking in the bare and dreary decor, the absence of ornaments and frills and flowers and silver-framed photographs like they had at home. Did children actually live here – without mothers and fathers? She could hardly bear to think of it.

A sick tide of panic rose in her throat.

She sensed that her parents were apprehensive. They kept looking towards the door and after some time the woman in charge came back. Behind her, like the rats following the Pied Piper, were all the children.

Elizabeth was truly terrified as they approached. She felt that she would be swallowed up into the body of them, hidden to the point of obliteration, so that her parents would never find her, so they would select another child and take it home, leaving her behind in this terrible, terrible place. Her heart began to beat very fast, and furred globules of iridescent pink light swam across her vision.

The woman took a little girl by the hand and led her up to them. 'This is Sally,' she said. 'She's just five.'

Sally gazed at them and smiled. She was very small and looked no more than three to Elizabeth. She wore a pale-blue dress and a lemon cardigan and wrinkled brown socks. Her hair stuck out spikily. She looked like an orphan in a story-book. To Elizabeth's astonishment she climbed up on her mother's knee and began to trace around her face with enquiring fingers as though she were blind. 'Are you my aunty?' she asked.

Her mother was clearly unnerved by this question. 'Well – no. Not really, dear.'

'Are you going to take me in the car?' Sally wanted to know.

Meanwhile the other children had gathered round and were staring brightly at all three of them. One or two of them stroked the fabric of Elizabeth's coat and touched her lovely new shoes. She was paralysed with helpless fear and the wild thumpings of her heart were now causing actual pain. She sat, rigid and quiet, outwardly perfectly calm, but inwardly screaming.

After a while the woman in charge came to disentangle Sally who was firmly entwined around Elizabeth's mother's neck.

In the car on the way home her parents did not speak a word.

In the week that followed, Elizabeth had horrifying nightmares. She prayed and prayed for Margaretha to come back and stop this mad and obscene thing that was happening.

The next Saturday the same torture sequence was repeated in another – almost identical – children's home with another little girl called Barbara. Barbara, like Sally, was undersized and drably dressed. She had sticking-out bunny teeth. She never stopped talking in a bold shrill voice. On the way home Elizabeth heard her mother murmur the words: 'precocious' and 'not quite our type'. She breathed a sigh of relief.

Things quietened down after that. The hunt seemed to be off. Elizabeth got on with the business of being a lonely, only child. She began to hanker after a dog. They had had a dog before, a wire-haired terrier called Candy. It was a kindly, docile, harmless dog. Elizabeth's mother was not, by her own admission, a dog lover. Dogs caused mess, dropped hairs and created dirt. You must never let them lick you on the lips as you might get a terrible disease.

'What sort of disease?' Elizabeth asked.

'Something dreadful.' Her mother paused to consider. 'A worm.'

'Could you die?'

'It could be very serious.'

Elizabeth reflected on the likelihood of catching a fatal worm and decided there was little risk – and anyway, she did not really care. She cuddled the dog in secret and kissed its lovely moist dog-smelling muzzle.

Now Margaretha had not died as a result of asthma or bronchitis, she had died of a virulent, unknown – and therefore untreatable – virus which had attacked her intestines and bowels causing her to dehydrate rapidly through constant vomiting and diarrhoea. Although the dog had had nothing to do with this, her mother began to distrust it. The dog became a focus for her guilt in allowing her child to contact a fatal illness. It had to go. It was packed off to live with Elizabeth's aunt and uncle who did not, she noticed, die as a result.

Elizabeth set about mourning its loss. One day she tried to walk to her aunt's house but it was twelve miles away and the police picked her up as she walked along the main road and took her home again. Her mother was weeping and distraught. Elizabeth never again went outside the door without telling her mother where she was going.

She bought magazines about dogs. She read stories about dogs and wept over the one where the faithful dog sits guarding its master's grave. The picture of the dog she herself would soon have was constantly in her mind: a labrador, golden and velvety with a big square head and tender brown eyes. It was her firm belief that this dog would one day be hers and she was quite prepared to wait.

Thoughts of the dog were comforting and healing. With the dog to think about there was less time to ponder on Margaretha's absence and the terrifying issue of dispossessed orphans and the caprices of adoption. The searching eyes and eager hands of desperate children in unspeakable institutions hovered incessantly at the gates of her conscious thoughts. She did everything in her power not to let them through. Fear would clutch at her throat, gagging and choking, if she permitted herself to consider the awfulness of being rootless, being hewn from unknown anonymous rock and having no rightful place in life – and even more horrifying – having no rightful parents. She understood what it was that she, as an adopted child, shared with those pitiful children. She understood that her kind parents had unwittingly inflicted unspeakable cruelty on those children by flirting with their most fundamental hopes and yearnings. How many times did these wonderful and desirable mummies and daddies come to view a child, bringing with them images of a home and a fire and a room of your own where your knickers did not come out of a communal cupboard? (She knew all about the cupboard; Sally had shown it to her at the same time as the lavatory.) How many times did those mummies and daddies go away and never come back, leaving the selected child's self-image even more damaged and shrivelled than before? What torment of loss and rejection was suffered?

For the first time in her life Elizabeth's security of tenure in her parents' home and in their affections lost its cast-iron certainty and became a thing of conjecture; another area of potential loss. Her heart began to beat very fast again. She dragged her thoughts back to the golden labrador.

But it was not a golden labrador that joined the household. Her parents, one Sunday – totally unexpectedly – went out for an hour in the car and brought a baby home with them. 'There,' said her mother, raising her voice over the baby's frantic yells, 'this is your new sister. We've called her Helena.' Elizabeth looked at the heaving, furious, red-faced bundle and was shocked and revolted.

'It's not right for you to be an only one,' her mother explained. 'It's too lonely for you.'

Her father did not like to hear the baby cry. He made them all a cup of tea and then went out for a round of golf because it was such a fine day.

Elizabeth's grandma nursed the baby whilst her mother prepared a bottle for it.

The baby would not suck. It spat the teat out and roared even more loudly. Purple veins stood out in its raging features.

'It's the teat,' her mother said. 'The hole is too small.' She made it bigger with a sterilised needle.

'It's the milk,' her grandma said. 'It's too hot.'

They both seemed to know everything about it. But the baby still went on howling. Eventually it dropped off into a short nap of exhaustion, but within the hour it had struck up again. Not one drop of milk had been consumed.

Elizabeth was disappointed. She had been looking forward to having a quiet chat with her grandma followed by their Sunday family tea of roast ham and pickles. But now everything was in confusion and disarray. No one had time to speak to her and wherever she went in the house the din of the baby's howling battered her ears. Even the golden labrador temporarily deserted her and she had to drive all her concentration into the business of luring it back into her imaginings.

That day Elizabeth presumed to judge her parents and find them wanting. They had done a terrible thing and all the family were to be punished for it. The baby would cry for ever and there would never be any peace. Moreover, where had this baby come from? Was it so easy just to go out and get one? Were children of such little consequence?

She became an eavesdropper behind doors, desperate for information.

'Poor little thing,' she heard her grandma say. 'She's just skin and bone. Three weeks early, did you say?'

'Twenty-five days,' her mother said, her voice already weak with loss of sleep. 'That's why everything was such a rush. The mother was only nineteen; just a child.'

'Tragic,' her grandma said. 'Poor girl.'

'I keep thinking about that girl's mother, what she must have gone through. It's a very good family. The girl's parents look quite aristocratic.'

'And the father?' her grandma queried.

'A local boy apparently. Again from an excellent background. His father's a lawyer. Very nice people.'

'Ah! Well there shouldn't be any problems then,' her grandma said, putting a final touch of mystery on this totally baffling conversation.

Around this time Elizabeth experienced a curious desire to

steal things. It only happened·twice, but it was a dangerous and heady desire whilst it lasted. First she took Patricia Pollard's new doll out of her desk and hid it behind her own coat in the cloakroom. Miss Grisdale – now headmistress – instituted a search. When the doll was eventually found Elizabeth was ready for once to be sulky and defiant. But Miss Grisdale was very kind. She seemed to understand things about the taking of the doll which Elizabeth herself did not.

'You wanted it and you really thought it was yours, didn't you, Elizabeth? But you see it's Patricia's doll and she's crying like people do when they've lost things and I think we must give it her back – don't you?'

Elizabeth had silently agreed and Miss Grisdale duly returned the doll to Patricia. At home-time she gave Elizabeth a toffee from her 'goodies' jar. None of the children were ever told the identity of the thief. Her parents remained ignorant of the incident. Elizabeth fell slightly in love with Miss Grisdale and, after some weeks of cogitation and longing, stole the headmistress's fattest grey rubber – a rubber which had erased many of Elizabeth's wrong sums and smelled nicer and better than any rubber in the world – and bore it home where she put it to bed in a handkerchief. A week later she unwrapped it and dropped it back into Miss Grisdale's pencil and rubber jar when she was not looking.

The golden labrador was ten months old now, his imagined brown eyes full of tender devotion.

Ten

Elizabeth, travelling at one hundred miles an hour up the A1, had just passed Stamford Bridge, and was consumed with thoughts of Colin.

Helena had said, as a parting shot, 'You could get married again now you're on your own.' She sounded faintly coquettish, as though it was all a bit of a lark, as though a good man and true would obligingly present himself at this convenient point in Elizabeth's life.

Elizabeth had looked around Helena's kitchen at the paraphernalia of a married woman's life, the bowls and plates and crockery waiting to be stacked in the dishwasher, the pile of boys' sportswear and the white business shirts waiting to be ironed. She thought of all the time eaten away through tidying up and cooking, through listening, understanding and sympathising – through simply being available. She said, 'If a woman is not prepared to serve, then perhaps she must be alone.'

'Don't sound so gloomy,' Helena said with a dismissive laugh, having no wish to become embroiled in one of Elizabeth's philosophical discussions. 'Just make the most of it now you're free.'

Elizabeth managed to stay on until mid-week. The noisy, busy household stirred-up the rhythm of her thoughts so that she could no longer follow them to a peaceful conclusion. Without the consolation of a complete inner life she felt herself beginning to crumble. She needed space to think – to think about Colin.

Driving was psychologically soothing. She had always found this, which was why her choice of cars was very carefully considered. Most of the stories for her books had been conceived behind the wheel, as she sliced through the atmosphere in her shell of steel, on the move, part of the flow of human life, yet at the same time cut-off, and, therefore, unassailable.

This infatuation of hers, this being in the thrall of another person, this opening up and reaching out which could perhaps be called loving – all of this she wanted to be rid of. Before Colin there had been a period of equilibrium, when she had discovered that the quiet procession of orderly, uneventful days, untouched by desire or obligation, had been a perfectly satisfactory mode of existence. She did not want to be needy. She was weary of neediness, drained and debilitated from whirling so long in the circle of another's need.

Her professional training dictated that she should separate out the elements of her misery into discrete portions so that she could examine them dispassionately and thus defuse their power through a process of demystification. Emotions were no more than magic. Just as one could reduce the evil thrill engendered by the demon in the pantomime through the process of switching off the green spotlights, taking off the make-up, removing the costume, so one could diminish the tyrannical power of undifferentiated emotions by teasing out their component parts for disinterested examination.

She tried. She drew up a mental list. It did not help. She forced herself to think in conventional terms – of the sheer silliness of it all – this being linked with a student half her age, a mental lightweight who could never match her intellectual powers or share any of her cultural interests. What future was there for her? But all this was completely beside the point. All this did not counteract the sheer awesome missing of him, the sharp heart-arresting terror that he might not come back. She wanted no more than the certainty that, at least on one more occasion, she would lie in his arms and draw such sweet refreshment and strength from the generous joyful lustiness of his healthy and exquisitely ordinary young maleness.

Colin represented all those good things that had been missing for her; the capacity to approach and lay hold on the good things of life with light-hearted acceptance as though they were no more than the rewards he rightfully deserved. He, for all his youth and rawness and ignorance, carried a life-fuse that seemed to have been long snuffed to smoky greyness within her.

She stood in the silent hallway of her house and missed the smell of cigarette smoke, the mound of jackets heaped over the banister rail, the background of Radio 1, the sheer sense of a pulsing, purposeful presence in her house. Yet in time surely she would come to detest all these things. She would long to return to her tidy solitude. Yes? Surely? No. Not so. Not yet! He had massaged her cool still heart and made it beat with hungry life. She did not know how to manage without him. The fundamental essence of him flooded through her, wave after wave of anguished wanting.

She roamed through her house scouring it for his discarded clothing. She found a pair of black briefs, washed them by hand, rinsed them in fabric softener and put them to dry on the radiator in her bedroom. She dug down the backs of the chairs and retrieved a half-smoked cigarette which she licked lingeringly and then placed tenderly in one of the ash-trays she had bought specially for him.

She made two coffee-cakes, a spotted dick and some beef casseroles and put them in the freezer. It was now two days before the beginning of term. She went into college and could not concentrate, so she returned to the house and occupied herself with wiping and polishing and vacuuming. It made her tired so that she slept better.

She had had no communication with Colin for over three weeks. She got into the habit of taking the telephone off the hook for long periods so as to persuade herself that he might be trying frequently to contact her but having no success.

She opened many bottles of wine.

On the evening before term started, she sat in her drawing-room and noted its spotless perfection. She knew that she must stop waiting, and initiate some action to change things. Perhaps I should get a dog, she thought – first of all half-heartedly, then with increasing intent. Yes, she decided, I will get a dog, I will adopt one, some odd unplanned-for mongrel that had no right to come into the world, one that has been rejected and is existing only by luck and the skin of its teeth, one that is despised by the pedigree-conscious majority. I shall love it and feed it and train it and it will not be dismayed by my need to be a carer. She poured herself a glass of Chablis and pondered over this pleasing image.

She had had a dog before, following some quiet, tenacious nagging extending over a period of almost three years: 'Can I have a dog? Please can I have a dog?' she would chant.

Just before her eleventh birthday, her father took her to see a litter of black labrador puppies at a nearby kennels. A few days later a puppy with paws as floppy as clumps of seaweed lay asleep in a basket under the kitchen table. Elizabeth fell besottedly in love with it. The reality of it was one hundred times more dizzily joyous than she had ever dreamed of with the imagined golden dog. She understood her mother's reservations about the animal and was filled with a surge of love at her generosity in permitting it to join the household.

The puppy, as it grew, seemed to be as much in love with her as she with him. He sat up on the window-seat and watched as she walked down the drive on her way to school and he was there when she came back, awaiting her arrival with eager eyes. When she took him for walks he was unrestrainedly exuberant, but even in the midst of his boundings he was watchful. As soon as she called him he came racing back to her, his paws going up on her shoulders, his eyes devouring her. At four months old he was big enough for her to clasp like a lover. She would sit with her arm around him in the evenings as she read or listened to music on her record-player. His heavy head would sink onto her knee, and as she stroked the moleskin softness of his pink and black muzzle she felt herself choked with love and happiness.

Around this time Helena had her third birthday and began at last to sleep through the night. Her mother, now in her early forties, had become so worn down with the care of this raging and fretful child that she was ordered by the doctor to take a month's complete rest. It was decided that Helena and her father should remain at home under the care of Elizabeth's grandmother, whilst she and her mother and the dog went to stay with friends on the south coast.

It was a time of redawning happiness for Elizabeth, a

time of restored peace with the days and nights free from
the jarring vibrations of childish wails, a time of renewal of
friendship with the much-loved mother who seemed to
have been lost forever to the demands of the small
tyrannical intruder into the family.

Mother and daughter went for walks along the cliff tops.
Just beyond the shoreline were clusters of great rocks lying
in the water as though tossed there by some playful giant,
their jagged heads thrust up against the sky. Inland, the
great Devon fields, anchored in their rich red beds of ball
clay, spread themselves as far as the horizon. Elizabeth,
town bred in the heart of the industrial north, marvelled.
She and her mother consumed coffee and sticky lumpy
cakes in cafés which had red-and-white checked table-
cloths on the tables, and old clocks with ripe fat ticks on the
walls. Then her mother sat on striped deckchairs whilst
Elizabeth, in her blue ruched swimsuit, paddled in the
frothed hem of the sea and the dog snapped at the frizzy
waves.

The dog was learning to be patient, and sat outside
tethered to drainpipes or railings enjoying the admiration
of passers-by, but inwardly he was impatient to be reunited
with his mistress.

'Mummy,' said Elizabeth, feeling herself to be almost
grown-up now. 'I used to think Margaretha would come
back – I really thought so.' The subject of Margaretha had
been approached very hesitantly. Elizabeth had circled
quietly around it as though she were playing 'Sleepy Jack'.
Her mother's grief seemed to be a thing of intense privacy
and she was unsure of her reception if she invited herself
to share it.

Her mother's eyes filled up. 'You're so young,' she said,
'much too young to have to think about such things.'

'I used to think,' said Elizabeth, 'that I would like to dig
her out of the earth and open up the coffin, just to make
sure she was there.' Her mother looked terribly shocked
and Elizabeth wondered if she had gone too far. But it was
no more than the truth. She had from the start insisted on
accompanying her mother on the weekly visits to the
grave. She loved the grave. She wanted to stroke the
engraved headstone and trace the precious name and the
brief story of that sadly truncated life. Margaretha

Christine it said, and then the dates of her birth and her
death, dates with a span of just ten years and two days
between them. Elizabeth trotted up and down the aisles of
graves, peering at the fresh ones where cheerful flowers
nodded, re-reading the inscriptions on the old ones. It was
the mingling of centuries and decades that entranced her, a
sharing across time, the curious ultimate kinship of death,
cutting across the barriers of wealth and social class. This,
even at only seven years old, Elizabeth clearly apprehended.

She knew all the names on the neighbouring headstones
by heart. To those names she had added faces and brief
histories. In her imagination they were friends protecting
each other from loneliness on this exposed hillside, which
faced a skyline of aggressively jutting black mill chimneys.

Elizabeth noted that the dead were like families – all ages
were represented – but most especially the very old and the
very young. On some family headstones there were several
dead babies recorded, sometimes as many as three or four
in successive years. She imagined these little bodies, now
miniature skeletons, and was filled with pity. She often
reflected on the issue of flesh rotting from bones; reflected
in a dispassionate manner, feeling little pain or revulsion.

In fact, for a while she had felt very little at all, except the
empty aching loss caused by Margaretha's having ceased to
exist.

The bond between Elizabeth and her mother drew tighter.
There seemed to be a naturalness about this to Elizabeth; it
seemed to her that the mother-daughter bond could never
be rivalled by anything that might be felt for a father.
Gradually her father was dying out of her life. He spent
more and more time at work or at play outside the home at a
time when Elizabeth was coming to learn that one gets on
with life and makes do with what there is. That which is
unobtainable has to be done without; there was no point in
fighting against that. Her mother, however, was an ever
present figure. She too had been absent for a while –
emotionally absent at any rate. But now she was giving
herself back to the world – and most especially to her
serious and sensitive eldest daughter.

'If it wasn't for you,' she told Elizabeth, 'I don't think I would have wanted to go on living.'

Elizabeth was overwhelmed, as though she were in church and the voice of God had spoken. She trembled a little with a sense of awesome responsibility.

As the year turned towards autumn the family were on the move. The business was forging ahead – it was a time of huge profits, of big new cars and holidays in five-star hotels. Her mother longed for a house with six bedrooms and a big garden which was not overlooked. She found just such a one. She was a dedicated house-hunter and mover. 'Family hobby', Elizabeth's father remarked rather caustically. 'Her mother could never stay in the same house for more than a year at a time, either.' But he, for all his outward reluctance, was charmed by the mock-Tudor house, with its external black timbering and its shiny leaded paned windows. He imagined important customers coming for Sunday lunch and being suitably impressed.

The people who bought their existing house began to press for early vacancy. Anxious not to miss the sale her parents put the furniture in store and went to live with her grandmother. There really was not enough room for them all. The dog had to sleep in the garage.

'It won't be for long,' Elizabeth's mother said re-assuringly.

He was quite big now and showing signs of being an excellent guard dog. During Elizabeth's hours at home he monitored her every activity with quietly unobtrusive allegiance. His purpose in life was to be with her and incur her pleasure. She was his leader, the mistress of the pack, the one who laid down the rules and was to be followed, obeyed and adored. His senses were geared to receiving signals about her movements and her moods; whenever she sat and was still, so he would be there, his head against her legs, the moist droplets from his breath misting her shoes. When she moved he immediately interrupted his sleep and was alert and following. He waited slumped outside the door whilst she sat on the lavatory, he watched her in the bath with grave eyes and when given the word he got up to lick the soap suds from her shoulders and back. She had only to part her lips in the faintest overture to a smile and his tail began to move with pleasure.

Having left puppyhood behind he developed into rather a serious animal, regarding life through wistful quizzical eyes. Already at only nine months old he seemed to have sensed something of the inevitable sadness of existence; or so it seemed to Elizabeth, who loved the animal and projected onto it her own conceptualisation of the nature of life, and her premature appreciation of the inevitableness of its termination in the empty finality of death.

She took the dog on long walks and talked to him of these matters, having learned that they were not things to be spoken of elsewhere. One was allowed to mention death once or twice, but then the topic had to be shelved and space given to cheerful things. On the whole Elizabeth saw the reasonableness of this social convention. And in any case she merely wanted to think out loud, she did not want to be distracted by any kind of verbal response, or any alternative way of construing the issue. There was a need for her thoughts to settle and solidify, undisturbed by outside interference. She imagined sometimes that the inside of her brain – the part concerned with thoughts and feelings – would be like the plaster of Paris with which she filled moulds to make models of people and houses and goblins, the setting plaster into which Helena put naughty touching fingers, creating imperfections in the smooth-ness which Elizabeth had carefully prepared.

When Elizabeth got back from her walks she would dry the dog's paws and then sit quietly with him in her bedroom, her homework spread on the table in front of her. She would be at peace – in touch with things spiritual – a state which self-sufficient children find comforting and not especially difficult to achieve.

Her father, increasingly puzzled by his solemn thoughtful daughter, would put his head round her door and make jokes to jolly her along a bit. 'Aha, Greta Garbo, likes to be alone.' And so on. Elizabeth understood that she disturbed him, that her playful extroverted father was at ease when people were laughing and kicking-up their legs and thinking frothy things to do with making money or achieving at sport. He was a little afraid of her, a little in awe. Sensing this, Elizabeth was sad because she did not know what to do about it. She was not unhappy any more, rather balanced on a fine edge of contentment from which undue hilarity or fresh sorrow could easily topple her.

The dog, living in the damp garage, developed a persistent cough. The phlegm rattled in his throat and his eyes were patient and resigned as he arched his body in attempts to hawk-up the source of his distress. Elizabeth was frightened. He had pink rims around his eyes, his nose was rough and hard and dry and his tongue furred. He sniffed listlessly at his food and ignored it.

They took him to the vet, who diagnosed distemper. The vet explained how he should be looked after. Elizabeth fastened her complete attention on him as he spoke. She saw in his kind eyes a gravity that spelled doom.

For three days she nursed the dog and willed him to get well. She scanned him anxiously for signs of improvement. She kissed him and cradled his head in the bowl of her stomach and thighs. Her mother said she would wear herself out and that she must have a break. She said that her grandmother would take her and Helena to the cinema. They went to see a film about a lost goat. Elizabeth thought the film was rather silly and was surprised that it moved her grandmother to tears on a number of occasions.

On the way home, as they got off the bus and began to walk up the road, Elizabeth looked at her grandmother's face and knew that she had not been crying about a celluloid goat. A terrible presentiment of tragedy engulfed her. She began to run, wondering if it was too late to avert disaster. But when she got back the garage was empty, the rug from the basket gone. Her mother, in the house, was subdued and a little fearful. 'It was for the best,' she said. 'He didn't feel anything. He was very poorly.'

After her third glass of Chablis, Elizabeth decided on a small to medium-sized mongrel, the kind that had the sharp muzzle of a fox and the soft eyes of a fawn. She would get in touch with the Canine Defence League or some appropriately noble institution regarding the adoption of such an animal. She would get in touch the next day; the thought of the new term and returning home to an empty house terrified her. It was as though Colin had reached up and taken her from her shelf of solitude and now she was sentenced to be put back there, the defences that had enabled her to manage before having been well and truly stripped away.

It was tempting to bring the day to an abrupt end by going to bed very early, having taken one or two of the Mogadon tablets which still remained in her mother's medicine cupboard in the little bathroom up on the top floor. She would not do that. There was the question of pride. She pushed buttons and found a film on television, fast-moving and vacuous. Then mercifully, in due course, it was past midnight and the day was ended. She could retreat to bed without shame.

She began to switch off lights, to draw back the curtains. Into her desolation the phone pealed. She stared at it. Tentatively she approached, lifted the receiver and spoke into it. The voice at the other end was strong and buoyant, quite unmistakably cheerful.

'Hi, it's Colin! Remember me?'

Eleven

Her innards churned, her hands trembled. 'Ah – Colin,' she said.

'I'm at the station,' he announced with confident expectation.

'Yes – I see. Colin my dear, I've had rather a lot to drink. I'm over the limit. In fact to be perfectly truthful – I'm drunk.' Her words were perfectly enunciated, no more than the merest fraction more precise than usual.

'Oh.' It was not often that she heard doubt in Colin's voice. 'Are you trying to tell me something? Shall I go back to Albany Road?'

'Oh no. I should like you to come back here to me. But you'll have to get a taxi.'

'Right, great. Don't go away.'

She put the phone down. 'Sweet Jesus Christ,' she said to herself softly.

And then his bags were in the hall in a chaotic heap and she was in his arms and wild with desire, rejoicing in the solid bulk of him, pressing her face into the rough reassuring fabric of his anorak.

'So,' he said, with tender and presumptuous paternalism, 'what's all this about getting pissed?'

'I was lonely and I missed you and you never wrote or phoned,' she said, aware that these were the words of a neglected and petulant mistress; words that a woman like Elizabeth should never say if she wished to preserve her dignity and her lover's esteem. But Elizabeth, seeing Colin again, and noting afresh his transparent and remarkable straightforwardness, chose to say them. She did not say them with the purpose of purging her anger or invoking his guilt; she said them simply because they were true. This was one of the aspects of her dealings with Colin which was so delightful. There was no discrepancy between what was said and what was intended. The explicit and the implicit were in perfect correspondence.

'Neither did you,' Colin pointed out reasonably.

She smiled at his lack of appreciation of the uneven balance of their need. 'No, indeed I did not.'

'Have I been a bad boy?' he enquired winningly. 'Have I to slink away to the bed in the spare room – deprived of my rights?'

'Rights! You have no rights!'

'No, I suppose not.' Momentarily he was crestfallen.

She gained the idea that he had not been at all certain for some time about his reception. She reached up and stroked his stubbly cheek and with the other hand reached down. 'You have no rights, my darling,' she informed him, 'neither of us has rights. But I have desires. Ah yes. Lust is not the exclusive prerogative of the male.'

He brightened up. 'Mmm – well that's all right then.'

Protected and reassured by the familiar solid nakedness of Colin's body lying over hers, Elizabeth was overwhelmed. She began to sob. There had been too much loss, too much abandonment, too much illness and sadness and death. Too much rejection. It had been more than one person could bear.

'Hey there,' said Colin, holding her tight and rolling her over so he could rub her back, 'it's all right.' He was genuinely startled by this unusual display of emotion. He had seen Elizabeth stripped of her cool composure and greedy with passion, had watched her pleading shamelessly for him to do this and that to give her pleasure, observed her positively playful in her desirousness on occasions. But he had never seen her let rip with feelings that were clearly outside the sexual sphere. He was both flattered and enchanted.

Even whilst the grief rushed out, a separate, rational portion of Elizabeth's brain was operating, reflecting dispassionately on the implications of Colin's return. Now that he had come back to her, now that he was a fixture and she felt sure of him, she feared that her personal freedom had been lost. She knew that she would not be able to stop herself being fastidiously careful with him, that she would have no choice but to submit to the temptation to set herself out to please him in every way possible.

'Come on, it's OK,' said Colin, rocking her in the manner of a mother. He felt as though he were trying to dam-up an unstoppable flood. When eventually she was calm and quiet he lay back on the bed exhausted. 'Christ, I'm hungry. I could eat a sodding horse.'

Elizabeth looked at him, then got up, put on her dressing-gown and went down to the kitchen to cook steak and chips – thinking perhaps that a four-course gourmet dinner might cause him embarrassment.

The Senior Common Room was cranking up for the new term. Elizabeth sat with her cup of freshly-ground coffee and observed her colleagues as they presented themselves for work following a four-week vacation.

They looked, on the whole, in the pink – as indeed they might after all that time off. The prospect of the summer term was hardly daunting, either – a maximum of five to six weeks' frantic examination and marking schedule followed by a pretty swift decline in pressure of commitments as the frolics of the end of the academic year took over (a programme including such events as Ken's annual naked plunge in the river with an assortment of drunken newly-graduated twenty-one-year-olds). The students, after all, were only young once; staff had a duty to join in the fun, and not to be killjoys.

Given a little luck, and competent organisation, there would not be very much work to do until September. All in all Elizabeth judged that being a teacher in higher education was both an agreeable and profitable pastime – provided one was intellectually up to it. For the ones who were struggling, the misfits and impostors like the unfortunate Ken, academic life was a minefield of hidden pitfalls and cunningly camouflaged disasters. Someone like Ken could just about manage to keep one step ahead of the students, but was not of the intellectual calibre to withstand the deviance and treachery of the hidden agendas which underpinned Departmental Heads' meetings, nor the cut and thrust of encounters with the staff from the local university, the college's parent insitution; a body ferociously powerful in determining overall academic direction.

Having herself made no more than fitful progress from late primary school days until she reached university, Elizabeth understood something of the torment involved in being thrown into situations where one was forced to be humiliated by one's brain. It was because of these past experiences that she was now enormously grateful for the fact that her own mental equipment seemed to be in excellent working order.

Elizabeth had passed her eleven-plus but had not done well enough to gain the scholarship which would enable her to attend the city's direct grant grammar school as a maintained pupil. She was fully prepared to attend one of the local education authority's grammar schools, but her mother said that the direct grant school had 'a very good name' and that education was an 'investment', so her father, who seemed not unduly concerned either way, had had to stump up the money for fees. It was also apparent to Elizabeth that her mother's liking for the school was to some extent influenced by the benefits it offered in being free from boys and also those 'ordinary' children who were 'perfectly nice' but 'not quite like us'.

Elizabeth was a good, solid, averagely achieving pupil, never revealing any signs of the sharp, quick intellect that her early school achievements had reflected. With Margaretha gone, she felt that it would be permissible to resurrect her cleverness, but the latter-day brightness seemed to have dribbled away.

Keen to achieve excellence in some sphere, however, she turned her attention once again towards good behaviour – *find out what others want and provide it for them.* The genteel scholarly ladies on the staff posed no problem as far as this was concerned. Their needs were so transparent, so easily satisfied. They liked their girls to be clever, that was not in dispute. They liked the clocking-up of O- and A-levels and Oxbridge scholarships. But equally they valued traditional middle-class qualities of femininity – goodness, obedience, gentleness, softness, compliance and politeness – all those qualities that would earn the approval of the men their girls would eventually set out to please. Elizabeth's finely-tuned sensing apparatus apprehended all of this, and, as she seemed no longer able to excel in cleverness, she determined to compensate by excelling in goodness.

When she was made head girl in the final year, Helena proclaimed her a prize prig. Helena, at eleven, was already rebelling by refusing to wear her woollen knee-socks and the regulation navy-blue interlock knickers with detachable linings, preferring nylons and frills.

It appeared, however, that there was no question of Elizabeth being entered for Oxbridge. Her mother voiced a protest. As her girls grew older she had become more and more keen on the notion of academic glory. The girl next-door was reading English at Cambridge and a distant cousin had just acquired a first-class degree in Law. There were standards to be maintained.

'I'm just not good enough,' Elizabeth explained to her.

'Rubbish. You can do anything you put your mind to,' her mother said.

'No – the staff know what they're talking about.' Elizabeth truly believed this because her mother had always instilled in her a sense of awe regarding the judgement of these academic ladies, had always indicated how wise they must be, how much Elizabeth must respect them, attend to everything they said and obey their every command.

'You're as clever as anyone at Oxford University,' her mother avowed stubbornly. 'I just know it.'

'Manchester and Sheffield are just as good,' said Elizabeth, equally stubbornly, thinking of her partially completed application forms for those institutions – although in her heart she didn't really believe it.

Elizabeth wondered if her mother would go up to school and make a fuss – many parents did. But she gave in gracefully and no more was said. When the A-level results came out Elizabeth surprised everyone – and herself – by doing exceedingly well.

On arrival at Sheffield to read English Literature, she chose subsidiary subjects of Economics and Psychology. A few weeks into the term the Professor of Psychology called her into his study. Her first essay 'Comparing and contrasting the analytical and behaviourist schools of psychology' lay on the desk in front of him. Elizabeth sat down, arranged her dog-tooth skirt carefully over her knees and faced him rather apprehensively.

He was of a physical type she much admired – with beautiful dark-grey eyes and brows and a substantial amount of thick wavy hair. He was around fifty. Elizabeth thought she would like him to take her to bed and introduce her to the secrets of sex. She was rather surprised to have this thought regarding any member of the opposite sex; it was not one that had previously been in her repertoire.

'Miss Gibson,' he said gently, 'why aren't you at Cambridge?'

Elizabeth stared at him transfixed and helpless. She had no idea what sort of response he required. She had never met a man like him before; he was completely uncharted territory. She had no way of knowing what answer would please him best. It never occurred to her to indulge in the luxury of telling the truth.

'This essay,' he said, tapping the sheets with gentle fingers, 'reveals an exceptionally mature grasp of the conflicting issues in modern psychology.'

Elizabeth licked her lips and permitted herself a tight little smile.

'Oh,' she said eventually, full of shame that she should appear dull and barren in an oral exchange, when this clever and knowledgeable man had been so impressed by her written work.

'Have you ever studied psychology before?' he asked kindly.

'No.'

'I see. Did you enjoy the books on the reading-list for the essay?'

She flushed. 'Well ... some of them.'

'Mmm?' He was staring directly at her.

She hated to tell him what she really thought. She hated to lie. She hated to appear dumb. At the same time she had been repelled by much of what she had read, had furiously rejected the notion put forward by behavioural psychologists that human behaviour could be experimentally examined in a laboratory and reduced to a matrix of laws couched in cold statistical equations.

He smiled. He seemed very kind. 'Miss Gibson, a student is entitled to a point of view – to put it forward and argue it out and then maybe modify it through reading and discussion. That is what a university education is all about.'

'Yes,' she said. 'Yes, I see.' His careful appraisal unnerved her a little but she listened intently as he went on to review her past achievements and her hopes for the future.

He exhorted her strongly to consider taking Psychology as her main subject instead of English. He told her that Psychology was a growth area, that it offered exciting new challenges, that he had high hopes of the prospects in this field for students of her calibre. He alluded to the strong possibility of the opportunity to study for a D.Phil. at Cambridge when she got her first degree. Elizabeth left his presence entirely satisfied. Now she knew how to please him. She enrolled in the Psychology Department without delay.

She anticipated the Professor's lectures with keen pleasure, longing to hear of the insights into the human mind that she had perceived to lie in abundance behind his shrewd, penetrating, yet benevolent eyes. In her ingenuousness, mixed with a hearty dash of breathless late adolescent admiration, she imbued him with most of the knowledge available to mankind. It therefore came as a crushing disappointment to discover that his lectures were to be almost entirely devoted to the subjects of learning theory and something termed 'human skills' – promising perhaps as a title, but in reality as devoid of human interest as a course in technical drawing or algebraic maths.

She had yearned to learn what stirred peoples' hearts, what prompted their minds to produce the miracles of music and poetry. She had hoped to explore and examine the cause and nature of passion and stare into the depths of human motivation. Instead she found out all manner of things that she had never wished to know about vigilance and fatigue in airline pilots and the differing rates of human reaction times in pressing a buzzer in response to a visual or auditory stimulus. Besides being keenly disappointed, she was puzzled that the Professor, with his undoubted capabilities and sensibilities, should choose to spend his time deliberating on such issues.

Bewildered and disillusioned as she was, however, she set diligently about becoming the mature and exceptional student that the Professor had indicated she should be. It was excellence that she sought. Only that was good enough for the Professor. The taste of his praise had been heady and intoxicating. She hungered for more. She set herself a punishing schedule of study. She was in the library by nine o'clock every morning and there when it closed at nine-thirty in the evening. She never cut a lecture or handed in an assignment late. She had no social life and joined none of the university's societies or clubs. Her one source of pleasure and entertainment was to attend the concerts given by the Hallé Orchestra in the Civic Hall. This she did regularly – and on her own. In the main she avoided her fellow students, finding them frivolous, lazy, spoiled and vacuous. Half of the Psychology undergraduates in her year spent their day in the student coffee-bar becoming proficient at bridge, whilst the rest were not to be seen around the university at all – presumably either in town or in bed. They were certainly never in evidence in the library, apart from the day before an essay deadline, when the peace of the vast oak-panelled room was rudely disturbed as they flocked in, cramming themselves into the Psychology stacks and riffling through the shelves. There was anxious searching for references, feverish whispered exchanges and frantic note-taking. Elizabeth, who would have completed that particular assignment weeks ago, looked on initially with amazement, later with mild scorn, realising that the piece of work to be presented next day would be hurriedly thrown together in the early hours of the morning accompanied by endless black coffees to neutralise the effects of the late evening's beer. Nevertheless, one or two of her colleagues managed to notch-up an 'A' even with that level of preparation, and Elizabeth knew that she could give herself no respite if she were to maintain her position at the top of the pile.

By the end of the term she knew the view from every one of the library's windows, could recall each detail of the industrial skyline and the way in which the afternoon sun glinted jaggedly on the uneven glass of the Victorian buildings which stood opposite. She accustomed herself to quietness and the companionship of books. She read conscientiously through her reference list of journal articles and research monographs and developed a truly phenomenal capacity to tolerate boredom.

She filled her hours with study, not only through the anxiety about her ability, but also in order to deaden the intense pain of her homesickness. She missed the rhythm of family life, the frantic breakfast times and the scramble for the school bus. Solitary in the library she thought longingly at four-thirty of previous homecomings, when the stresses of the day would fall away as she walked up the long lane to the beautiful mock-Tudor house, where there would be a fire burning in the 'snug' and hot tea and crumpets to be consumed before the evening's homework was commenced. But most desperately of all she missed her mother, missed her in the manner of a much younger child – as though emotionally she were still in primary school. On several occasions, in her dreary lodgings, where hot water was rationed by the basinful and the smell of cooked sprouts clung constantly to the stairways, she wept under the bedclothes, miserable and humiliated because she was crying out for her mother – and she was nearly nineteen.

Towards the end of term Elizabeth was summoned again by the Professor. He complimented her warmly on the excellence of her term's work and asked whether she would be prepared to carry out some simple routine experiments to help him with the completion of some personal research. The nature of her task was unexciting to say the least and the topic was something of unbelievable dreariness connected with fatigue and reaction times. Nevertheless she was delighted to be of service and overjoyed to be the chosen handmaid.

'Have you enjoyed your first term?' he asked her, those dark eyes causing a weakness behind her knees.

'Oh yes,' she said brightly, avoiding eye-contact for the split second in which the lie was actually on her lips.

He smiled. She was sure that he could see into her heart, that he would understand all and forgive all.

'You mustn't work all the time, Miss Gibson,' he informed her gently. 'You must play a little. That is one of the principles of learning theory, you know – the most effective retention and recall results from those learning sessions where work is spaced and rest periods intervene.'

Elizabeth could not believe that he thought *life* was like that.

He walked across to the door and held it open for her. 'Have a good holiday,' he said in that low soft voice of his. He surprised her by extending his hand. She took it and shook it warmly. It was dry and hard and firm and she did not want to let it go.

When a fellow Psychology student invited her to the Christmas going down ball she decided not to refuse, and much to her relief her one friend, Joanna, also received an invitation, and moreover, she cheered up to the extent of writing home and requesting that a long dress and her charm-bracelet be despatched instantly by registered post.

Elizabeth enjoyed herself in a mildly pleasant way at the ball. Her partner was a kindly friendly lad who had a lot to tell her about his struggle to reconcile the teachings of behavioural psychology with the teachings of the Roman Catholic church of which he was a devout member. Elizabeth, currently lapsed Church of England, listened with politeness rather than enthusiasm. Joanna drank numerous gin-and-tonics and became flushed and silly and quite wantonly amorous.

At the end of the evening Elizabeth followed Joanna's example and allowed her partner the kisses and squeezes that she felt were his due. In her mind she was in the Professor's arms, drinking him in, savouring his words and his wisdom, adoring him with the soft fullness of her lips. She imagined her hands plunging into that thick springy grey hair, saw herself white and naked on a satin-draped bed, inviting him to take whatever pleasure he wished from her firm young body.

Twelve

When Elizabeth arrived home after her first term at university she found that her family had changed. It was like coming back from a holiday and being surprised to discover certain aspects of the house not quite as one recalled; the lines of an armchair more angular or curved than one had thought, the dimensions of a room altered in some way so as to make it quite unfamiliar for a few moments.

She fell upon her mother, almost weeping with joy. It was late and Helena was already in bed. Her father was playing in a league billiards-match and was not yet home. Elizabeth had her mother all to herself and was gratified to discover how pleased and proud she was to hear of her daughter's academic success.

'There's nothing to beat education,' her mother said. 'My father always used to tell us that. And to go to a university – such an opportunity.'

She was thrilled to hear Elizabeth's accounts of the praise she had received from all her tutors, learned with pride of the high marks she had received for her essays and her recordings of experimental work carried out in the psychology laboratory. Elizabeth was struck by the fact that her mother had no idea of the drudgery and boredom of academic work, no inkling that to be an undergraduate was nothing very special, that the life of a student was not at all glamorous – in fact quite the reverse. Her mother would be shocked at the shabbiness of the average student's lodgings, at the squalor of the students' union coffee-room and bar, not to mention the slovenly get-ups of the students themselves.

Eventually her father arrived home. Elizabeth embraced him and smelled cigarette-smoke on his coat, whisky in his breath. His face was flushed and his eyes glistened with the effects of alcohol. Her mother went off to the kitchen to make supper.

Elizabeth, looking at her father as he sat on the other side of the fire, was shocked to see the beginnings of an old man's slackness about his features. He was, she reflected, almost sixty, but she had never ever thought of him as being anything but maturely debonair.

'We won tonight,' he said absently. 'Could be in the running for top of the league.'

'That's nice,' Elizabeth murmured, having no real interest in sport herself.

He lit a cigarette and coughed bronchitically. 'Time I gave it up,' he said, thumping his chest with a clenched fist. He was agitated, fingers drumming on the arm of the chair. He got up suddenly and switched off the big central light, a pretty curved wood affair with nine peach-shaded bulbs. Six lights still shone from the walls. 'Every single light in the house on when I drove in,' he said, two angry spots of redness in his cheeks, 'like Blackpool illuminations. Your mother thinks money grows on trees. Spend and God will send!'

Elizabeth stared at him and felt a faint rumbling tremor in the foundations of her life. She did not know what to say to him.

'Well! I think I could do with a nightcap. Join me?' he asked her abruptly.

She paused, uncertain.

'Whisky?' he said. 'You're old enough now, aren't you? Not a schoolgirl any more?' The derision in his voice was faint but unmistakable.

Elizabeth had never before considered that staying on at school was one of the things she had to feel guilty about. Her mother had insisted on it. Suddenly, she realised that those extra years in the sixth form had been a heavy financial burden on her father. Most girls of her age had been out in the world working for several years by now. Her hand trembled a little as she held it out to receive the glass from him. She had not drunk whisky before. It was laced with ginger ale and it was delicious.

'I hear you're doing great things,' her father said, his well-being returning as the whisky did its work. 'We should be proud of you.'

She smiled, pleased but embarrassed. She had never discussed academic or literary subjects with her father. As he often boasted that he had never read a book in his life, the pursuit of such topics seemed rather bad form.

'You're well out of the rat-race here,' he said bitterly, 'the darkies are taking over. The mills are full of them.'

Elizabeth had attended a number of consciousness-raising lunchtime lectures and debates on the immigration topic and was therefore of a liberal persuasion regarding the influx of Asian people to the manufacturing cities in the north. Her father's words seemed raw and brutal.

'They're doing the jobs that no one else wants to do,' she ventured as respectfully as possible.

'There'll soon be no jobs for the locals if the government doesn't come to its senses and stop them all flooding in. You ask anyone round here,' he said, glaring at her as though she were a stranger, 'the vast majority want England for the English.'

Elizabeth was nonplussed. She did not know how to begin to counter his over-generalisations, his appeals to 'common sense' at the expense of informed reasoning. Speaking with her father now, she was sharply aware of the transformation that had taken place within her. She wanted him to share in her widened horizons. 'Perhaps one could view it as a valuable opportunity for the races to mix together, to develop harmony through the sharing of work experiences.' She had been rather charmed by these phrases heard at a recent debate.

Her father glared angrily at her. 'These fellows getting together with our girls and spawning half-castes that nobody wants. Is that what you call harmony? There'll be a blood-bath.'

By the time her mother came in with supper their first full-blown row was in full swing. Her mother served out the coffee and sandwiches and appeared not to notice what was going on. But before Elizabeth went to bed she took her on one side and said quietly, 'Don't argue with your father, Elizabeth. Even though you are no longer a child, parents still deserve respect.'

Elizabeth journeyed cautiously around her father for a few days. She noticed that he was setting off for work very late in the mornings, taking very long lunch-hours and retiring to bed for a 'snooze' before returning to work in the afternoons. He seemed shrunken and worried and old, and he was smoking fifty cigarettes a day. She asked her mother if he was ill.

'No – he's got a lot on his mind with the business at the moment.'

'Why?'

'Oh, one or two staff problems. Men have these sort of things to worry about.'

Elizabeth was seized with anxiety. 'Oh dear.'

'It's just a bad patch. We'll soon turn the corner,' her mother said. 'You get these bad times in business. It's not secure like a profession. My father was always turning a corner, but we never went without anything. It was so exciting.'

Exciting: Elizabeth did not think so. Her grandfather had died very painfully of cancer at a comparatively young age, leaving her grandmother so poor that she had to rely on the charity of her children to maintain her standard of living.

As her mother seemed disinclined to be overcome with gloom and worry, Elizabeth thought she had better follow suit. In any case it was difficult not to be bathed in happiness simply by being at home again – enjoying the warmth and brightness of the big house, its gleaming paintwork and pretty knick-knacks, the freshly-cut flowers and the tasty home-cooking. Her father built huge fires in the grates, heaping on vast lumps of coal which threw out such heat that the family had to retreat to the far corners of the room.

Helena had changed from a twiggy schoolgirl with sparrow's knees to a coquette with long blonde curls and nylon stockings. She was constantly being visited by friends who filled the house with happy squeals and loud rock music. There was so much going on and always someone to talk to. Elizabeth tried not to think about returning to her lodgings after Christmas, to the cold attic and the breakfasts of limp bacon and tinned tomatoes that her landlady kept warm in the oven for two hours before it was time for breakfast.

Over Christmas, in addition to the lavish family parties

held at their house, there was the neighbourly round of drinks parties to attend. Her parents' house was the middle one of five standing in large gardens on the shoulder of a grassy hill, overlooking fields, with not a mill chimney in sight, for whilst the mills were no more than a few miles away they were completely obscured by the hill. The houses were all owned by local businessmen and were quietly perspiring under their burden of money. This was an area where re-fitted kitchens, bedrooms and bathrooms were a constant source of conversation, an area providing generous employment for decorators and plumbers, handymen, gardeners and cleaners. Getting staff had not yet become a serious problem, although the signs of insurgence in the ranks were there – as noted by Colonel Clyde, their next-door neighbour, who after dispensing and drinking several sherries remarked upon the fact that their cleaning-woman had just had a telephone installed. General shocked disapproval was expressed despite the fact that all those commenting possessed an ivory phone and at least two extensions (possibly of differing colours).

'Now then, dear, what is it you're studying?' Colonel Clyde asked Elizabeth, not pausing to be informed. 'You're looking jolly nice and pretty, anyway. That's what I like to see. Don't go spoiling yourself and coming back a "lefty" blue-stocking, eh? You won't let her do that, will you?' he said to her mother, raising a coyly admonishing eyebrow.

Elizabeth's mother laughed charmingly, smiling at Elizabeth with an indulgent conspiracy that she understood to be of an entirely female nature. Her mother had always stressed the desirability of feminity – and here was a chance to put it into practice. Elizabeth understood that she was expected to smile and be a nice, pretty, good, not-too-clever, non-argumentative girl. The men would expect her to want to be like that – because that was the way to make them like her. And her mother would expect her to be like that, because that was what she was used to, because that was what had worked for her.

Elizabeth looked around at the assembled company. The men were all grey- or navy-suited and when they were not braying with confident laughter their faces became closed and solemn. They clearly had weighty and

mysterious matters on their minds. There was a quality of
elusiveness and inaccessibility about them, because every
day they vanished into an unknown world of decision-
making and dealing, and the heavy matters of tax and
profit. The men were to do with the creation of money, and
in this world money was accorded the same respect as God.
The females in contrast were lightweight and colourfully
clad. Their world was known and open to Elizabeth, a world
both sparkling and predictable. The women were to do with
the frivolous disposal of money – but only in carefully
prescribed areas, as approved by their husbands, and only
in return for domestic services which the men considered
basically too demeaning to perform, services which they
secretly despised the women for carrying out. The women
were really rather like children, Elizabeth thought, an
entirely new rebellion rising suddenly in her throat.

There were many things Elizabeth wanted to say but she
knew that she must not say them. Her parents seemed to
like the Clydes quite a lot. Her mother said she had never
seen a carpet as beautiful as theirs anywhere.

'Indian,' said the Colonel's lady. 'We brought it back from
Bombay. You can't buy that kind of quality here.'

'We were in India for ten years, you know,' the Colonel
said, introducing a topic of conversation which rapidly and
nastily turned to the subject of emigration from the Indian
continent to Yorkshire. Elizabeth felt her heart beginning
to thump against her ribs. She felt slightly dizzy and wondered if the sherries were affecting her. Murmuring
excuses she walked from the large ornate drawing-room
and wandered off into the house, through the maze of the
study and snug, the sitting-room and breakfast-room, until
she found the cool quietness of a conservatory overlooking
the manicured gardens and the wood beyond. A solitary
figure sat there – a man of around her age with a cheery
boyish face and a mass of bright ginger hair.

'Oh!' she was startled and annoyed not to find solitude
for a moment.

'Hello. Come and join me. I pinched a bottle and a glass
and got the hell out of it. The Colonel's a boring old fart, but
his whisky's good. Who are you?'

Elizabeth recited her name dutifully. She felt rather stiff
and disapproving, suspecting that he was tipsy.

'Oh – I know your Dad – he's an ace at billiards!'

'Really!'

'Yeah – I'm just a learner. He's taken me along to some of the matches. I'm Mike Lashley. We just moved in round here a couple of months ago.'

Elizabeth's mother had mentioned the Lashleys. They were reported to be extremely well set-up. Their new kitchen had over two hundred miniature spotlights sunk into the ceiling. 'Just like stars,' her mother had commented in awe.

'So you're the brainbox of the family then. I've heard all about you. I thought you'd be frightful – horn-rimmed glasses and looking like the back of a bus!' He grinned mischievously.

She burst out laughing at this double-edged compliment.

'What is it you're studying – English Lit. or something?'

'No – Psychology.'

Momentarily he looked genuinely interested. 'Wow – can you see into the workings of my filthy mind?'

'No.'

'Are you going to psychoanalyse me?'

'No. I'm not doing that sort of psychology,' she said primly.

'That's the only sort I've heard of,' he told her. 'I wouldn't let them push me into university. What a drag – all that studying. I put my foot down, left school at fifteen.'

Elizabeth was full of admiration. 'What then?'

'Oh, this and that. Buying and selling. I had my own business but the bank manager got a bit shirty. I made quite a nice little bit though, invested it wisely. So now I'm just enjoying the fruits for a while – getting in the misspent youth, practising billiards.'

What was it about some people, Elizabeth thought, especially men, that made them good at this sort of thing, squeezing the juice out of life without all the drudgery and application that seemed necessary for people like her? She longed to be a free spirit like Michael, instead of being so slavishly acquiescent to what was expected of her.

On the night before her return to university Elizabeth was surprised to be taken into her father's confidence. 'How are you managing for money?' he asked abruptly. 'I wish I could give you a cheque to supplement your grant, but ... things are a bit tight at the moment.'

'I'm quite all right,' she assured him hurriedly. 'I'll get a job next vacation – pay for my keep.' In actual fact she was quite poor and existed mainly on lunches of cauliflower-cheese and an apple.

He laughed, and again she felt a little dismissed, a little destroyed, as she had years before one Sunday afternoon in the factory. The laughter soon died away. 'I'm tired,' he said. 'Haven't the energy I used to. Can't keep the turnover increasing every year.'

Elizabeth felt as though she had been struck dumb.

'The outsize market is shrinking,' he joked grimly. 'The large ladies are on reducing diets. It's all thrown-together cheap stuff now – buy this week – throw it away next. That's not what my business is about. But it's all I know. I'm too old to change. I need new ideas, young blood.'

Elizabeth looked at him longingly and was ready to give everything up, the informed debate, the high essay grades, the prospect of a first class degree – even the tender regard of the Professor. She would become her father's right-hand girl and learn everything there was to learn in order to make his business sing with life again. When she was young and quizzed him about the business he used to say that everyone who started there had to do a stint of making tea and picking up the pins. 'Even the boss's daughter,' he would say slyly. Well, that was all right. She was quite prepared to do her share.

'What do you think of young Michael Lashley?' her father asked suddenly.

'He's very nice,' she said, surprised at this change of topic.

'He's just the sort I need,' her father said reflectively. 'I've asked him to consider joining me. I think that lad could just turn things around – make my business hum.'

Thirteen

'All right for some,' Ken said, sitting down beside Elizabeth and disturbing her perusal of the *Guardian*. 'You're looking lovelier than ever, tranquil and serene after a month's doing what you like. You single women; you've got it made. What did you do with yourself – fly off to the sun?'

Men had been saying this kind of thing to her for years – 'You working wives – must be nice having two salaries to go at.' 'You bachelor girls – having as much fun as the lads, I'll bet!' 'You divorcees – a job *and* the maintenance – you know which side your bread's buttered!'

'Redhill, actually. It rained.' She could see that the vacation had done little for the re-charging of Ken's spiritual batteries; he looked raddled and rough-edged – and a trifle menacing, like an ill-treated dog who might just break his chain and run amok savaging people.

'Our beloved Principal informs me that two of my courses are cancelled – not enough takers. He's a devious bastard under all that perfect gent act.' Ken's face was red with anger.

'I have a great regard for Herbert, and I never discuss colleagues,' Elizabeth observed sharply.

Ken fumbled with his coffee and cigarettes. 'This bloody place!' he said bitterly.

'There are far worse ways of earning a living,' she informed him briskly. 'If you worked in a bank you'd have to clock in and out. Self-pity is very unappealing, Ken, and it sweeps you into a downward spiral of deeper and deeper gloom.'

'I think I'm ripe for a bit of excitement,' Ken said, rallying and changing the topic like a scolded adolescent. 'A bit of living dangerously wouldn't come amiss. Might as well be hung for a wolf as a lamb. If this job folds up I can always hire myself out mending washing-machines. There's a national shortage. Doreen can't get anyone for love or money.' He fell silent. Gloom seemed to have overtaken him again. 'Doreen's got a job,' he said finally.

'Ah.' Elizabeth was less surprised than Ken seemed to be.

'She hasn't been in employment since before the kids were born.' He was clearly bewildered.

Elizabeth looked up and noted that the Principal was heading in their direction with his gliding yet purposeful gait. He moved softly around the Senior Common Room, a velvety cat-like stalker, whose arrival would invariably catch one unawares. He would stand, courteously awaiting a gap in the conversation, his quietly brooding presence having the compelling effect of bringing whatever other matters were in hand to a speedy conclusion, so that full attention could be afforded to him. Ken dropped his spoon onto the saucer with a clatter and looked up at his boss with a mingle of awed respect and sulky defiance.

'Ah,' said the Principal, 'just the two I was looking for.' His eye-contact was all with Elizabeth, his smile quite openly affectionate.

Her heart leaked a drop of blood for Ken, so clearly being dismissed by the Principal as a man of little worth. She had a staunch and warm respect for the Principal, in fact he was probably one of the few people she loved just a little; she wished he would unbend into a small display of hypocritical sentimentality and show some friendliness to Ken, for whilst his discreet ignoring of the Head of Community Studies was not an act of deliberate cruelty, it was one of which he was well aware.

'I have a meeting with the University Senate next week,' the Principal announced, pursing his lips slightly and rocking on his heels, mannerisms which Elizabeth had come to associate with the more serious side of him. 'Rather momentous decisions are afoot. I'd like to talk to you both informally beforehand.' He raised his eyebrows.

Elizabeth knew that a space in the diary would have to be made. This was a summons, not a request. She speculated on the nature of the topic the Senate were to discuss.

A mutually convenient time having been agreed, the Principal seemed disinclined to leave. What a very attractive man he was, Elizabeth thought admiringly, as she always did on observing his dark eyes and brows and his thick wavy grey hair. It was rumoured that he was near retiring age and, if so, he was certainly wearing well – could knock spots off most of the Senior Common Room's forty-year-olds for straight sex-appeal, before one even began to consider the awesome charisma that emanated from a mind that was sensitive and expanded, that had accumulated not only exceptional knowledge but also remarkable wisdom – qualities which Elizabeth had not often noticed existing together. She remembered that his wife had been admitted to hospital before the vacation. 'How is Hannah?' she enquired.

He looked towards the windows through which could be seen the suave decorum of the college's lawns, then turned back and said, 'She's dying. It can't be very long now.'

Elizabeth gazed at his departing back, stirred with shock and compassion. 'Oh God!' she whispered.

Ken sighed, stopped short from making some sharp comments about the momentous decisions of the Senate. 'He's a cool customer,' he said wonderingly, 'carrying on as normal when his wife's at death's door.'

'What else is there to do? Should he be wailing and wringing his hands, or leaping forth into battle brandishing a sword at the Angel of Death?'

Ken shot her a look that said, 'You're weird, you're not like normal people.' She knew that was what the look said, because it was exactly the kind of look her mother used to give her when she trotted out her newly-acquired psychological theory – except that her mother used to say out loud what she felt.

'Mmm, well … this Senate business,' Ken ventured, having given due acknowledgement to the other business. 'Sounds like a head-roll job to me.'

Elizabeth feared that it did. And it'll be 'thee or me' she thought, reminded of one of her father's little sayings. She took a covert glance at Ken's strained, uncertain features and felt that familiar mingle of compassion and vexation.

*

Unashamedly, without any misgivings or reservation, Elizabeth set herself out to please Colin as he had never been pleased before. He had gone away from her and he had returned – of his own free will – thereby giving her all the happiness she could expect. He would go away in the summer and most likely *not* return, but that prospect she felt now that she could bear. They would part with sadness and wistfulness and she would grieve a little. But there would be no regret or bitterness on account of a job only partly done. Their business would be completed.

Out of her own new-found sense of fulfilment, her joy at being reunited with him, she began to understand a little more about Colin's capacity for being pleasured and cared for, to appreciate how this stemmed, not from selfishness, as she had originally and simplistically thought, but rather from that quality that had first drawn her to him; that conviction of being a part of things, that cheery unruffled savouring of life as though it were his right. She was sure that Colin had never been perplexed and troubled with the issue of being Colin – nor was ever likely to be – whilst she, regarding the issue of being Elizabeth, was even now in a state of confusion, the reasons for which were embedded in her history.

She reflected on the origins of Colin, on how his parents would have created and wanted him in a climate of joy, on how he had sprung from the loins of a loving mother who had cared for him so tenderly; flesh of her flesh, bone of her bone. But her own parents, those unseen, uneventuated figures of whom she knew virtually nothing – beyond the fact that they had been no more than children themselves when they made the terrible mistake of conceiving her – those young parents would have reacted with fear and horror when they discovered that a new life had been activated by their pubertal experimenting. Her mother, her natural child-mother, had made the simple kind of mistake that today would most likely end in abortion. She had had to endure the shame and terror and pain of pregnancy and childbirth, had been delivered of a baby – and then given it away. Maybe she had torn her heart out in doing so – but for the child, for all those ill-conceived children, the primary rejection must surely have been crucial. The child's first most primitive questions would undoubtedly have been concerned with the notion of being a trespasser at the great party of life – with the right to exist at all.

Ah, Colin, Colin, thought Elizabeth, stretched beneath him, her flesh covered by his, how much you are giving me, how grateful I am.

Colin raised himself from the drugged state into which she had reduced him and began to stroke her from her shoulder-blades to her long white thighs. 'Is there *anything* you wouldn't do?' he asked curiously.

'With you, probably not.'

'You're amazing.' He supported his weight on his elbow and looked down at her. 'How many lovers before me?'

It had always surprised her that he had not asked before. 'Too few,' she replied, not flippant – deadly serious.

He chuckled. 'Were they any good?'

She knew there was no need to answer. He was clearly perfectly confident of having beaten the lot of them into a cocked hat. He threw himself onto his back and stared up at the ceiling. 'I'm turning into a lazy slob,' he announced abruptly. 'Improvements are long overdue.'

She simply laughed at him. 'Really?'

'Mmm. In mind and body. Starting tomorrow!'

'Oh my dear!' Her voice was ripe with indulgent fondness. Lazy, loutish, laughing Colin. Her only true fleshly link. She kissed his face and shivered with the naked tenderness she felt towards him.

Fourteen

In her second undergraduate year Elizabeth, now twenty, was hard-working, self-sufficient, lonely and troubled by a constant latent anxiety about the financial situation of the family she was absent from.

Michael Lashley's incorporation into the business (going straight onto sales and management and not being required to pick up a single pin) had done a lot to cheer her father up, but done nothing to halt the alarming progress of the decline in profits.

Arriving home at the start of each vacation, Elizabeth's heart sank as she noted the steady decline in the state of the house and grounds. Some of the mock-Tudor beams were rotting and perilously near to falling from the high gables, the paintwork was flaking and peeling and the gutters choked with moss. Inside the house, things were wearing out and not being repaired and replaced. Only three rings on the cooker worked and a hinge had fallen off the front door so that only the side entrance could be used. Her father's once beautiful Rover car stood on the drive, unwashed and rusting, and beyond it the huge garden stretched wild and rampant. The hundreds of rose trees, once strapped neatly to stakes by the part-time gardener, now sagged untidily, their stems throttled and quenched by greedy creepers.

Her father persisted in the optimism and good spirits occasioned by the presence of his new young co-director, and her mother, whilst irritated by the increasing idiosyncracies of the fabric of the house, seemed to hold to the view that they were simply in that tricky process of 'turning the corner', that soon things would be on the up and up and prosperity return.

Elizabeth did not share their optimism. Although

ignorant about the details of the dwindling sales and turnover, she had a bad feeling about the way things were going. She was now beginning to be rather frightened.

Her academic studies ground on, still, in the main, tedious and of little apparent relevance to real life. The closest she got to gaining an insight into the human psyche came in a course entitled 'Abnormal Psychology' which consisted of a brief series of lectures and a number of visits to the local psychiatric hospital, a grim Victorian pile – filled with hollow, fetid corridors where rocking, grey-faced figures sat in hunched, drugged lifelessness and sinister with locked doors beyond which an assortment of scuffles and moans could be heard. Elizabeth's nostrils filled with the gamy-sweet fragrance of pathology and she was nauseous with horror and pity.

She supposed that now, at last, she was being shown *life* – but it was like being lowered to the seabed without an oxygen mask or any preparation. On the evenings of the visits to the hospital she was never able to eat any supper.

Elizabeth's mother had been most perturbed to hear of her daughter's exposure to what she considered 'the sordid side of life'. 'I think it's wrong for young people to be concerned with that kind of thing. I hope you're not in any danger?'

Elizabeth understood that her mother liked to think of her as being on the brink of some shining and dainty existence where there would be no greyness or squalor or pain – nor any of the bitter rapture connected with the discovery of reality. She was beginning to apprehend that there was an ever-widening discrepancy between her own gestating aspirations and those her mother cherished on her behalf. This was only dimly perceived by Elizabeth who did not, at this stage, link it up with her occasional unexplained feelings of irritation and displeasure regarding her mother's views.

Widening the aperture of this self-illumination was a new friend called Hilary. Hilary had temporarily joined the second-year psychology course on a grace-and-favour basis, her husband being Professor of Physiology and a close friend of Elizabeth's own admired and beloved Professor of Psychology. 'Oh dear, I'm an impostor,' Hilary would say apologetically, 'I hope no one will mind.'

Far from minding, none of the students seemed to notice
Hilary's presence. She was separated from them by an age
gap so large as to render her invisible. She had four
children ranging from twenty-four to twelve. She
belonged to that older generation who were sagging and
wrinkled and not connected in any way with the
beer-drinking, lecture-cutting, bridge-playing undergraduates who were having difficulty hauling themselves out
of their teens.

Hilary was tall and fresh-faced and big-boned and wore
unsmart tweedy clothes of the most compelling appeal.
Elizabeth wanted to throw away all her hobble skirts and
tight sweaters and stiletto heels, all her clumsy attempts at
black-stockinged, flat-heeled intellectualism, and start all
over again so she could look like Hilary. Except you
couldn't buy Hilary's clothes or her 'look', any more than
you could recreate a drawing-room of the past from an
assortment of period pieces. Hilary's clothes were what
they were because *she* had lived in them, because whilst
they had surrounded her body her brain had teemed with
all the thoughts that came spilling out in abundance on
Elizabeth's fascinated ears. Hilary talked about everything:
childbirth, politics, poetry, natural history, physiology, sex
– oh most especially sex. 'I loved having the children,' she
told Elizabeth as they sped towards the psychiatric hospital
on the upper deck of a lurching, roaring bus. 'Giving
birth, breast-feeding. In fact I loved everything to do with
sex.' Her firm, clear voice carried down the length of the
bus and she flushed, realising that she had caused a small
stir. 'Oh dear,' she murmured, rueful but still smiling.

Elizabeth was charmed. No adult in her social circle at
home ever mentioned sex. It was an activity which hovered
beneath the surface of niceness and cleanness, something
which clearly occurred – witness the little dynasties to
prove it – but which was hidden, mysterious and
distasteful. Elizabeth herself only knew what she did by the
piecing together of third form biology notes on
mammalian reproduction with the information in a
woman's magazine pamphlet which she had sent for in the
reassuring knowledge that it would be despatched to her
in the inevitable plain brown wrapper. She had never
touched or been touched by a boy. She longed for that

touch – but knew that it would make her mother displeased
and unhappy. Even the minor misdemeanour of smoking a
cigarette in her room in the last vacation had caused her
mother some distress and heavy mention of idols with feet
of clay. But here was Hilary; wise, informed, sensible,
grown-up – giving permission not only for the partaking,
but for the enjoyment of sex just for its own sake.

Hilary had such an appetite for life. She shrank from
nothing, shirked no issue. She and her husband seemed to
exist in an atmosphere of rich communication. Hilary
would report on their conversations. 'Vernon and I were
discussing the bloodbrain barrier in bed this morning,' she
said, 'and I was wondering how one could apply that
concept to these poor mutilated psychiatric patients ...'

Elizabeth was aware of being afforded another glimpse
into a life totally different from the one she knew.
Uncomfortably, traitorously, she concluded that for an
undergraduate a trade background could not help but
constitute an educational handicap.

Hilary invited her for dinner. She lived in a Victorian
villa filled with draughts and the wholesome fragrance of
beeswax polish which came from tins, not aerosols.
Elizabeth had not experienced a house like Hilary's
before. In Hilary's house all the outlines were blurred and
softened, magical and exotic like fur in front of a light.
Whereas, in her own house, everything was sharp-edged
and splashed with colour, here everything was in the tones
of nature – brown and rust and pond-green. The lighting
was soft to the point of dimness, no more than isolated
pools of gold falling from bronze-shaded brass
candlesticks with not a central fitting or wall-bracket in
sight. Elizabeth stared around her and knew that her
mother would have condemned the place as dark and
dowdy, would have stared appalled at the lumpy, faded
chairs and sofas with their covers of old silk and tapestry
bedspreads, would have longed to roll up the assortment
of dark-hued rugs and mats and cover the gleaming
wooden floorboards with a thick layer of silver wall-to-wall
Wilton. Staring at an Edwardian jug bursting with a
randomly placed nodding bunch of daffodils and palm,
Elizabeth, thoroughly schooled in the arrangement of stiff
chrysanthemums in laurel and Oasis, felt herself falling in

love with the place. She longed to feel at ease there. She understood instinctively, that the things in Hilary's house were valued for other reasons than their being smart or fashionable or new or expensive.

Hilary's husband Vernon (he who discussed the blood-brain barrier over his morning tea) gave her a large sherry in a fluted Victorian glass. Whilst Hilary was in the kitchen, appearing occasionally for more sherry and an up-date on the conversation, Vernon spoke with Elizabeth on a variety of topics, giving every indication that he considered her to be able and well-informed, and by implication inviting her to express opinions which he showed every sign of respecting.

He shared some of the qualities of her Professor but was quieter, less charismatic, less handsome. She felt no desire to work hard to please or entertain him. He made her feel good enough to be just as she was.

An assortment of young people came in and out of the room — some of them, presumably, being Hilary and Vernon's children. They all seemed to lead independent lives.

Over dinner it became clear that reasoned discourse played a large part in Hilary and Vernon's relationship. They talked to each other in a way that struck Elizabeth as man to man; the wife's opinion, even on quite serious topics, having equal weight to the husband's. She knew intuitively that Vernon would never make denigrating or indulgent remarks about the female sex, that it was unthinkable to consider his ever rising to his feet and proposing a toast 'to the ladies, God bless 'em.'

She drank a lot of his *Sunday Times* Club wine and began to entertain bold plans about her future. She saw it opening up before her, heady and intoxicating, filled with choices, freed from the constraints of tractability and assent. In a flash of insight she understood that compliance to the will of others is an option, that there are alternative ways of behaving which are perfectly moral and acceptable.

'Did you say you had just the one younger sister, Elizabeth?' Hilary asked as she cut into a cunningly constructed pudding of ice-cream and meringue.

'I did have another sister. She died when I was seven.'

The memory of Margaretha stirred like a sleeping adder. Elizabeth wanted to tell Hilary and Vernon everything. 'I'm adopted. We were all adopted. My mother couldn't have children.'

Hilary and Vernon exchanged glances. 'Oh my dear!' Hilary exclaimed, as though sympathy was required.

'It doesn't seem strange to me,' Elizabeth said defensively, 'I've never really thought about it. In fact it seems quite normal!'

'Yes, yes. It was a wonderful thing that she did – to adopt three babies,' Hilary said. 'But not to have babies of her own and then to lose a child ... Your poor mother. How very very sad.'

Elizabeth wanted to reach over and close Hilary's lips. She did not want to hear Hilary's voice talking of sadness. She had felt elation a few moments ago and she hated to feel it slipping away so soon.

'You must be such a joy to her,' Hilary said reflectively. 'How much she will miss you. Do you get home at all during term time?'

'Well, no. Not at all, really.' Elizabeth had always considered that the enduring of misery for a complete and unbroken term was the correct way to live an adult life.

Vernon and Hilary were both staring at her.

Hilary said thoughtfully, 'Children are such a wonderful gift. I cannot think of anything worse than losing one.'

Elizabeth felt all shot through with misery. Only moments ago she had stepped from the cool sobriety of the shade into a disc of sunshine. The brightness was now snuffed out – so soon. 'I don't think she's ever been really happy since,' she said, suddenly realising.

'Ah – and now you are growing up and leaving home. That is a very difficult time for a mother. There will be times when she will feel so lonely for you.'

Vernon reached over and filled her glass up. Elizabeth's stomach rocked a little. She had no more taste for the wine.

'What is your mother's profession?' Hilary asked, seemingly unable to leave the topic alone.

'She's just at home,' Elizabeth said, instantly over-whelmed with the guilt of having betrayed her mother in some way. And then a new thought came to her. If only her mother *did* have a job; what a good thing it would be for everyone.

'It's easy to get depressed at home,' Hilary said with a laugh. 'Vernon thought it was time I got round to using my brain again – and here I am studying psychology at my advanced and menopausal age. I've been *such* a lucky person.'

Elizabeth declined Vernon's offer of brandy, already feeling drugged and heavy from her consumption of sherry and wine. It was an effort now to join in the conversation, to make a pretence of being as lively and stimulated as she had felt at the beginning of the evening. Her yearning to open up to Hilary and Vernon had abruptly vanished – and that dismayed her. A burden of vaguely perceived restraints and responsibilities was settling on her, pulling her down like tightening guy-ropes.

Hilary and Vernon had gone on to discuss the locus of learning in the nervous system of cats; Vernon, as a physiologist, arguing hard for the role of the associational areas in the temporal lobes, Hilary, as a budding psychologist, putting forward more abstract and cautious hypotheses regarding cortical functioning.

They did, indeed, belong to another world, a world Elizabeth seemed unlikely ever to join. A small stab of panic pierced her heart. She felt alarm now, fear, like a bird trapped in a room where the sun shines brightly through sealed windows.

Fifteen

'Am I glad to see you!' Helena exclaimed, as Elizabeth, home from university on a weekend break, hopefully free of anxiety, dumped her case on the kitchen floor, her arms internally quivering and jerking with the effort of having carried it from the half-mile-distant bus-stop. 'Why didn't you get a taxi?'

'Economy.'

'Huh. There's not much of that here. A lot of talk about it. Dad goes berserk about Mum having the heating on full blast, rampages round switching lights off everywhere and then pushes off to the off-licence for cigarettes and whisky; then she goes into town to cheer herself up running-up big accounts in the department stores.'

'Are you worried about it?' Elizabeth wondered, noting that her sister seemed to be getting prettier and more sexy by the week.

'No – it'll come right, won't it? They must be OK, still keeping this keeping this house going and everything.'

'Where's Mum?'

'In bed.'

'But it's only half-past eight.'

'She's always in bed these days.' Helena inspected an immaculately varnished nail and plucked some schoolgirl dirt from the base of it. 'Feeling a bit low-spirited,' she said in a strained mimicking voice, passing a hand over her brow. 'Dad's playing billiards as usual but who can blame him? She's always moaning about how he's not the right one for her.'

Elizabeth felt as though she had been struck by the sword of doom. Anxiety and pity seized her.

'Look,' Helena said, 'do you think you'll be able to sit with her? I've got a date. He's picking me up around nine.'

'Do they let you?' Elizabeth asked, shocked. 'Go out this late?'

'Heavens, Liza, you're such a goody-goody. How can they stop me?'

Elizabeth had not thought of that.

'You were so bloody perfect. I could never live up to that – and I'm not even going to try.' Helena stared hard at her. 'You've never had a boyfriend, have you? You never had one when you were at school, I'd have known.'

'No – I suppose not.'

'You were always being such a nice good girl for Mummy,' Helena said wickedly. 'Slaving away for exams and doing the washing-up after her super high teas when the boring relations came.'

'Well they did pay out a lot for me in school fees. I suppose I owed it to them to work,' Elizabeth said, feeling priggish and uncertain.

'That crap school. They might as well not bother as far as I'm concerned. I couldn't care less. I hate the place.' Helena began to knot her blonde hair up into intricate shapes, spraying each edifice with hair-lacquer. This task completed, she smoothed a thick layer of pancake make-up over her face, pausing a little on the cheek-bone where there was a purplish mark. Her eye-shadow was bright green and at least four coats of mascara went onto her eye lashes. 'Try and keep Dad occupied as well, will you, when I come back. He's always out there shining torches and rattling milk bottles while we're necking.'

Helena was just thirteen. She looked sixteen and acted somewhere between three and twenty, depending on her mood.

Elizabeth went upstairs to see her mother who was propped up on a wedge of pillows lying quite still and unoccupied. 'Hello dear,' she said faintly, 'I'm sorry for you to come home and see me like this.'

Elizabeth kissed her, full of sympathy and concern. 'You can't help it. We all just want you to get better.'

Her mother sighed. She looked drained and disordered without her make-up and with her hair in a mess. On the table beside the bed were three or four empty glasses, white-rimmed and cloudy, two bottles of capsules and some indigestion mixture. There were cups half-full of

cold tea and crumb-strewn plates that looked as though
they had been there for days. The effect was distressingly
squalid and Elizabeth longed to clear everything up. Her
wayward, disloyal brain unexpectedly chose this moment
to conjure up an image of Hilary. A small voice in her
heart was crying out for strong, healthy, happy Hilary:
'You be my mother, I'm still a child.' Her eyes widened with
horror at the thought. The rejection of it was fierce and
instant. She looked at the woman in the bed and her heart
turned over with tenderness. This was her mother whom
she loved, her mother who cooked roast lamb and mint
sauce and wonderful apple-pies, who was gay with gossipy
titbits about clothes and celebrities. Whoever wanted to
spend all their time pondering on the blood-brain barrier
for goodness sake?

'I'm so glad you're here,' her mother said. 'You're not
missing any studies, are you, or gay times with your
friends?'

Elizabeth smiled. 'No.'

Her mother moved a hand across her forehead.
'Helena's not old enough to understand, and your father's
out nearly every night.' Tears glittered beside her
eyelashes.

Elizabeth was horribly distressed and overwhelmed with
compassion for her ill, unhappy mother. Years ago, as a
child, when she herself had been ill and miserable, her
mother had been like the sun dispensing the clouds on a
sullen spring morning. She had cared for her with such
attentive tenderness and dispensed all manner of
medicines and been so strong and knowledgeable in the
ways to make a sick child well again. Elizabeth would lie in
bed and hear her footsteps coming up the stairs and her
heart would swell with grateful love and the certainty of a
rapid restoral to health.

Elizabeth was aware of the doorbell pealing insistently.

'Liza, can you go?' Helena yelled from her bedroom.
'I'm not dressed yet. Make him wait in the kitchen.'

Stricken and shaking, Elizabeth went down to answer
the door and embarked on a polite and mechanical social
ritual with the young man who stood there. He looked
around eighteen and was carrying a set of car keys which
he inspected from time to time in the manner of a proud

girl checking up on a new engagement ring. Elizabeth's heart was thumping as she absorbed the shock of her mother's deep unhappiness and the crumbling of her parents' marriage. She felt desolate with her own power-lessness to do anything to make things better. Obviously she would have to come home more often.

Helena appeared at last and eyed the young man flirtatiously.

'Wow, you look terrific!' he breathed eagerly – and who could disagree?

When Elizabeth returned to her mother, she found her making a brave effort to be cheerful. She had mopped her damp eyes and dabbed on a little lipstick. 'Forget what I said, dear. I shouldn't burden you with that. Young people like to be gay and having fun. Now I want to hear all the news. Everything you've been doing.'

The next morning her mother was still in bed – promising faithfully to be up at lunchtime. Her father was politely welcoming, but distant and withdrawn. Helena was the only one in excellent spirits.

'The next time you go out, young lady,' her father informed her, 'you'll be back in good time.'

'Good time for what?' Helena inquired cheekily.

Elizabeth found herself appalled at this lack of respect. How could Helena be so *rude?*

Her father, amazingly, seemed not to notice. 'Good time not to make your mother sick with worry.'

Helena bent over her cornflakes. She was trying desper-ately not to laugh. 'Can I have a quid, Dad?'

'You've had your pocket-money already.' He dug in his pocket and assembled some loose change. 'There you are.'

'Thanks.' Helena shot Elizabeth a look of naughty triumph. 'That's the way to do it.' She finished her cereal and got up.

'Where are you going?' her father asked sharply.

'Out. Round to Rosie's – we're off into town.' Everything Helena said was bright and assertive.

'You're not going anywhere until you've cleared this lot up.' His glance indicated the breakfast crockery.

'Why should *I* do that?' Helena asked with undisguised insolence.

A vein in her father's temple began to throb. 'Just do as

you're told for once!'

'Dad!' she protested. 'I haven't got time. I've got to get changed.'

Elizabeth saw her father's faced become ugly with rage. He got up and pursued Helena as she made for the door, swung her round by the shoulder and shouted at her in fury, 'It's time my voice was heard in this house.'

Elizabeth sat paralysed with fear, sensing the mood of violence which had invaded the room. But Helena stood her ground and stared boldly into her father's face. He hit her hard, very hard – the blow striking the exact spot of the purple mark on her cheekbone.

Elizabeth cried out in distress. 'Oh, I'll do it!' She started to gather up plates and cups in feverish desperation as though that would make everything all right.

'I hate this house,' Helena yelled, breaking into noisy, childish sobs. 'I wish I'd never been born.' She rushed from the room and flew upstairs.

Her father sat down heavily on his chair and glared into the newspaper. He showed no sign of sharing any of his feelings with Elizabeth and she crept away with the dishes into the kitchen, feeling in some way implicated in Helen's defiance.

In the evening they went round to the Lashleys' for drinks. Elizabeth's parents got all dressed up and drank shorts and began to smile again. Being 'charming in company' as her mother called it, was effortless and automatic to both of them. They looked like a settled, affluent, self-satisfied couple. Helena had a new dress and some red high-heeled shoes and never stopped laughing.

'Your father is such a good boss to Michael,' Mrs Lashley observed to Elizabeth. 'We're so glad to have got him settled, you know.' She spun away, radiant and carefree, queen of her immaculate territory; the gold taps in the bathroom, the flocked silk on the walls, the miniature galaxy on the kitchen ceiling.

Elizabeth looked on at the two families, noting the smooth flawlessness of their social skills. She too knew how to charm, how to present an impeccable social surface. She listened and she chatted and she listened again so that everyone thought she was delightful. Yet she was simply an observer, standing on the perimeter of the group; an outsider, crippled by her internal solemnity.

She knew that things were deeply wrong.

The Professor called her into his study and asked if she would be interested to work again as his assistant on a new research project. Elizabeth was well aware of being regarded in the Department as the Professor's pet, the one chosen for his special little jobs, the one who would fall in with whatever he required.

But this time she really wanted to say 'No'. She wanted to ask the Professor to devise a project full of human interest, something, perhaps, with a bearing on the problems of families coming unstuck as a result of diminishing financial resources and the withering away of passion and affection. Just as she was preparing to frame an answer around the word 'no', she heard herself saying, 'Would you like me to draft out an experimental design – maybe run a pilot project first?' She thought of all the interminable statistical calculations and felt the weight of future boredom settle dully upon her.

'Excellent.' He smiled and hesitated a second before adding, 'I'm afraid there's no payment available.'

That was a pity. She could do with the money – and in any case it was usual for students to receive some remuneration for out of hours research work. So why not me, she thought, a slumbering adder stirring inside her. She had a vague sense of being used. Should she protest? Would Hilary protest? Her mother, she knew, would advise total compliance. She would consider it an honour to be asked, think it churlish to complain or express one's own view.

Maybe I'm just weak, she thought, a soft touch, a push-over. Maybe I should cultivate the brash, carefree selfishness I see all around. Instantly she rejected the notion, realising that she could never be comfortable in that role. There seemed to be no middle road between submission and wilful obstruction. The very idea of denying others what she thought they wanted caused her to seize up with anxiety. 'I'll start work on the design straight away,' she said slowly.

*

It was a raw, chill Easter that year. The daffodils trembled in the east wind; horns of yellow brilliance under a surly sky.

On arriving home for the four-week vacation Elizabeth found that her family had moved into a cheerful phase once more. Her father said that young Michael Lashley had some interesting new ideas to put into practice, that things were going along nicely and generally looking more promising. Her mother, on the strength of this, went into town and bought two spring suits and three pairs of leather court shoes on the account.

Helena breathed a sigh of relief and got on with a new round of boyfriends – mainly untroubled by her parents.

Over the Easter weekend it was decided to return the Lashleys' recent hospitality. Elizabeth's mother prepared a dish of ham in wine and peach sauce, made several creamy desserts and put on one of her new suits. She was happy because she loved entertaining and spending money on lavish supplies of luxury foods. Expenditure on entertaining she regarded as a requisite rather than an extravagance.

'Are you going to wear *that* outfit?' she asked doubtfully, looking at Elizabeth's Hilary-style tweeds and flat shoes which she had purchased from a nearly-new shop. 'Don't you think it's a little drab?'

'No,' Elizabeth said, proud and hurt.

Her mother looked unhappy. 'We ought to be giving you a dress allowance.' All the neighbours' daughters had one. They had 'little jobs' and huge allowances from their parents who wanted their offspring to look a credit to them.

Elizabeth held some vague, undefined anger in check. 'No, I'm all right. I can manage.' Sympathetic to her mother's unease, however, she changed into something more colourful and rooted out some stiletto-heeled shoes.

Mrs Lashley, in the event, outshone both of them in a dress that had clearly not been purchased in a provincial department store. She wore a queenly necklace of rubies and pearls which, in the context of the Gibsons' daintily crumbling drawing-room, had a certain ostentatious vulgarity about it.

Michael Lashley was as cheerful as ever – outrageously

so in the circumstances, Elizabeth felt, for she now carried around with her a constant and terrifying premonition of catastrophe. Nevertheless she was soon happily anaesthetised with his jokes and chat and laughter and, with the aid of a few glasses of sherry and some table wine, she allowed herself to believe in his vivacious optimism. It was a curious and tantalising security that he offered; when Michael said that things were going to be, not just all right, but super, great and simply not true, one could not totally dismiss it – however improbable and fanciful it appeared. She stared at him in fascination, dazzled and frozen into immobility. Maybe, just maybe, things *would* turn out all right. The business would pick up, the money would start to flow again, the house would be repaired and the big hedge girdling the garden would be trimmed into submission once more. She went on gazing at him, hypnotised by those pale blue eyes in their hem of ginger lashes. The merry, untroubled words tumbled from his mouth like water over shifting pebbles and she longed to believe. Yet beyond, dimly, she sensed emptiness, a dark void where she would fall and fall as though she had toppled into one of those black and terrifying mill chimneys which had filled the skyline of her childhood.

Michael noted the attention he was getting from the Gibsons' serious, academic, elder daughter. He was gratified and stirred. His audiences were not usually so conspicuously spellbound. He manoeuvred her into the empty snug at the back of the house, pinching a bottle of wine from the drinks tray *en route*. He told her of his bold initiative in taking her father's business into the mail-order arena. There would be substantial investment money necessary of course, but the profits would be phenomenal; they were quite simply onto one great big colossal winner.

Elizabeth was lulled and reassured as though she were a baby being rocked in a cradle. She was not at all surprised when he pulled her onto his knee and put his arms round her. 'Why didn't you go into your father's business?' she asked, reflecting on the silver-crowned Mr Lashley senior whose skilful management of rich landowners' accounts seemed to be lining the Lashley coffers very nicely.

'Oh, accountancy's dry stuff,' said Michael, reaching up to kiss her and placing a free hand on her padded nylon bra. 'It's exciting being in with your dad. He's terrific! Wish he were *my* father.' He made everything sound deliciously light and playful – even the desperately grey and worrying things.

Michael undid the long zip at the back of her dress and slid his hand inside her bra. The merest touch of his fingers – fingers not in any way skilled, but courteous and gentle – sent a great bolt of lust from her breast down into her thighs. She could hear the adults in the next room – parents, the older, wiser generation. Her construction of the order of things told her to obey them implicitly. Sexual urges, she knew, would be disapproved of – for her, at any rate. She understood in some vague way that Michael would be excused. 'No,' she said, pushing his hand away, whilst very much wanting it to continue its activity. 'No, no. I mustn't.'

Sixteen

Elizabeth was surprised to find things taking a turn for the better in her final undergraduate year. The Department put on a course in Social Psychology which offered some actual human interest, although she did not seriously believe that any direct analogies with life could be drawn from the little games played in the experimental laboratory. It was a great improvement from what had gone on before with buzzers and lights, however, and she felt one should be grateful.

What was more gratifying and exciting was the Professor's recent reiteration of his high hopes of her obtaining a First in her finals. Gradually she began to believe in such a wonderful eventuality herself. She stepped up her already punishing programme of study as though toning herself up to a peak of academic fitness like an athlete training for a track event.

The messages from home continued to be light-hearted and optimistic. Her mother's letters were filled with reassuringly gossipy news and a clearly discernible undercurrent of excitement about the new prospects in the business. Michael Lashley was so full of drive and energy, she reported, so keen, so ambitious – so modern. He seemed to have a knack of spotting up-and-coming trends and detecting gaps in the market just waiting to be filled. Mail-order was definitely the coming thing. Michael said that everyone would be shopping by post soon. He said that once they got a toe-hold in that area things simply couldn't go wrong – and she was inclined to believe that he had a point. They were keeping their fingers crossed.

Elizabeth attempted not to reflect too deeply on what was going on in the business, and, in any case, she was mainly out of touch with it now, not able to judge the wisdom of the plans that were being made or their likelihood of success. Her father had shown no inclination to share his hopes and concerns with her and she, not invited, had not wished to intrude. For Elizabeth the words 'can't go wrong' had a spurious ring to them, but she chose to hope rather than doubt.

Preparations for the finals examinations began to take over her life. The degree classification depended almost exclusively on the eight three-hour examinations at the end of the year; her research dissertation being the only piece of previously prepared work which would be taken into consideration. She became like one driven and possessed. The notion of a first-class honours degree obsessed her. It became the only thing of importance and reality in her life. Things of massive importance were at stake – far more fundamental issues than the gaining of the highest award the university could offer at this stage. This award, this recognition conferred by the outside world, was to do with the whole essence of her, was intimately bound up with those deep and intuitively perceived sensations of worth, was linked with those most hidden and most furiously suppressed anxieties about being a part of things – about being like everyone else. To gain this qualification would prove to her that she was a person of value, would give her permission to begin to exert her own will rather than always considering that of other people.

She hardly left the library. She rushed her meals. She never went out for a drink. She avoided friends and conversation; they were an encumbrance, an intrusion on her inner world of feverish ambition. She was like someone in love, except that the love object was not flesh and blood but a fragmented, only partially apprehended, abstract concept.

Her reservations and basic distaste for the subject matter of psychology ceased to be of importance. The subject itself became an issue of complete indifference. Psychology, as it had been shown to her, could go by the board. Psychology was no more than the vehicle by which she would gain entry into the élitist world of the clever and academic, a world about which her parents and their powerful circle of friends had no knowledge. Admission to that world would demonstrate to them beyond doubt that she had currency of her own outside the confines of being their child. Through the mastering of the teachings of psychology she would gain something that was solely and exclusively for her. It troubled her to think like this.

The week before finals commenced she could hardly eat. She lost half a stone from a frame that could ill afford to lose a pound. Sleep began to evade her. She knew that co-students were taking a heady mixture of stimulants and tranquillisers. She scorned medication. She had seen the results with her mother; a temporary improvement and elation, followed by prolonged spells of low spirits and tearfulness and a need to step up the dosage.

The exams, once they started, were enormously reassuring. They seemed to be well within her grasp and she attacked them with the zest and confidence of the well prepared. When they were all over she returned home for a few days before the results came out. Looking back, she saw those days as a brief idyll, a small oasis of untroubled happiness – lazy hours spent in the garden under a hot, early June sun (the lawns were clipped again, as Michael Lashley had convinced her father of the wisdom of investing in a power mower), drinking coffee with her mother and the neighbours by day and iced Cinzanos in the evenings when her father was at home.

Michael Lashley lured her out for one or two late drinking sessions in country pubs. He told her all about the growing mail-order initiative and she felt at ease in his company because he knew all about her family and the business and the problems. She let him kiss her in the spacious grandeur of his father's Jaguar Mark X – and quite enjoyed it.

The list of results was already on the board when she arrived at the university. The small group clustered around it broke apart to let her through. They fell silent, watching her as they would watch someone who is to be informed of a death. Elizabeth's heart shifted painfully in her chest, then began its familiar, sickening pumping. She could see that there was just one name under the First Class Honours section – all the others were under Second or Third. It did not look like the shape of her name. She knew even before she reached the board and the print came into focus that she must prepare herself for failure. And she was right to do so; her name was in the Second Class group. The highest award had gone to one of the stalwart bridge-players.

Elizabeth hid in the ladies' lavatory, huddled in one of the stainless steel cubicles and trembled with the bitterness of disappointment. When, eventually, she emerged and went down to the Union bar she was told that the Professor was looking for her. It sounded urgent. She went straight to his room.

'Elizabeth,' he said, causing her heart to lurch again, 'you mustn't be disappointed.'

She sat silent, bowing her head both literally and figuratively against the crushing blow. Second-class, second-rate she thought, consumed with self-pity and hating her own weakness for feeling that way.

'I've been talking with one of my colleagues at Birkbeck College in London,' he said quietly, fixing her with his wonderful clear grey eyes. 'There's a research project coming up there – a study on the development of twins. I have a feeling that would be more to your taste than the work we're doing here?' He smiled questioningly.

So – he had guessed. He had bothered to consider her preferences. Gratefulness welled up.

'There's a Ph.D. in it,' he added.

'But don't I have to have a First to do that?'

'You have a good Second – and my warmest recommendation.'

She sat with a bowed head, staring at the floor for a few moments. Then she allowed the joy to surge up and devour the pain and humiliation. She imagined herself as a research student in London, saw herself in the throbbing capital, a member of its great university – contributing to the growth of knowledge in the field of human development beneath the awesome gaze of the Palace of Westminster and the British Museum.

She would have a little room close to the college and although she would not have much money, she would organise it with care so that she could attend concerts and West End shows and dine occasionally in darkly romantic foreign restaurants. She would invite her family up to town sometimes and take them along – Michael Lashley also perhaps.

Reflecting on her time as an undergraduate she knew that she was very much changed from the girl who had started out on her course three years ago. Yet still she clung to the reassurance of home and family; that anchor still held firm. But with this opportunity she saw that it was now the time to cut loose. The prospect of freedom fizzed in her head.

And at the end of all this adventuring she would be a Doctor of Philosophy. Doctor Elizabeth Gibson. She could feel the triumph now, see the hands reaching out to congratulate her. There would be admiration and recognition and respect ...

'Why not take a few days to think it over?' the Professor suggested.

She shook her head slowly and smiled. 'There's no need. It's exactly what I want.'

He nodded, used to the impulsiveness of youth. He promised to send her further details through the post and then he made his farewells – holding her hand most delightfully for just a fraction longer than was necessary.

Elizabeth, exhilarated and carefree, telephoned home. She got a very bad connection and could hardly hear her mother's voice at all, it was so faint.

Her mother said, 'Oh, it's you, dear. Did you pass?'

Elizabeth knew that to her parents any kind of degree at all was somewhat magical and unreal. The fact that she had not got a First would make little difference to their pride in her achievement. She said a little about the research project, not by intent – she would have preferred to save the news until she saw them in a few hours' time – the words just came gushing breathlessly out.

'London?' her mother said, then, 'Are you coming home?'

'Yes of course. I'll be on the next train. I wanted you to know the news. I didn't want you to worry.'

Some faint murmurings came over the line and then the pips went.

Elizabeth sat in the train and watched the June afternoon roll across her vision. The sky was like stainless blue glass and the sun seemed to leap from it and touch everything with a brilliance that mirrored her own internal landscape.

For the first time she felt that she was in control of her life. From now on she was not going to allow herself to be used in a way that did not concur with her own will and desires. She was going to be in charge of her own fate, not buffeted about in ignorant helplessness. She smiled to herself. She felt that she was truly happy.

At first she thought the house was empty. She had expected her parents to come to the door to greet her. Instead they were sitting in silence in the drawing-room. Michael Lashley was there too – but not Helena. They were all still and withdrawn and stricken.

Elizabeth swallowed down the saliva that had rushed to her mouth. She was filled with terror. Where was Helena? What had happened? Oh God!

Her mother came to embrace her. 'Well done,' she said, more in politeness than conviction.

Elizabeth stared down at her. 'What is it? What's wrong?'

After a long pause, her father looked up and said simply, 'It's the end.'

She staggered against the sofa. Michael Lashley stood up and came to stand beside her, placing a steadying arm around her waist. 'The bank has foreclosed, called in all the loans,' he said evenly.

She did not understand. 'What?'

'The business has gone into liquidation,' he explained.

'We'll have to sell the house,' her mother whispered. 'What shall we *do*?' She started to weep very softly.

Elizabeth was horribly frightened. Her heart beat so hard it felt as though it would burst.

'Don't worry,' Michael said soothingly. 'I'll look after things.'

Elizabeth knew better than to be comforted by these words but she was touched that he should say them nevertheless. 'I've got my degree now,' she said firmly, 'I'll be able to work and help out. It's not the end, Dad. It's bad – but it's not the end.' Inside she was weeping for all of them, for all the lost hopes and yearnings and aspirations. Birkbeck College and West End theatres dissolved from her imaginings. She was aware only of the funeral quietness of the room and of the rampant garden beyond the windows where creeper-choked roses struggled to bloom.

'We don't want to stand in your way,' her mother said uncertainly. But Elizabeth had seen the relief that passed swiftly across her features.

'Where's Helena?' Elizabeth asked, already assuming responsibilities.

'We arranged for her to go out,' her mother said. 'We haven't told her yet.'

Elizabeth's mind was full of questions but she knew the answers were of little importance. What had happened in the past had happened. There was a future to get on with now.

Seventeen

The Principal's room was on the north-facing side of the college. He had elected to vacate the grand high-windowed salon on the sunny south side – previously most graciously and majestically occupied by his predecessor – a silver-haired maiden lady of the old school – in favour of this unpretentious and more sober office which was quiet and hidden away, with an atmosphere of industry and reflection rather than leisurely discourse over lemon tea from bone china cups.

Today, in honour of Elizabeth and Ken, there was coffee served in the standard Senior Common Room earthenware cups – with milk not cream. It was good coffee though, freshly ground, and there were crisp sweet biscuits to go with it. The Principal was not a man of ostentation, but he valued – and expected – the highest of standards, both in material and abstract matters. Elizabeth regarded him with solemn sympathy. He sat behind his desk, self-possessed and imperturbable as usual, but she was aware of the stern, quiet stillness of him, a demeanour adopted by those who wish to grieve in the most intense privacy. He was living through that terrible period between death and the funeral ritual when the emotions are impounded and very little can be knowingly experienced. Hannah had died three days ago. He had been at the hospital constantly in the final forty-eight hours of her life. Quite clearly he was starved of sleep and weary. But still he was alert. Ah yes, Elizabeth thought, there will be no question of slackness, no decline in awareness of exactly what is going on, no possibility of anyone taking advantage whilst he is laid low. There were slaty smudges beneath the clear grey eyes, but the gaze was as steady and penetrating as ever. In sadness he seemed to her quite disturbingly beautiful.

Ken, sitting beside her, shifted restlessly, communicating his unease. He had earlier indicated to Elizabeth his disapproval of the way the Principal was carrying on as though nothing had happened. 'Why can't he stay at home and lick his wounds like ordinary people? Does he think the College will grind to a halt without him?' Ken had paused and been unable to restrain himself from adding maliciously, 'He's a cold fish – no real feelings. That's what's at the bottom of it.' He assumed a firm and fixed expression, defying Elizabeth to offer one of her psychological explanations. There were times when a spade should be called a spade – a bloody shovel even.

'Perhaps he needs the distraction of work,' Elizabeth suggested, 'the reassurance of a daily routine.' She herself had certainly found it necessary to carry on with the mundane details of existence when staring into the face of death; it gave life a reality and tangibility that might otherwise slide away. She knew that Ken had no direct experience of death; his parents were both still alive and there had been no lost siblings. She knew this because she made a point of getting to know such things about those with whom she had regular contact. It was necessary information to help her gain an insight into their way of viewing the world.

Her current reading of Ken was that the Principal's state of grief troubled him in the way that one is disconcerted by watching a news report of those starving in the Third World when one's own stomach is contented and full. It is more restful and comfortable simply not to be confronted with that sad sight. To Ken, the Principal was behaving with indiscretion, flaunting his wound in public, like a man displaying the cauterised stump of a fresh amputation.

And, of course, grief gives one a certain status, a certain mysterious charisma. It commands respect. In Ken's book the Principal had all of those in abundance at the best of times. He had no need of this extra bonus. Elizabeth was uneasily aware, however, that the Principal was about to lay a blow on Ken which would more than even the score.

The Principal made some gentle murmurings about such harmless and innocent issues as the extension of the students' coffee-lounge and the newly-acquired collection of prints depicting urban nineteenth century industry which now graced the main corridor. Ken made boisterous rejoinders and emitted one or two loud laughs as though they were in the pub relaxing over a pint.

Whilst this exchange took place Elizabeth occupied herself in watching the Principal's fine long-fingered hands moving reflectively over a document on his desk ominously entitled 'The Way Forward'.

Eventually, the topic of the fabric and adornment of the building having been exhausted, the main agenda was embarked on. Opening his hands out on either side of the document as though blessing it, the Principal observed that change was in the air, that the College was in the position of having to work hard to justify its existence, that accountability loomed large, that cost-effectiveness was the latest war cry of those who administered government funds. He talked of the most efficient use of resources, of pooling expertise and considering viable alternatives to the present teaching arrangements.

Even Ken was quiet and still, such was the soft, compelling holding power of the Principal's voice. The words in themselves were merely euphemisms, means for cushioning the blow of the harsh reality of falling numbers in the student body, rapidly diminishing funds and ultimate cuts in staffing. Eventually the Principal got around to mentioning the word manpower – at which point he paused.

Elizabeth smiled at him. She was impressed with the performance and understood that it had been almost exclusively for Ken's benefit. Realising that the Principal knew that she knew this it was hard to keep an element of complicity from their shared glance. 'So, in practical terms – from the point of view of Ken and myself – where does the way forward lead?' she enquired evenly.

Things were not usually conducted as directly as this in the College. Senior Management spent a lot of time in meetings – that was what they were for, that was why they had few other commitments. There was a need to draw things out and not to reach conclusions too soon.

The Principal pursed his lips slightly, which had the effect of making him appear pinched and prim. A convenient façade, Elizabeth thought, sensing much of the

raw and primitive in her boss. The question of sex rose up
suddenly and irreverently in her imagination and a shaft
of lust trembled within her.

'It leads to the conclusion,' the Principal said,
responding to her frankness, 'that the College can no
longer support two separate Humanities Departments.'

'Christ Almighty!' Ken cried, entirely forgetting himself
and causing Elizabeth to wonder whether he could truly
have been so unprepared for this unpalatable eventuality.

Ignoring Ken's lapse into impropriety, the Principal
went on to observe that, most regrettably, the situation
would arise where there would be two Department Heads
and only one Department.

'So, we'll have to fight it out,' Ken said.

Elizabeth felt his eyes on her, felt the starkness of his
hostility – head-rolling was one thing, jockeying for
position with his genteel colleague was quite another. He'd
rather be thrown tragically and nobly on the scrapheap,
she thought, than have to compete with me.

'We may be obliged to advertise nationally,' the Principal
informed him calmly and without mercy.

Ken made a show of mirth. 'We'll be on the dole
together,' he told Elizabeth, making it sound rather
smutty.

The Principal lifted his chin in a gesture of reproof.
'Neither of you will be made redundant. There will be a
place for both of you on the staff – but perhaps not at
Department Head level.' His glance lingered a little over
Ken, marking him out for demotion.

Elizabeth had the feeling that Ken might die if he did
not have a cigarette and she was not surprised when he
made a hurried departure. She imagined him scurrying
away from the hallowed precincts of the Principal's office
and inhaling deeply in the corridor like a furtive
schoolboy.

'Oh dear,' the Principal said in tones that were more dry
than regretful. He stared reflectively out of the window
where the fickle and frisky spring weather was flinging
down hard white beads of hail on the cars in the staff park.
Half an hour previously a fierce sun had glittered over
well-polished bonnets. Elizabeth maintained a tactful
silence. She would have got up to go herself if she had not

sensed the Principal's wish that she should stay. He asked
if she would join him in a pre-lunch sherry. 'I've been
indulging rather more than usual in the last few weeks,' he
told her.

She tilted her head, gave a little shrug as though to say,
there is nothing to be ashamed of in that.

'Elizabeth ...' Again his hands moved in a graceful
gesture of supplication: 'There is a matter that is causing
me concern ... a matter of some delicacy.' He looked at her
with sad, troubled eyes.

Elizabeth sat perfectly still, her hands resting loosely
entwined on her knee. Into her mind came an image of
herself and Colin clasped together naked on her bed that
morning, moving together with slow, voluptuous rhythm
– doing exceptionally well that which perhaps should
never have been done at all. But her heart was entirely
quiet and steady as she waited for the Principal to expand
on his hesitantly introduced theme.

'There is, I know, no question of your discretion,' he
told her, 'and therefore I am permitting myself to seek
your judgement. I have the feeling that my own is not at
the peak of its objectivity just at the moment.'

She had never seen him like this, uncertain, vulnerable,
seeking support. She licked her lips apprehensively; how
she would hate to feel that she had failed him.

'Miss Baxter,' he said thoughtfully. 'One of our
second-year students. She is, I believe, in your Personal
Tutor group.'

It took Elizabeth one or two seconds to process this
information as her mind had been proceeding along a
quite different track. 'Yes, she is a steady hard-working
student. Is there some problem?'

He pursed his lips again. 'Clearly she has not thought to
go through the appropriate channels in communicating
her current distress. I was hoping she would have talked
with you ...'

Elizabeth had had several discussions with the wide-eyed
Miss Baxter recently. They had all been of an academic or
chattily superficial nature.

'I value your opinion, Elizabeth,' the Principal continued evenly. 'You see clearly and you judge with wisdom
and compassion.'

She stared into the grey eyes and said, 'I do not judge, Herbert, in fact I dislike the term quite intensely.'

'We all judge, Elizabeth.' His eyes kindled a little. He always enjoyed the diversion of verbal sparring.

She shook her head decisively, 'I prefer to think in terms of assessment – and maybe even that is disagreeably god-like. Perhaps the notion of appraisal is the one with which I could be most comfortable.'

'Semantics,' he smiled, 'terminologies.'

'Our lives are governed by semantics. What other code do we exist by?' Elizabeth loved talking with him. It was a luxury and an indulgence – one of life's bonuses – like making love with Colin.

For a moment they smiled into each other's eyes, then he said baldly, 'Miss Baxter has been putting it about that she has been receiving unwanted attentions from the Head of the Community Studies Department.'

Elizabeth recalled Ken's misquote about how one might as well be hung for a wolf as a lamb. He could hardly have contributed more effectively to his own downfall if he had consciously tried. Oh Ken ... 'Putting it about?' she murmured, seeking clarification.

'The clerical staff have sharp ears and keen noses in respect of these matters,' the Principal remarked in detached tones. 'When Mrs Parker draws something to my attention I feel bound to initiate some follow-up ...'

Elizabeth wanted to make her position perfectly clear. 'You spoke of judgement,' she reminded him.

'And you repudiated the notion most fiercely.'

'I would not presume to pass judgement on Ken,' she said. 'You must not ask that.'

'I would not presume to expect you to do so – I am fully sensitive to both his position and yours. You should know that.' The firm gaze was not without a leavening of self-mockery, playfulness even.

'But you might expect me to have a view, to take a stance.'

'My dear Elizabeth, what a member of academic staff does with a student of an age to make legal and moral decisions, is a matter entirely of his or her judgement – and I use the word now in its capacity to describe choice and discrimination.'

'You would take no stance then? You would have no opinion?' she murmured insistently.

'Ah, that is another matter. I would naturally have an opinion – and so, my dear, would you!'

She smiled. 'Touché. But you would not,' she said softly, 'expect it necessarily to agree with yours.'

'Ah ...?' He shrugged mysteriously. A spark of mischief enlivened his grave and weary features.

Values, Elizabeth thought. She recalled that disturbing period after her graduation when she returned home and found that the old values were so seriously wanting that they required dismantling. But there had not been the experience and wisdom to create a new system to put in their place. She had existed in a wasteland, a state of gentle anarchy. And had things really changed? Was she still a moral drifter?

The Principal stroked his sherry glass with a slow and rhythmical finger; silences caused him no anxiety. She looked up and smiled at him affectionately. They had forgotten all about Ken. They were simply enjoying each other's company.

Instantly she felt the old familiar stab of guilt engendered by having a pleasant time when someone else was having a bad one. 'I'll have a word with Miss Baxter,' she said, 'advocate a little ... discretion.'

He nodded. 'Good.' The matter was instantly dismissed. He filled her glass up. 'Hannah so much enjoyed her sherry before lunch,' he mused. 'I didn't always join her. I suppose I've always taken rather a hard line on lunchtime drinking.' He refilled his own glass. 'Life does go inexorably on, does it not?'

'Hmm,' said Colin, on hearing that she had been sinking Tio Pepes in the Principal's office. 'You better watch it. These lonely old widowers ... I bet he fancies you.'

She shook her head. 'Grief is a very effective means of stifling libido – at least temporarily.'

Colin sighed and raised his eyes heavenward, an amiable smile on his amiable features. 'Elizabeth,' he said, delving into the curve of her neck with hot and rapid kisses so as to reassure himself that he, at least, was still young and lusty, 'let's just stop talking for a while – OK? Oh, and by the way,' he added, coming up for air, 'what's for supper?'

Eighteen

On the day after she came home with her Second Class Honours Degree, Elizabeth went down to the local town hall and put herself on the job market.

The Senior Primary School Adviser – responsible for the recruitment of staff – looked at Elizabeth's pale and wary features and brought her in for interview immediately. She sensed the desperation of the girl sitting before her and guessed that whatever terms and conditions were offered would be accepted. The Adviser had a little desperation of her own. Teaching staff in the areas of inner city deprivation were currently so thin on the ground that it was rumoured that any person applying for a post would be taken on providing they had a head and four legs and could stand upright. Her scope for exercising personal judgement and power in selecting personnel were thus somewhat limited; a situation she deplored. Sometimes she went home in a state of bitter enragement, having been forced to engage staff whom she considered totally unsuitable for the job. Compared with some of the people she had taken on recently this girl looked to be of an extremely high calibre. However, she was in no mood to be giving anyone an easy ride. She frowned at the uncertain-looking applicant and said, 'You have no teacher-training. You do realise that that puts you at a disadvantage, don't you?'

Elizabeth found this woman who held the keys to her immediate salvation extremely severe, daunting and guilt-producing with her iron-grey chignon and her steel-framed half spectacles. She felt that she was back in school herself, asking for privileges which she did not merit. 'I'm willing to study while I'm teaching. Perhaps you could recommend some books.'

The Adviser permitted herself to be a little impressed. She disapproved of a system that allowed graduates to be let loose in schools and entrusted with the education of children having had no preparation for the task, but she also knew, from experience, that good, well-educated middle-class girls invariably did splendid work in the grimmest and most run-down schools. They had a tremendous sense of vocation, were like latter-day crusaders sallying forth into battle to right the world's wrongs. They would get married, of course, to doctors and solicitors, and drive all their energies into producing and educating children of their own – but whilst they were in service they gave excellent value for money. She informed Elizabeth of her starting salary.

Elizabeth was most pleasantly surprised. She had not known before that her graduate status entitled her to a substantially greater amount than was received by a college-trained teacher. She was sure that it was not fair, but that day her own need was such that she elected not to be troubled by guilt.

The Adviser looked through Elizabeth's qualifications. 'A psychologist,' she said with interest, regarding Elizabeth with fresh and genuine curiosity over the top of her glasses. 'We haven't had a psychologist on our books before.'

Elizabeth could tell that her status had rocketed in the older woman's estimation. This was the first occasion on which she was to find that people ignorant of the subject-matter of psychology were enormously impressed by it.

'The education service needs psychologists,' the Adviser commented. 'Once you've gained some experience in teaching you'll be able to take some further training and come back to us in an advisory capacity.'

Elizabeth stared at her. She had no knowledge of all this.

'Excellent career prospects,' the Adviser commented.

Elizabeth couldn't believe her luck. Ambition stirred again within her: career prospects, a socially valuable job, status, money!

She went home and reported on her successful afternoon. Her mother was delighted. She reflected, not for the first time, how her own parents had always stressed the value of a good education and the qualifying for a profession – even for girls; it was something to fall back on just in case. Elizabeth hugged her. She was ecstatic – drunk and dizzy with her new-found significance in the world. The imminent crisis regarding cash flow in the family would be significantly decreased – perhaps even solved – once her salary started coming in regularly. She would have the means to save her parents from poverty and disgrace.

Her father was not at home to share in her good news. He and Michael Lashley were busy at the factory, sorting out all the material assets that could be sold to produce a little ready money. Her father had warned them all the night before that he intended to honour all his outstanding debts and that there would be very little capital left over once that had been done. Michael had been openly opposed to such a noble way of carrying on. He said the family should come first; let the creditors go to hell. Her father declined to respond to these stirring words. He had gone away quietly into another room and drunk a lot of whisky.

At the start of the next week Elizabeth arrived to take up her duties in a school sited in the crumbling centre of the city where the crime rate was higher than most other places in the country and where a majority of the children looked forward to Monday mornings and showed a reluctance to return home on Friday afternoons.

Elizabeth had never seen such squalor and privation; had never had an awareness that it existed. She had heard Colonel Clyde and her parents' Tory friends nodding together over the whiskies and dry gingers and commenting that no one in this country was poor these days. She had listened but taken no view herself, not having access to the information that would enable her to judge.

She looked at these children, born in the affluent late fifties, and understood that whatever was the reason for their parents' lack of ability to feed and clothe them adequately, the result was that the children themselves were existing in a state of severe material impoverishment.

Many of them were dirty and smelled strongly of sour urine and stale faeces. Elizabeth sat with them at dinner-time and watched with amazement as they fought like wild animals over the second helpings of thick yellow custard. For the first few days she was revolted and outraged until eventually she realised that the naked greed on their faces sprang solely from the fact that they were very hungry. Fridays were particularly ferocious days when blatant stocking-up for the weekend went on.

Elizabeth returned home each evening drained and exhausted from the clamour and demands of these starving children. She came to learn that they were hungry, not only for a hot cooked dinner, but also for any crumb of adult attention – either positive or negative. Some of them seemed to engineer trouble time and time again. Elizabeth found herself constantly sorting out fights, bullying, extortion, stealing, destruction of classroom equipment and all manner of generally provocative behaviour. For these children anything was preferable to being ignored, and as most of them could not earn the teacher's attention through their academic prowess (many could barely string more than three or four spoken words together; the skills of reading and writing were completely barred from them) they would engage in a variety of deviant activities which they knew from experience would not pass unnoticed. They were shrewd and manipulative, and Elizabeth, for all her intelligence and education, found herself struggling hard to keep one step ahead of them.

She told Michael Lashley about the problems she was having. Michael was around at her family's house nearly every evening. During the day he was still occupied in helping her father with the practicalities of winding-up the defunct business. He had a knack of keeping her father reasonably cheerful and amused. Elizabeth had noticed that a large amount of whisky and cigarettes were consumed in this process and she worried a little about where the money was coming from. 'I've got to find a way of handling the children better,' she said to Michael, after a particularly harrowing day sorting out who had slashed a new anorak in the cloakroom. The culprit had been sullen and noisily defiant. The parent of the child whose coat had been damaged was so angry that Elizabeth thought she would have struck her if the Head had not arrived to intervene. 'In some ways they're so poor and limited,' she reflected, 'but in other ways they're really quite ... clever.'

Michael smiled knowingly. 'Native cunning, my charming innocent. You shouldn't need me to tell you that. Who's the psychologist round here?'

During this period of exploring new territories in the outside world, Elizabeth was anxiously aware that on the home front things were in a state of accelerating decline and deterioration.

At the start of the new school term, as the white Autumn mists laid themselves like smoke on lawns and roofs and balding trees, the house was put up for sale. Elizabeth knew how much the house had meant to her mother: 'The palace of my dreams,' she used to call it. She could not bear to reflect on how her mother must be feeling as the estate agents sized it up, their contempt barely concealed as they noted the tired, chipped paintwork and smelled the telltale fragrance of dry-rot coming from the timbers. In this affluent area they were used to pouring forth smooth compliments on delightful and luxurious appointments that had been made with no regard to cost. They valued the house at a distressingly low figure and ventured to express the gloomy view that the vendors would be lucky to get even that.

Both her parents seemed adept at outwardly ignoring the full horror of what was going on. To Elizabeth it seemed that they were witnessing the destruction of an empire – or the sacking of a city at the very least. But her father simply settled into a calm routine of drinking endless cups of tea, smoking almost constantly and making sure the fires were stoked up so there was somewhere comfortable to sit, and her mother continued to bake her splendid fruit pies and egg-custard tarts.

'I'm happy to take a back seat now and let other people

do the worrying,' her father remarked on more than one occasion. 'My needs are simple.' Some of his old sparkle resurfaced on the nights when Michael called and took him down to the Conservative Club to play snooker, but for the rest of the time he seemed to Elizabeth vanquished and diminished, shrivelled and rubbery-looking like the inside of a mussel-shell.

Some semblance of social life continued. Convivial occasions with the Lashleys were initially somewhat strained, as nobody quite knew who to blame for what. But after a few whiskies and gins-and-tonics things went on pretty well as they had before.

Mrs Lashley thought it was very jolly for Elizabeth to have a little job, although she was dismayed to hear of the problems with which she was having to deal. 'That such things should happen in this day and age,' she said, hearing with disbelief about the privations of the children in Elizabeth's class. 'I blame the parents, you know. People shouldn't have children if they are not prepared to look after them.' She spread her forceful, pampered, self-righteous hands in the air in despair. Elizabeth thought she heard the word 'feckless' mentioned. 'It's all these welfare state handouts. People get slack. They don't have to strive any more. And then, of course, mothers go out to work,' Mrs Lashley concluded, shaking her head sadly.

Mr Lashley was pretty sporting about the failure of the business. What could one expect with a Labour government in power, he enquired gallantly. He spoke in his customary jovial way to Elizabeth, but she could see that he was wary of her now, that for him, she was more heavily tarred with the brush of her father's failure than her own modest success in keeping the family afloat financially.

Michael, however, was unflaggingly breezy. 'Cheer up,' he would say to Elizabeth, 'it may never happen.'

But it has happened, she thought, and there will be worse to come. Sometimes she glimpsed the road ahead, long and dreary, filled with work and responsibility. Perhaps it would be better after all to embrace her mother's fantasies of dancing and glamour and romance – with a barrister or a company director to provide the wherewithal.

*

The house took a few months to sell. Eventually contracts were drawn up. The original price had to be dropped substantially and when the buyers had their survey done, they required a further reduction because of its dreadful state of disrepair.

Elizabeth began to hate their visits; the newly-appointed consultant in gynaecology, his wife who had private means, and their clever, healthy children who sniggered at the weedy garden.

The problem of where to live now became pressing. Elizabeth had taken her mother to look at a number of houses; all of them found unsuitable for some reason. Elizabeth wondered if they were not a bit on the pricey side as well. Her father declined to be involved.

When the money from the house was eventually received, he informed them that it was all required to honour the final debts from the business.

Elizabeth's mother staggered against the table. 'You mean there is nothing left,' she whispered.

'Well, just a bit. Not enough for a house.'

Her mother began to weep very quietly.

Elizabeth experienced a surge of strength as though the Holy Ghost had lit upon her. 'I'm earning a good salary now. I shall go to the building society and get a mortgage.' She felt a trifle dizzy with power. 'We'll have a lovely little new house with central heating and a manageable garden.'

It never occurred to her that there was any other option; did not cross her mind that she might choose to cut loose now and have a life of her own – that this was probably her very last chance.

A few weeks later her father suffered a massive and fatal heart-attack whilst he was out playing snooker with Michael Lashley.

Michael came to break the news. He was shocked and crying. He had been truly fond of his former boss. 'It was very quick,' he said, 'honestly. I don't think he felt a thing. He just collapsed over the table ....'

Elizabeth sat on the lavatory and expelled all the contents of her bowels and then she was very sick.

When she returned to the sitting-room Michael was

sitting with her mother, stroking her shoulders. 'I'll look after you both,' he said, making a brave attempt at being manly and protective.

It turned out that her father had rather overestimated his assets. He left her mother precisely eleven hundred and fifty pounds – hardly riches even in those days, certainly not enough to put her mother in the same league as her genteel widowed friends who had fallen on hard times and retired annually to Tenerife to discuss, over the Tequila Sunrises, the difficulties of living on a fixed income.

Nineteen

Elizabeth married Michael Lashley and took him and her mother to live in the tiny semi-detached house for which she had managed to raise a loan.

She married Michael because he had shared in her family's disasters, because he was amiable and kind and because she felt, that as one of those fleeing from the sinking ship, he had a right to be saved.

Michael was ever optimistic about starting a new business venture. 'We'll soon be out of here,' he reassured Elizabeth, 'get somewhere a bit bigger.' He had one or two irons in a number of fires: buying and selling antiques, renovating vintage cars, flogging life assurance in a big way. If the worst came to the worst he supposed he might have to take a job, but really being employed was only for those not daring and bright enough to squeeze some goodies out of the system on their own.

He was invariably cheerful, and unfailingly warm and considerate in his attitude to Elizabeth's mother. In fact the two of them got on extremely well, drinking coffee and pottering around the house whilst Elizabeth was at school. They often had the sherry out by the time she arrived home around five-o'clock.

Relationships with the Lashley seniors were cordial but little more than that. Michael could hardly be said to have made a glittering marriage – unlike his sister who had picked herself an extremely wealthy peach and settled in an eight-bedroomed house in Buckinghamshire. The happy couple were visited very regularly by their parents. Elizabeth was overwhelmingly glad for Mrs Lashley to be devoting her attentions to her daughter and basically leaving her and Michael to get on with their own lives.

She was also aware of a coolness between Mrs Lashley

and her own mother. This seemed to have some connection with a conversation they had had prior to the marriage when Elizabeth's mother had taken the bull by the horns and informed the Lashleys that Elizabeth was adopted. 'I had to do it,' she told Elizabeth in some distress.

Elizabeth shrugged. It was not an issue that mattered to her.

'You see, if it came out from some other source,' her mother continued unhappily, 'it would look as though we were trying to hide it – as though there were something to be ashamed of.'

'Oh good gracious, I don't give a damn what the stupid woman thinks.'

'There's the question of children ...' her mother went on uncertainly.

'There is absolutely no question of children at present. I've got to keep on working.' Elizabeth could see that her mother was a little afraid of her in this fierce and determined mood. 'And anyway, what about children? Are you saying that the Lashleys might be concerned by their offspring's blood being contaminated by unknown factors?' She thought it all highly silly and amusing, but she could see that that was exactly what her mother had been saying – and that she did not find it at all funny.

She put an arm around her mother and hugged her warmly. 'Oh Mum, to me it's normal to be adopted. It's all I've ever known. It simply doesn't matter. And what other people think about it matters even less.'

'Do you know what she said?' A pink and angry spot appeared on her mother's cheek. 'She said "Oh my dear, you love them like your own, I'm sure. What difference is there?" '

The mimicking of Mrs Lashley's queenly voice was so accurate that Elizabeth burst out laughing. 'The silly old cow!'

'Oh! Dear me! Well, yes I suppose she is. I mean she wouldn't have said that if she didn't think entirely the opposite.'

'Quite,' Elizabeth said, who did not need it explaining to her.

*

Regarding the having of children, Elizabeth had been perfectly serious when she told her mother there must be no question of it. Not having children for at least two years had been one of the conditions of her obtaining a house loan. Whilst trying to get a mortgage she had found herself exposed to the most humiliating and blatant sex discrimination. Men in suits (Ah – how well she knew men in suits) gave her the feeling that she was a child seeking a grand favour. She had to keep reminding herself that she was exceedingly creditworthy, that she must ignore the impression given by each suited man that he was being required to finance the loan from his own pocket, and that any one of the companies in question would be damn lucky to get her as a customer. It was hard to convince herself, of course; her father had always given the impression that the ladies were a bit scatty as far as money was concerned – and her mother had confirmed that view in her own actions and philosophy.

They said, 'Why isn't your husband applying for this loan?'

They told her that only one quarter of a woman's salary could be taken into account.

They could not contain their surprised disapproval when they learned that her husband had no job or income and means – and was being supported by his wife. She felt herself much punished for Michael's inadequacies.

They had to agree that her salary was good and her job safe. 'But you'll have a baby,' they said, 'and how will our loan be repaid then?'

'I won't have a baby,' she said, mildly enough. Despite being the Swinging Sixties it was not yet fashionable for women to tell men to get lost and mind their own business regarding these matters.

'But how do we know?' they said – some with undisguised and triumphant satisfaction. 'What guarantees do we have?'

What did they need, she wondered? Should she have her reproductive organs hacked from her body to present to them in a glass bottle, pickled in formalin like the dead leverets in the biology laboratory at school?

At last she found a sympathetic face. It was a round,

pink and good-tempered face, the sort of face her mother
called homely because one could hardly call it handsome.
The body belonging to the face was soft and plump, and
though clothed in a suit, was not at all intimidating because
the bulges gave the game away that it was only human
after all. 'You see, love, there is a problem, because young
ladies like you do tend to get pregnant and old societies
like us tend to be very jealous of our money. Give me
something to work on with my superiors and I'll do my
darnedest to get you the readies.' Clearly he loved a
challenge.

She had already considered a possible avenue of
approach. 'Is being on the pill all right? I'll get my doctor
to write you a note.' Unaccountably she blushed. The
degradation of it all rose in her throat.

He coughed and looked away tactfully. 'You're on – and
if I don't get you that money by this time next week, I'm a
monkey's uncle,' he concluded, using a popular and
baffling little saying.

The whole experience was a salutary one. Elizabeth saw
no point in railing against a system that would take
decades to change. In the face of prejudice against
working women (a prejudice which came just as strongly
from other women as men) she felt that the only option
was to grit her teeth and carry on. The important thing
was that she was earning good money – and getting equal
pay with men. She knew that this was a relatively new
situation for women teachers and she was heartily grateful
to those people who had fought to make it happen.

Her mother and Michael were easy to live with in that
they preferred happiness to gloom if at all possible.
Sometimes her mother was low-spirited and lamented the
loss of her beautiful dining-room and elegant drawing-
room. She furnished the tiny through-room in the semi in
a style that reflected lost grandeur. There were all the old
familiar things – many pieces which had belonged to her
grandmother – so the place looked quite like her old
home, and Elizabeth sometimes wished for something
completely different to express her own personality. 'It's
all good solid stuff, you know,' her mother would say,
plumping up cushions and laying a linen cloth on her
gold-plated trolley in preparation for the visit of a friend

from the old days. She hated to think how her standards must seem to have slipped. But she was putting up a good show. Her friends never guessed at her true destitution. They just thought it was such a lovely arrangement for the newly-weds and mother to live together so amicably.

Michael was becoming rather hopeful of persuading an old school pal of his to pull strings and get him in as a partner in a second-hand bookshop that a friend of a friend was planning on starting up. 'It could be just what I'm looking for,' Michael said enthusiasticially. 'Could make a bundle of money – and I've always loved books.' This was quite true; he spent a considerable amount of the day reading adventure stories.

'But won't you have to put some money in?' Elizabeth wondered, practical and concerned. 'I thought the whole idea of having a partner was to bring in some capital.'

Just for a moment Michael was deflated, but instantly rallied. 'I'll ask Dad,' he declared, and on the strength of this bold plan he took Elizabeth and her mother out to dinner at a very nice Italian restaurant and paid by cheque from their joint account.

Nothing more of a definite nature was said on the subject but Michael kept dropping hints of good news around the corner.

He and her mother drank more sherry together and looked at house adverts in the *Yorkshire Post*.

When the electricity and gas and phone bills came in Elizabeth started to get worried. She asked her mother very politely if she could please remember to switch off lights when she left rooms and also be a little more strict with herself as regards the telephone. It was her mother's habit to leave lights on in empty rooms so that they looked more welcoming when one returned. She also liked to get her calls all over and done with in the high-rate morning hours as most of her friends went out after that, busy with afternoon teas and shopping and, later on, the theatre and concerts – activities which Elizabeth was sad to note were much missed by her mother who could no longer afford them. 'Oh dear, oh dear,' her mother said, terribly contrite, 'I'm afraid I'm such a burden to you. I think I shall have to try and find a place of my own.'

Inwardly Elizabeth was torn apart with pity. Her mother

could never support herself in a place of her own. Her life
had been most cruelly truncated and diminished. No one
should be expected to bear what she had borne. Death,
disgrace, loss of independence, poverty – well, relatively
speaking.

'And, in any case,' her mother continued pathetically,
'it's nice for young couples to be together – just the two of
them.'

Elizabeth could not deny this, but verbally that is just
what she did. She hated it that in addition to all her other
misfortunes her mother might feel that she was
unwelcome.

That evening she said apologetically to Michael, 'I really
think we shall have to economise – just a little.' She felt bad
having to say this to him because he was so good-tempered
and so kind to her mother. What other young husband
would put up with his wife's mother being around every
minute of the day? 'The bills are rather alarming.'

'Don't worry, sweetheart,' he said, 'there's soon going to
be a lot more money coming into the old coffers. You'll be
putting your feet up and having a well-earned rest.' He
took her out to an oak-timbered pub and bought her a few
gins-and-tonics to emphasise the point. And for the next
few weeks he entered into the spirit of economy by
choosing South African sherry in preference to the Dry
Sack on which he had been brought up.

Helena called in from time to time, dashing up from
London or Bristol where she was promoting cigarettes.
Her 'rep's' job carried with it a fat salary, commission on
sales, a company car, three scarlet uniforms, a leather
make-up case and a variety of sexual opportunities.
Helena had left school at fifteen, got herself a job, and
escaped from the sinking ship just in time, before it finally
went down.

She walked into the bright all-purpose room and took a
quick glance round. 'Nice little set-up,' she told them
cheerfully, but her eyes, directed in Elizabeth's direction,
said rather you than me.

Helena seemed to be thriving, much to Elizabeth's relief;
she did not think she could take on another hard-luck case
just at the present. She seemed to her sister quite
unbelievably smart and glamorous. She was very bosomy

and had shapely legs which looked gorgeous in the new short skirts. Her hair was still palest blonde and she wore it in a stunning range of adventurous styles. Michael and she swapped risqué stories and got on famously together. Helena took them all out for a drink and was exceedingly generous, prompting Michael to be even more lavish in his ordering than usual.

Helena was heavily into sexual innuendo. At first Elizabeth was inclined to agree with her mother who was feverishly reassuring herself that it was just a 'lot of talk'. But after a few opportunities to talk to Helena on her own she became aware that her sister was becoming more than a little sophisticated as far as sexual experience was concerned. 'What about pregnancy?' Elizabeth wanted to know. 'Are you on the pill?'

'On and off. And I feel a hell of a lot more sexy when I'm off.'

'Yes?' Elizabeth was intently interested.

'It suppresses desire in a high proportion of women. Haven't you read about it?' Helena chuckled at her sister's innocence.

'No.'

'Yes. There's masses of research going on. But in the meantime there's always the sheath and *coitus interruptus*.'

Elizabeth was quite amazed. She was the one who had been good at Latin in school.

'But think of the risk.'

'Think of the pleasure.'

Elizabeth wondered whether to confide in Helena that she had never had any. Michael was very gentle, very quick, very unarousing. He moved economically and swiftly within her and always had a climax. She did not really know whether she had or not. Perhaps it was because their room was next to her mother's; she had read in women's magazines that this could be a factor in female frigidity. The main problem seemed to be that Michael did not really like the warm moist parts of her body – certainly he seemed disinclined to linger there with hands or lips. Gradually she was becoming to dread his reaching for her and had even, on one occasion, resorted to the old cliché of a headache.

She was inclined to think that Helena knew what she was

talking about. She fingered her plastic envelope of *Conuvid-E* thoughtfully, wondering whether to throw its contents away. Then she took a pill out and placed it on her tongue. The risks were too great.

A week or two later she consulted Michael. After all he was the main party concerned.

'Of course you're not frigid,' he said gallantly. 'You're doing just great. Some women can't manage it at all,' he said with the mystery of authority.

'Really?'

'Mmm – can't manage to ... let him in,' he said delicately. 'Tighten up and so on.' He gave her a knowing look.

'I didn't know that.' Sometimes she felt ashamed of her ignorant innocence.

Michael gave her an affectionate chuck under the chin. He felt masterly and just a trifle lofty; heady and unusual sensations for him these days. 'Look, let me take the responsibility, I'll make sure it's OK.'

Elizabeth had the vague feeling that many women through time had been caught on this one, but she felt, also, that Michael had a right to be trusted.

'We'll get really randy,' he murmured lasciviously, nibbling at her ear. A sharp shaft of lust trembled within her.

She finished the sachet of pills and did not seek a further prescription.

For a while she managed to avoid love-making altogether through a variety of ingenious strategies.

The next time Helena came home Elizabeth overheard her and her mother talking in the kitchen. 'Elizabeth's very good you know ... but I hope you never find yourself in the position I am,' she heard her mother say. 'It's terrible to be a charity child. If I really allowed myself to think about my life I'd scream and go mad.'

That night Elizabeth drank half a bottle of Michael's sherry and then seduced him rather soundly in her black see-through nightgown.

Twenty

Elizabeth was frightened of the baby.

It was not solely its representing of new responsibilities, its being another mouth to feed, when she was hard pressed to keep her two current hangers-on in the manner to which they still dearly yearned to be accustomed, but rather its unpredictability, its mystery and remoteness. It cried and she did not know why, it took varying amounts of milk from her breast and there was no way of checking to find out if it was the right amount. Everything with the baby was alarmingly hit-and-miss – yet at the same time awesomely important. Making mistakes with a baby could be a matter of life and death. She told herself that some infants survived in the most perilous circumstances of neglect. For example, many of the children she taught had clearly withstood dirt and infections and gross neglect, but she felt nevertheless that she could never relax her guard, thinking that she was more than likely to be one of the unlucky ones who did her best and still ended up with a dead baby.

She had loved being pregnant. The initial shock had been bad and she and Michael had had some sharp words.

'You said you were going to take care of things,' she accused him hotly.

'Well, these things aren't foolproof.' Michael had looked stubborn and sulky, found out in an error for which he knew he was responsible. 'Anyway, I'm pleased. Aren't you?'

'My God – haven't we enough on our plates already?' Haven't *I* enough, she thought selfishly.

'We'll manage. It'll all be OK. You'll see.' Michael was so

eager to be happy. He looked after her most tenderly. He was hugely proud to have been involved in procreation.

Elizabeth went on teaching. She felt enormously well. She felt full of purpose. She felt as though she were part of a miracle, for inside her was this hidden, secret being. For the first time in her life she felt unconflictedly important, that what she was doing was praiseworthy and right and good. There was a sureness about things that had never been there before.

The actuality of the baby as a newcomer to the outside world was as yet unreal, too far into the future to consider. The baby's internal existence was the true reality, and that existence and the knowledge and feelings surrounding it were exclusively hers. They gave her the most intense experience of joyous possession she had ever had.

Nurturing this baby in her body was to do with the very stuff of life – flesh and blood and matter. And those were things which Elizabeth, as an adopted child, had been deprived of.

There had been no conscious sense of deprivation; she had not realised until now what had been missing.

The notion of heritage, of blood and line, had always been one which had held a fascination because she had been debarred from participating in it. For her there was no line. She had sprung from unknown loins and her origins were unspoken of and unacknowledged. She heard talk of flesh of flesh and bone of bone (as a child she had been subjected to much religious education and extensive consideration of the Bible, a document filled with blood and line and branches and begetting), but these were issues on which she could have no say, rather as a legless man demurs from entering into any discussion of the running of races.

Ancestry had been denied her – but now she would start her own genealogy through this seed growing inside her. She was the fertile ground in which the seed would swell and develop to create a whole new network of lives.

She began to feel very sure of herself. She was serene and cheerful and radiant and when she looked in the mirror she saw that the normally pale, thin face was now amber-cheeked, rounded and verging on prettiness. Is that really me, she wondered.

'Are you sure you're all right?' her mother asked anxiously. 'Oh, isn't it a pity you have to go on working.'

But Elizabeth felt strong enough to tackle a class of thousands, never mind the forty who confronted her each morning. She seemed to be gaining even more satisfaction from her work than usual. She was decisive and forward-planning, finding out about maternity leave and making the necessary applications.

She discovered that the condition of pregnancy conferred on her an entirely new status – for if all the world loves a lover, all the world positively adores and reveres a mother-to-be. But more important and unexpected than the approval of the outside world was the respect Elizabeth found herself commanding from her mother. This state of fecundity awakened in her mother an almost hallowed esteem that was far in excess of anything she had demonstrated in connection with her daughter's academic success. Elizabeth sensed that her mother was standing back from her a little, strangely hesitant and in awe. She was not able to pour forth the usual barrage of advice based on her own experience – because this was something entirely outside her province.

Elizabeth basked in the sweetness of previously unknown filial power. She felt a little sorry for her mother, some tender pity that she had not been able to conceive and nurture a baby in her body, that she had had to go out and acquire someone else's – for it was hard to deny that that must really be no more than second-best. She treated her mother kindly, took delight in sharing the experience with her, but never for a moment omitted to enjoy the fact that she was in an indisputable position of supremacy.

It occurred to her that she had, in the past, made the assumption that she would never bear a child, that she would be barren like her mother. She had a sudden flash of insight into the way in which she had existed in a pathological state of identification with her mother. She knew that motherhood and the baby would change all that.

In her mind, doors guarding smotheringly airless rooms seemed suddenly to be opening. In the shimmering fresh air beyond, little jewelled birds darted and sang freely amongst the high branches of trees.

'Look,' said Michael, 'by the time this baby comes along I
really will have something on the go.' His plans to further
an involvement in the bookshop venture did seem to be
progressing more hopefully than most. Certainly this was
the longest period of time that any one project had held his
interest. From what Elizabeth could gather, suitable
premises had already been acquired in a desirable area of
York, and the purchaser and his daughter were working
out how to fit the shop up and what stock to fill it with. She
also guessed that the father was extremely well-heeled and
was indulging a pet interest with an artistic and cherished
daughter. 'Paulette's just down from Cambridge. Got a
First in English Lit,' Michael had told her admiringly. 'But
what can you do with that? ... except teach of course.' It did
not sound as though there would be much likelihood of
Paulette's burying her bright talents in some fusty school,
getting herself covered in the fine dust emanating from the
chalk-face.

'Where do you come in?' Elizabeth asked him kindly.

'Public relations, sales directing ... you know the sort of
thing. Just up my street.'

Elizabeth thought it sounded like long hours serving in
the shop – which would not be up his street at all. She
refrained from saying so. She no longer regarded Michael
as a likely earner. He was a spender, not a getter.

She herself was earning a very respectable salary and
though it was quickly eaten up by the commitments and
extravagances of the household, there had never been a
time when she had been overdrawn at the bank or needed
to seek extra credit. She had even managed to save a little
and as the Lashleys had generously undertaken to furnish
them with all the costly paraphernalia needed by a new
baby, she decided that she would use the money to buy
another car. Her current vehicle was an ancient,
split-windscreen Morris Minor, rusting and idiosyncratic,
expensive to repair and not yet old enough to be of
interest to collectors.

Michael was most enthusiastic about the venture but
scornful of her low aspirations. 'We can do better than
that,' he said, observing the four-year-old Mini Country-
man she was negotiating for. 'We want something with a
bit more go in it.' He took her to another garage and eyed

an Austin 1300 GT.

'No,' said Elizabeth, using a firm tone with him for once.

She saw his eyes glisten as he observed the silver Jaguar standing beside the GT. For Elizabeth, dreaming of a silver Jaguar was a sweet and pleasant fantasy. For Michael, not being able to own such a vehicle seemed like a denial of that which was rightfully his due.

The baby came suddenly. Elizabeth woke one night to find herself and Michael drenched in warm amniotic fluid. The ambulance came straight away to take her to the hospital and Edward was born ten hours later.

There was no screaming, no searing pain, just a wonderful sense of being so much a part of things. She was exhausted at the end of it all and quite happy for the baby to be taken away so she could rest.

They called him Edward Michael. He had a squashed, rubber-dolly face and a glow of orange fuzz around his egg-like head.

Elizabeth took him home when he was ten days old. Her mother stood at the door waiting, tears in her eyes. 'Oh I hope he hasn't been cold in the car. Did you wrap him up properly? Is it safe for him to travel in the back on his own? I always used to sit with you and steady the cot. Has he had his feed? Perhaps you'd better give him it now. It's always best when they're in new surroundings to give them a little something, makes them feel secure.'

Suddenly things had changed. Suddenly her mother was in control again, her experienced child-rearing hands firmly on the reins. The balance of power was shifting; Elizabeth could feel it draining away from her by the minute.

Ah – now her mother was strong again, more so than she

had been for years. She may have known nothing of pregnancy but she knew everything about babies and she spared Elizabeth none of her wisdom and expertise.

Elizabeth had no weapons with which to fight back. Her ability to analyse, to maintain a distance and appraise objectively, to use her knowledge and professionalism, was of no value in this new situation. Motherhood was a highly complex and baffling business. Those who had mothered must stand as models for those who had not. The novices must heed the accumulated and proven wisdom of the good mothers who had gone before them.

Elizabeth, her body empty, shrunken and strangely still once more, felt as though she had served her purpose. She chose not to fight.

She was overwhelmed with the presence of the new being in the house. She did not understand it, and she hated the way it sucked greedily into every waking and sleeping minute. She allowed her mother to take the creature over. In any case she, herself, would be returning to work in seven weeks and her mother would have to manage on her own then. Gradually she came to feel that the baby was rightfully more her mother's than hers. Her mother loved it in such an unconflicted and unfailingly tender manner – and in doing so she radiated a happiness Elizabeth had never seen in her before. It was as though she had been given the most wonderful gift possible. New and endless supplies of energy flowed from her.

There were one or two arguments. The main one concerned the issue of breast-feeding. Elizabeth's mother thought it was a very unsatisfactory and basically outdated method of feeding a child. She, of course, had bottle-fed all her three and it had always been reassuring to know how much they had 'taken' at each feed. Elizabeth made a faint protest. Breast-feeding was one of the baby-care activities she quite enjoyed. She felt close and protective towards the baby at those times and was charmed with the liquidy sucking noises he made which told her that she was an efficient milk producer. Still, as her mother pointed out, she would not be able to breast-feed regularly when she went back to school and it would surely be best to get him used to the bottle now.

After a few days Elizabeth got some tablets from the doctor and bound up her full throbbing breasts. Within a week the milk had vanished.

The Lashleys came, bearing many gifts. Elizabeth's mother asked if she could be allowed to get the baby ready. He was in her arms when they arrived and Elizabeth stood back a little as though really the baby were not hers. 'Absolutely gorgeous,' Mrs Lashley said. She peered at the baby with proprietorial curiosity. She was clearly searching for something. It did not take long to find it. 'Those eyes,' she announced with satisfaction, 'just like my great-aunt Alice's. Isn't it amazing?' She plucked at her husband's sleeve, 'Look, the eyes, exactly like Aunt Alice – don't you think?'

Mr Lashley shrugged politely. He couldn't even remember an Aunt Alice, but if it entertained his wife to make these speculations he saw no reason to spoil her fun. He was really rather more concerned about his car. He had touched it on the gate-post when they left home and the scratch was quite bad. And he wished Elizabeth would be a bit more jolly. She was so terribly serious and tragic-looking. A strange girl altogether. But then she was putting up with Michael who, let's face it, was a bit of a disappointment. Mr Lashley senior never stopped thanking his lucky stars that he had been strong enough to put his foot down about Michael's joining his firm – standing out against all the motherly pleas.

'Definitely takes after my side,' Mrs Lashley decided, throwing her husband a playful and apologetic glance in case he should be troubled by his side having been passed over. With much regret she returned the baby to his maternal grandmother in order that she could graciously accept the champagne Michael had bought for the occasion.

Elizabeth was to find that whilst everyone adored a pregnant mother, no criticism was too harsh for the woman who goes out to work and abandons her child.

'I don't know how you can bear to leave him,' her colleagues said. 'I always stayed at home with mine for the first few years.' And so on. The school secretary was more blunt. 'Women shouldn't have them if they can't look after them.'

Elizabeth grew a horny coat of protection and got on with the ferocious enjoyment of her work. Job satisfaction was just about the only sort she was getting at present.

Her mother worried about Mrs Lashley's remarks concerning the unknown Aunt Alice and the implied message of the significance of inheritance and genetic factors. She spoke to Elizabeth on the subject whilst Michael was out. 'It isn't as if you haven't a family background as well,' she said to Elizabeth indignantly. 'And you have only to ask.'

Elizabeth stared at her. She did not believe it was as simple as that. To ask would be a betrayal of this mother who had loved her through her baby years, through childhood, adolescence and young adulthood. To ask about another mother must surely hurt her unbearably. She declined the invitation firmly, yet at the same time something stirred within her, something too vicious and unpardonable to admit to consciousness. It was not until years later that she confessed to a psychotherapist her bitter anger that her mother should have this exclusive knowledge of her roots, that she should know from where her soul sprang, that she should own everything about her – even her past. The rage festered inside and was outwardly manifested in her habitual uncertainty and generalised guilt.

'They were very nice people ... the ... your parents,' her mother volunteered insistently, 'from good upstanding families.'

Elizabeth felt her face become all set and stony. 'Nice people'. She remembered the phrase from childhood, heard clearly now the hidden message. 'Nice people – but not quite like us'. What did that mean? Social Class v origins? Should she feel shame? She smiled. Inwardly she saw the funny side and she really did not mind; in fact she thought it quite exciting.

It became interesting to speculate on that humble fleshly mother. How had she felt when she was pregnant? Terrible, presumably, as she would have known from the start that she must give her baby away. Elizabeth knew that this fleshly mother had been very young, no more than fourteen or fifteen; that gem of information her mother had let drop when she, Elizabeth, was still a child. It had had the effect of making the flesh mother unreal – like a character in a story. She must have been on the lusty side though, Elizabeth thought, to have taken such dreadful risks. The thought gave her a warm feeling of satisfaction.

Edward was growing steadily but by the time he was six months old Elizabeth began to suspect that something was wrong with him. He was not quite like the other babies at the early infant clinics, not as demanding or noisy or alert. In his eyes she saw a blank and dead look.

She said nothing of this to Michael or her mother.

She took the baby to the doctor and expressed some vague unease about him. The doctor tested the baby's heart-rate, took his blood pressure and checked his eyes and ears. Then he took a small rubber hammer and tapped his knees. Elizabeth dimly remembered things from her physiology lectures about the knee-jerk being an indicator of the efficiency of the spinal reflexes. She watched very carefully and tried to convince herself that it was only her own fearful conjecturing that made the responses seem slow and feeble. Even so, her heart began to bump about within her ribs.

The doctor repeated the exercise, stood in silent reflection for a few moments – and then said, 'He's OK. I can't find anything to be concerned about.' He looked at the mother's white and stricken face and told her that she should not worry.

But she worried. She worried that the baby might be ill, and that she would not be able to cope with her mother's chronic anxiety. She worried that the baby might be damaged and handicapped in some way and that Michael would be devastated. She worried that the baby might die because of something she did or did not do – and that her mother would never forgive her.

Two months later Edward had a convulsion after his evening bottle. He became still and frozen and his eyes assumed a fixed and unseeing stare. Then his body began to contort and saliva fizzed in his mouth. Terrible watery gurgles came from his throat. Her mother leapt up from the chair where she had been reading the evening paper and could not stop herself rushing across the room and snatching him from Elizabeth's knee. 'He'll choke,' she cried in despair, laying the baby on his side on the floor and hitting his back. 'Find a pencil,' she shrieked, 'to stick in his mouth.' Mercifully, before this superstitious and dangerous ploy could be carried out, the drama was suddenly over and the baby dropped off into a deep sleep.

'You must call the doctor immediately,' Elizabeth's mother said authoritatively to the shocked young parents, as though they would not have thought of it themselves.

The doctor referred the baby to the consultant paediatrician at the local hospital who explained that it would be necessary to carry out certain investigations, one of which would involve taking readings of the electrical activity in the baby's brain.

'You mean an electroencephalograph?' Elizabeth asked. She had been doing some background reading – once again drawing on information from her physiological psychology course.

'Yes.'

Beside her, Michael was drawn and silent. Elizabeth touched his arm comfortingly, feeling his great need for her to be strong.

She remembered the rats in the experimental laboratory with electrodes clamped to their heads in order that electrical shocks could be administered and resultant brain damage monitored. Edward, of course, was not to receive any shocks, but the idea of his odd little head being covered in electrical apparatus was frightening and repulsive. Protective and motherly love stirred strongly inside her. It was with sickening self-loathing that she acknowledged this to be an entirely fresh experience.

When the investigations were completed the consultant formed his conclusions carefully. 'The pattern of activity

in the brain is a little unusual in certain areas,' he said
cautiously.

Elizabeth frowned. 'What are you telling us?'

'At this age any reading of brain activity is subject to a
degree of unreliability. We shall need to take further
readings in a year's time ... then I shall be able to tell you a
little more.'

Michael sighed. He was ready to get up and go.

'What exactly do you mean by "a little unusual"?'
Elizabeth asked insistently.

'Just that,' the consultant said. 'It doesn't necessarily
mean anything.'

Elizabeth could tell that he had said all that he wanted
to. He was squaring off papers on his desk, glancing at the
clock on the wall. A great determination seized her. 'But if
it did mean something – then what exactly should we
expect?'

The doctor paused thoughtfully.

'I'd like to know the very worst,' she said quietly.

'It could mean physical disability.'

'Mental handicap?' she went on probingly, conscious of
the shock that had passed through Michael's body as the
words hit the air.

'Possibly ... Yes.'

'Is there anything we can do?'

He met her eyes directly for one brief second. 'No.'

Her heart was very still for a moment. A terrible sadness
shot down to the root of her. So be it. So be it.

Her mother held Edward tightly in her arms and refused
to believe that there was anything wrong with him. 'And
even if there were,' she said, 'I should love him all the
more.' She took him over almost completely, lavishing
affection on his heavy, listless little body as though to
compensate him for the blows that had been laid on him
by his creator.

The Lashleys had to be told. They came along and
regarded the baby with a concern that could not conceal a
heavy element of suspicion. They stared at him, clearly

stunned and bewildered as to how things had gone wrong.
There was no mention of Aunt Alice. Both of them were
impeccably polite and restrained, but there was a need to
apportion blame, and Elizabeth felt her mother-in-law's
eyes on her, read the silent accusations that spoke of bad
blood and inferior stock. Mrs Lashley took Michael on one
side and Elizabeth imagined her reassuring him that he
was not to blame. The blood on his side was
irreproachable.

When they had gone Michael said uncomfortably, 'We
could get a another opinion, have a private consultation.
Mother's offered to pay.'

Elizabeth's mother was instantly supportive of the idea.
Private medicine had been one of the family's taken-for-
granted luxuries in the good old days.

'It won't help,' Elizabeth said.

'It might. You never know. These doctors are very
clever.' Her mother looked at her accusingly.

'You mean they are more clever because you pay them?'
Elizabeth asked.

'Well ... you'll get very good attention. They might just
find something the other doctor missed.' She turned and
appealed to Michael. 'Don't you agree?'

Michael, whilst hating to take sides in domestic
arguments, had to admit that he did.

Elizabeth was consumed with anger. 'You two,' she said
with cold imperiousness, 'you think that money will solve
everything.' And neither of you earn it, she added silently.

'I know all about your funny ideas,' her mother replied,
equally heated, 'and I'm sorry that those children you
work with have such dreadful lives – but you can't sacrifice
Edward because of your high-minded principles about
them. Surely you have a duty to get the best for your own
child?'

Elizabeth's deliberations had not, in fact, been travelling
along this particular path, although her mother was
perfectly correct in suggesting that this was an issue that
might trouble her. Her heart was now rattling so
frantically in her rib-cage that for a moment she feared
that she would be overcome with some premature attack.
'Another opinion will not make Edward normal. Whatever
is wrong with him is not yet clearly identifiable or treatable

– and it probably never will be. We have to come to terms with that. All the opinions in the world will not alter that fact.'

'That you should deny your child any kind of opportunity,' her mother said admonishingly. 'I would not have believed it of you.'

Elizabeth turned to her husband. 'You do what you like. Use your mother's money to try and bring about a miracle. But it won't work and all you'll do is put the poor child through a lot of extra suffering.'

She walked from the room leaving the two of them shaken and subdued.

Michael made no further mention of the matter and no further opinion was sought.

Edward had no more fits until he was a year old when he suffered two successive and major convulsions. At fourteen months old he suffered a further two and almost died. After that he seemed to improve. There were no more fits. But as his second birthday approached, he was not yet up on his feet and he was saying no words, and Elizabeth knew that all the most dreadful things that had been predicted were going to come about. Being accustomed to think things through, she was miserably aware that having a handicapped child represented an iron clamp around the parents' feet for ever. She did not, however, ever find it possible to voice that gloomy forecast to Michael.

Michael was currently in an optimistic frame of mind. He had finally landed the job in the bookshop and was actually earning money. Elizabeth could see that he was happy and she was glad for him. He got on famously with Paulette and her father, and often Paulette brought him home herself in her racing-green MG Midget. On one occasion she loaned him the car so that he and Elizabeth could attend a wedding in style. 'It'll all be all right,' Michael said suddenly as they were driving back from the reception, he contentedly tipsy and delighting in having his foot on something which responded with a cheery roar. 'It's all going to be all right.' He reached over and squeezed her knee. Tears sprang to her eyes. They never

seemed to express open affection these days, never seemed
to make love any more.

When they got home her mother was sitting contentedly,
rocking Edward and crooning to him. He was big now and
lay passively in her lap like a pillow of stones.

When Edward was twenty-six months old he toppled from
his high chair as Elizabeth was lifting him out. He became
limp, and then the familiar shaking and writhing started,
gathering force and speed as though something crazed
were trying to escape from him. He had never suffered
anything as bad as this. Nature, having been cheated once,
did not make another mistake. Within minutes his squirming body was still, and he was dead long before the
ambulance arrived.

In the autumn of that year Elizabeth was asked to take on a
temporary post as Acting Head of a tiny school on the
outskirts of the city. It was quite a few miles from her home
and on darkening November evenings she took a sombre
enjoyment in driving back in the soft drizzle. Not long
before, Michael had confessed to her that his relationship
with Paulette was more than platonic. They had been lovers
for some time and he would like to marry her. He had been
most contrite and apologetic but Elizabeth had not found it
difficult to be kind. In many ways she felt relief. Michael
represented yet another area of failure in her life. She had
done little for him; been a pretty dull sex-partner, given
him a sub-standard child and burdened him with an ever-
present mother-in-law. She did not blame him for wanting
to leave.

Sometimes, as she was driving, she felt herself to be so
gentle and still and of such little substance, that there
seemed to be something pleasant in the prospect of simply
dissolving into the November fog and not troubling the
world any more.

Sometimes she felt far less gentle and much more self-
punishing. She railed at herself for making a complete mess
of things. She had married an ineffectual man and produced a defective child. She had been a disappointment to

her mother who longed for· a story of happiness and success to cheer her dull days.

'A charming boy – but weak,' her mother had said regretfully when the news of the separation broke, and Elizabeth felt that she, as a daughter, had not come up to the mark by being chosen by a man who had permitted her to support him. By being self-reliant and taking on responsibility she had contravened the natural order of things.

She was a failure.

She and her mother continued to live together as neither had anyone else to cling to.

The tension and rivalry that had surrounded them when Edward was alive very soon vanished, for the question of which of them was to forge the primary bond with the child was now no longer an issue, and in its place there developed a strong bonding together of mother and daughter in shared sorrow.

Twenty-One

Elizabeth's employers were exceedingly generous. They gave her every possible assistance in order for her to gain the qualifications that would enable them to employ her in an advisory capacity as an educational psychologist.

They offered to place her on an adviser's salary scale whilst she trained: a rate of pay far in advance of her present one, one which carried with it all manner of fringe benefits like travel expenses (first-class rail fare if she chose to travel by train), meal allowances, a book allowance and all academic fees paid. In return she had to do no more than agree to let them employ her as an advisory psychologist on an even higher salary for a minimum of two years after completing her course.

'It sounds almost too good to be true,' her mother commented.

Elizabeth was inclined to think the same. Where was the catch, the bitter pill amongst the sugar? She did have some faint regret about leaving teaching, but after three years in cramped classrooms with around forty wild and gamy-smelling children she thought that a fresh challenge would be appreciated. She saw no reason not to go ahead.

She spent a year at Manchester University becoming reacquainted with the subject of psychology and that of psychology in education as a speciality. She wrote essays on the social, emotional and educational needs of children and visited all manner of special schools and units catering for children with learning and behaviour difficulties. She felt as though she were on the frontiers of new thinking, gaining insight into all the modern and enlightened ways of dealing with those children who had the misfortune to be the also-rans of the education system.

She could not wait to finish the course and put what she

had learned into practice. The fervour of the hero-innovator surged within her. She shared much of her excitement with her mother who looked forward to hearing the day's news as they sipped their bedtime drink. 'It'll be nice when you're home again,' her mother said. 'The house is so quiet during the day.' It was, indeed, a long day for her, mainly on her own. Elizabeth had to set off from the house at six in order to catch the early train to Manchester and did not arrive back sometimes until after nine. But she was glad that it had been possible to manage with this arrangement. To have taken lodgings close to the university and left her mother entirely on her own would have been unthinkable.

She completed her course and returned to her home city in her new and exalted capacity as an adviser. There was only one other educational psychologist working for the local education authority, and the two of them shared offices on the second floor of a crumbling Victorian villa in a somewhat doubtful district of the city, where much business behind drawn curtains went on for most of the day.

Her new colleague, Albert Bentall, was an extra-ordinarily timid man who had a Cambridge First in Psychology. From what Elizabeth could gather he had never actually taught in a school, nor had he taken any post-graduate training to prepare him for the demands of an advisory job. It seemed as though he had just, somehow, ended up working for the education advisory service, without really intending to. It was very soon apparent to Elizabeth that he was hideously miscast in his current role, which demanded a good deal of going about and spreading the word of innovative thinking in education and psychology to a basically sceptical audience.

As Albert Bentall hated even to encounter the secretary in the corridor, it seemed likely that the job of visiting schools and homes would be only one stage removed from torture for him. He was so chronically shy and hesitant that he could hardly bring himself to approach Elizabeth in her tiny office on the morning of her arrival. She heard the footsteps coming down the corridor, fearful, shuffling footsteps which paused outside her door for what seemed an age. A timid scratching on the panels followed and when she called for him to come in he slid between door and frame without appearing to displace any particles of air.

He would be around mid-fifties, she thought, and looked as though all the life had long gone out of him. Physically he was of a solid and yet spongy texture. Elizabeth was to discover later that his wife kept him on a strict diet and often, before he departed for his three-hour lunch-break, she was to see him in his car solemnly relishing huge cream-buns.

This morning he spoke to her very courteously and with much self-deprecation before handing her a neatly-typed list of all the schools in the area. Beside the name of each school he had pencilled in his or her initials to show which of them had the responsibility of following up requests from the schools for the opinion of the psychologist on individual children who were causing concern. Immediately she noted that her initials appeared nearly twice as frequently as his.

'You'll see,' he explained helpfully, 'that I've given you all the central schools so that you won't have to spend so much time on travelling – as I shall have to, of course, looking after the schools on the outskirts.'

Elizabeth was too amazed to speak for a moment.

She stared blankly at the list, realising that the share-out of work was scandalously unfair and the issue of travelling a total irrelevance.

'It's always been arranged like that,' he continued mildly. 'Your predecessor seemed to manage all right. She left to have a baby,' he added, as though to stave off any suggestions that she might have collapsed from overwork.

'But surely the inner city schools throw up the worst problems,' she suggested gently, not wishing to appear unco-operative or aggressive – especially at this early stage.

A look of unmistakable anger passed briefly over his features and she understood that he was not a man to cross. 'There are a lot of problems in my schools – and of course I have a good many administrative responsibilities to deal with as the senior person here.'

She had no wish to cause trouble. 'Yes, yes – of course.'

He produced another list; this time with the names of

about a hundred children on it. He coughed. 'I'm afraid
there's a bit of a waiting-list.' He handed over the sheet,
which represented a backlog of three or four months'
work.

Elizabeth knew she should simply refuse to take on that
kind of load. But she was handicapped by her ingrained
habits of niceness. She had been taught to be a nice child
and a nice young girl and now she was a nice young
woman. She did not know how to proceed without being
unpleasant – and so she simply gave in.

It was really no problem at all for men like Albert
Bentall to throw women like Elizabeth to the wolves.

She found the work interesting despite the pressure of
numbers to be got through. She interviewed dozens of
children and parents and teachers and tried hard to come
up with solutions to the problems they posed. She had
been trained to be a problem solver, to pick out where
difficulties lay for a child or family or teacher and to advise
on ways of improving matters. She soon discovered that
people did not want to hear about improvements, they
wanted to hear about nothing less than the miraculous.
They thought her job was to make the non-readers read,
make the restless concentrate, make the uninterested full
of enthusiasm, and more important than all of those –
make the wayward and naughty good.

They brought out their most difficult, deprived and
emotionally damaged children and said to her – 'There!
Over to you. You're the expert, *you* sort them out.'

For a year or two she flew around her patch in a frenzy
of earnest commitment, being badgered to bring about
changes in the human condition that only God could be
expected to attempt. Timidly she approached Albert
Bentall on the subject of the impossible heaviness of her
case-load. With much hesitation she pointed out the
unequal share-out of work. He stared at her with a fixed
gaze and for a moment she felt a twinge of fear at the
strength of his will. 'I have to take things steadily,' he said.
'I have very high blood pressure.' She saw in him an
awesome invincibility, directed to one end only –
self-preservation.

She abandoned any idea of making him change.

There was one particular aspect of her work that she began to hate; namely, directing dull and disruptive children into special educational establishments to get them out of everyone's hair. Normal schools preferred not to deal with the problems thrown up by the limited, the unlucky, the black and the non-conforming. Elizabeth, cajoled and bullied by headteachers who assured her that rejection from the mainstream system was for the 'child's own good', would reluctantly visit the children's struggling, down-at-heel parents to tell them that their offspring was a sub-grade egg and must be deprived of normal educational opportunities to attend a school the local authority called 'special' and the other children called the 'dummy-dump' or the 'funny-farm'. Standing in the parents' cramped houses where the carpets were tacky with years of filth, she felt herself to be an intruder, an interferer, a patroniser; an old colonial bringing standards to the natives. Who am I, she wondered, in my navy suit and my nice white car, to tell these people that their child is a dud? Sometimes she wondered if they would break into a rage and attack her, but no one ever did. They were all so weary and defeated.

Gradually Elizabeth herself grew weary, drained and disillusioned, worn down by her constant dashing round the crumbling innards of the city's decaying schools and squalid houses listening to endless tales of misery and poverty and failure. Her pioneering spirit began to ebb away. She was full of confusion and uncertainty about what she should be doing, whether she should make a stand against these distasteful tasks she was required to perform which went against her nature. And it distressed her too that whatever she did, she could never please everyone.

In a moment of weakness she voiced some of her reservations to Albert Bentall. He stared at her blankly, cold as a fish. 'We do what is best for the children. We are professionals. These parents have low standards and slack methods of child-rearing. It is right that their views should be overridden in the child's interests.'

So sure was he that she was almost convinced that he was right, that her own stance of permitting everyone their unique, individual freedom was nothing more than moral sloppiness.

Despite being a bearer of bad tidings, Elizabeth was glad

to find that she got on well with even the poorest and most limited clients. She had a way of speaking to them in soothing, convincing tones which lulled them into the belief that what she was suggesting was compasssionate and worthy.

She realised that she had the capacity to command respect and she grew to have a taste and a need for it. That, and the prestige and money that went with the job – money that was making her mother's life immensely more pleasant – stopped her from thoughts of leaving and trying something a little less contentious and stressful.

The Advisory Service was expanding and Elizabeth acquired some new colleagues. A lively and enthusiastic young man called Clive was appointed to work with her and Albert. He wore a fluffy beard, tight denim jeans and one gold earring. His hobbies were ballet-dancing, Indian cookery and dieting; the latter being necessary in order that he could continue with the two former. Elizabeth speculated with interest on the dash he would cut in a leotard, given the generous proportions of his buttocks and thighs.

If Albert had any misgivings about the flamboyancy of this addition to his staff, he did not show it. Albert, of course, rarely showed any feelings about anything as long as it did not impinge on him directly – and, in any case, Clive had proved himself as entirely satisfactory by accepting with amiable unconcern all the fieldwork responsibilities Albert loaded onto him.

Clive was immensely cheerful and never bowed down with despondency about the nature or volume of the work.

After he had been in harness for a few weeks, whilst he and Elizabeth were eating their lunchtime sandwiches together, she was prompted to ask him, 'Doesn't it worry you to be in such a powerful position in making decisions about children's educational future?'

'No,' said Clive.

'But think of the moral responsibility,' she insisted. 'Think of the awfulness of getting it wrong.'

'Getting it wrong?' He smiled and shook his head.

'Well ... recommending a child for special education and ... it being the wrong thing for the child,' she concluded lamely.

'Statistically,' Clive said patiently, 'one has a fifty-fifty chance of being right or wrong when making such a decision. You make a decision to move the child to special education or you make a decision to leave him where he is. Simple.'

'But we're dealing with children's futures, their whole lives might be at stake.'

'We're not responsible for that. We're paid to make an informed decision, in the light of the knowledge available to us, which, of course, is very little in terms of any given person's total circumstances. If we do that, with precision and disinterest, then we have done a good job and that is that. End of problem. Go home and forget about it.'

'But children matter,' Elizabeth said in desperation. 'We can't be disinterested, like mechanics or technicians.'

'If we are not,' he smiled, 'then we are playing at being God.'

Elizabeth found herself wanting to be convinced. If what Clive said was right then a weight of crushing responsibility could drop from her shoulders.

She kept a close eye on Clive's working style and noted that he practised what he preached. He was not troubled in the least when required to become involved in the tinkering about with people's most private emotions regarding their children, seemed never happier or more energetic than when plumbing the depths of human misery. Gradually it dawned on her that he did not see what he was doing in those terms. He did not see 'misery' or 'confusion'; he saw problematic issues which required to be examined dispassionately and a variety of alternative coping strategies to be suggested. He did not perceive himself as being in the business of attempting to make amends to the clients for the wrongs the world had heaped on them.

Elizabeth's problem was simply that she felt so sorry for them all.

The team were later joined by a child psychiatrist called Janet and a social worker called Tim. These two and Elizabeth and Clive took to having case-discussions every week. They would save up their thorniest problems to share with each other in order to gain support and advice.

Janet and Tim had both worked in a number of other services up and down the country. Elizabeth was only too prepared to learn from them. Janet went on lots of in-service courses to learn about new ways of working and new approaches to the problems they all had to tackle. She would come back and try out her new knowledge on the unsuspecting public.

When she first joined the team she was in her 'non-directive' phase. Using this approach, the clients would be allowed to express whatever worries came into their head, and the professional worker would simply reflect it back to them, thus encouraging them to see their difficulties objectively. So if the client told Janet, 'Well, you see, love, the problem is, he wets the bed,' she would come helpfully back with, 'I can see that you are concerned about him wetting the bed.' This had the effect of Janet's having a good many failed appointments when she invited clients for follow-up.

Later she moved into a diametrically opposed 'directive' phase, which involved telling the client straight how she viewed the problem. 'I have to lay this firmly at your door, there seems to be a good deal of parental collusion here in what your son/daughter has been doing,' she would tell the hapless parents of delinquent teenagers. A similar pattern of failed follow-up appointments ensued.

Janet was happy to talk at length, so dazzled by the ingenuity of her insights that she appeared not to see the people she was assessing at all. Clive would have his feet up on the desk, a lazy and quizzical smile on his face. Occasionally he would quote one or two pertinent and controversial research findings and Janet would falter for a second. But then, on she would go, undeterred, seeming to be positively buoyed up by her reflections on the lamentable ignorance and failings of her clients.

Tim would receive her words with earnest thoughtfulness. He never challenged Janet. He would be dependent on her for a good reference when he applied for a senior post.

Elizabeth was fascinated and repelled by the things that were said at these weekly meetings. Janet put forward the view, couched in professional not personal terms, that people conspired to create their own fate. An abandoned

mother with no money and children with emotional
difficulties and learning problems, was seen as having
chosen disaster and ill-luck. Janet went on to illustrate her
argument by pointing out the number of women, who,
having been beaten up by one man, instantly selected
another mate who would do just the same. Janet talked of
'colluding with your own destiny'. There was no such thing
as simple bad luck, no such handicap as drawing the short
straw of restricted opportunities.

Week after week Janet propounded her theories and
Elizabeth listened with full attention. She became deeply
troubled by what she heard. From the lips of an educated
and knowledgeable person were pouring all the old
reactionary, conservative views dressed up in psychological terms: one had a duty to get on one's bike and make the
best of things, one got as much out as one put in, one had a
duty to haul oneself up by the bootstraps if things were
bad. It seemed like the old maxim of the weak, the
put-upon, the ill, the weary, the feeble and the inadequate
having a duty to pull themselves together and show a bit of
spirit.

One week Tim brought a case up for discussion which
especially interested Elizabeth. It was the case of a child, an
only one, who lived with his divorced mother and his
grandparents, one of whom was terminally ill. The
problem seemed to centre around the grandmother's
insistence on challenging the mother on her child-rearing
techniques, the child gaining attention through specta-
cular acts of defiance against his two mother-figures and
the mother being uncertain about how to handle things so
as to preserve as calm an atmosphere as possible for her
father to die in.

Janet leapt eagerly into the discussion. 'This mother has
a problem with ego-strength,' she said. 'I should be
wanting to ask why she ever permitted the grandmother to
assume any kind of rights over the kid in the first place.
And why hasn't she separated from her own parents yet?
What is the source of her need to remain a child herself?
Why is she still living in the parental home?'

Tim consulted the file. 'There is a financial problem,' he

said. 'The mother has no source of income and the father has failed on the maintenance payments.'

Janet shook her head vigorously. 'This mother has a right to every state benefit going. You can help her find out about that, Tim – but more important I think we should be working towards giving her the ego-definition to split from these parents.'

Elizabeth listened and a bleak dismay seized her. She saw how Janet would judge her own situation, would see her fettered by her own weakness, would define her filial duty as a form of cringing feebleness.

I am inadequate, Elizabeth told herself. I have failed in marriage and my child is dead. I am stuck in a job which gives me no joy and I have allowed my mother to act as a ball and chain on my freedom and ambition. She bowed her head and stared at the floor in shame.

She looked again at Janet. Janet with so much knowledge, yet so little wisdom, Janet with no uncertainties about her usefulness in the world, Janet with her lively mother who sculpted and painted and travelled abroad and would eventually leave her a great deal of money.

Elizabeth suddenly wanted to cry and had to leave the room abruptly.

She stood in the corridor and reflected that when you were down on your luck the only kind you were likely to attract was the bad sort. Was not the wisest course just to accept that? Was not the best thing one could do for the clients to sit with them and weep and say, 'My God, your life is a disaster and I can't begin to imagine how you survive'?

Twenty-Two

'I think I shall go and stay with Helena for a week or two,' Elizabeth's mother said. 'It'll be a nice break for you without me and I'll be able to help with the new house.'

Helena, recently married, and miles away down in Surrey, was about to move from the attic flat she and Philip had been renting into a brand-new two-bedroomed detached. Helena was a dutiful daughter and telephoned her mother every week. Often she would speak to Elizabeth first.

'Are you bearing up, Liza?'

'I'm fine.'

'Mum sounds a bit grotty. The old low spirits and a bit of tummy trouble. All the usual stuff she's been saying for years.'

'I think she's OK. She's in her seventies, after all,' Elizabeth said loyally.

'God, I don't know how you stick it. You must be a saint. Look, send her off to me for a bit. I'll keep her busy and you can have a bit of fun on your own.'

'She'd like to come anyway. She misses you.' Elizabeth did not want Helena to feel like the less-favoured sibling.

'Right. Now you'll be sure to make hay while the sun shines, won't you?'

Elizabeth laughed.

'Come on, Liza, no messing, how's the love life?' This was a favourite topic of Helena's. She hated to think of Elizabeth, or any woman, being without a man.

'Nil, I'm ashamed to report.'

'Well don't you fancy anyone? You can't live like a nun forever.'

'The field does narrow down rather when you're getting middle-aged.'

'Rubbish, you look terrific!'

'Mmm, but the men don't. And anyway they're all married, all the decent ones – and I've no intention of getting mixed up with a marriage.'

'Lonely divorcées?'

'Too fragile and damaged. And it's always so easy to see what went wrong for them the first time.'

'Oh dear. How about "the younger man"? It's all the rage down here. Nobble yourself a nubile.'

'Well,' Elizabeth said, wanting to amuse her sister, 'let's see: there's this young man who's set up a smart restaurant down the road. He does always smile very nicely at me – and he's really rather beautiful ...'

'I'm slavering with lust. I shall be wanting to hear a lot more about him. Absolutely no excuses for not acting fast and loose while Mum's away.'

Elizabeth thought seriously about what Helena had said. She recognised that her body was neglected, that she was hungry and needy to be caressed by a man – and that time was flying by. She thought about sex and love and decided that, in the circumstances, it was permissible to discard the notion of love. She would allow herself to behave in a modern and unsentimental manner.

The day after her mother had departed to Surrey she went to have dinner in the smart little restaurant and eyed up its young proprietor in a gently predatory manner. Instinctively she knew that he would be available for what she required. With much courage and greatly accelerated heart-rate, she ventured to invite him out for a drink. His lack of hesitation in accepting was most encouraging. This occasion having passed off successfully, she invited him round to lunch, the purpose of the rendezvous being quite clear, although not spoken.

She made an effort not to be too prepared, too organised. She failed. The creamed prawn and salmon flan was warming in the oven, the wine – an exceptionally fine Chablis – was chilling in the refrigerator, and the house was orderly and spotless, shown off to perfection in vivid golden sunlight. Just a nick below the surface and a housewife's blood would flow, she thought irritably, as she checked her appearance in the mirror, searching for slackness and wrinkles.

He was forty-five minutes late. She saw him at the gate, smiling, seeing her straight away. She led him into the dining-room, fussing with glasses and plates, offering him a drink, talking in a fluttering voice.

Then his arms were around her, pulling her close, and she knew that he was experienced at this sort of thing: he, fifteen years her junior.

He was very tall, of beanstalk slenderness. He leaned down and kissed her, a wide-open kiss, close and warm and wet, with tongues intertwining. His hand was assuringly caressing her bottom. He leaned up against the wall, confident and at his ease. She wanted to go on and on kissing him. The insides of her thighs felt warm and melting. She pulled away.

'Have you got planning permission for your extension yet?' she asked.

'Mmm.' He smiled seductively, bent his head for another kiss.

'When will the work start?'

'Soon enough ...' He raised his eyebrows in amusement.

'Will it be a long project?' As if it mattered.

'No idea.' He muzzled into her neck.

She turned and looked out into the garden. Suddenly she wanted to explain things to him but she did not know what to say. She felt the wine on her breath. She had had a couple of glasses whilst she was waiting for him. 'Do have something to drink,' she said. 'I must taste terrible.'

'No – but I'll have a little wine.'

She moved away from him. Why? Much better to be close.

'What shall we do?' he asked, gently provocative.

'Have lunch,' she said, ever the good hostess, truly her mother's daughter.

She began to lose her nerve as she took things from the oven. Words came scuttling out of her. He sat at the table waiting, tenderly reassuring, tolerantly amused – so very, very relaxed. She busied about, touching him softly as she passed his chair, moving her hands over his shoulders and downwards to stroke his chest. He had beautiful silky brown hair which she brushed with her lips. She wanted him most desperately, a great physical yearning pulsed inside her.

'That's nice,' he said, leaning his head back against her breasts. He was giving all the encouragement she could wish for.

She sat down. The food seemed to multiply on the plate. She could not chew it. Her voice went on chirping endlessly about her forthcoming holiday, his forthcoming holiday, about cooking and wine and her new suit which he had admired.

Suddenly he took her hand. 'You're shaking!'

She was ashamed. 'I'm in rather a state,' she confessed. She knew she should get up and place herself on his knee and just keep on kissing him. That would put it all right.

She started to fuss with the apple-pie she had made. He said he would have some. Then he changed his mind. He insisted on her having some. She declined unless he joined her. It was ridiculous.

'Shall we have coffee?' she asked. 'Now ... or later?'

'Later,' he said. 'Let's go somewhere more comfortable and sit down.'

He chose the sofa. She sat close to him. 'This is a nice airy room,' he said. 'These Victorian houses are very elegant.'

She told him of some of her plans for alterations.

'You mustn't spoil the character,' he said gravely.

There was a pause.

She took his hand, admiring the slender fingers, the white-rimmed nails. He wore a ring on the wedding finger.

'Are you going to make love to me?' she asked, alarmed that the occasion appeared to be slipping away to nothing.

'Am I going to make love to you?' he echoed lightly. 'Well, shall we go and relax somewhere and take things as they come?'

'I'll show you my house,' she said. That, at least, she could be proud of. They walked upstairs holding hands. She showed him her study, the place where she kept and wrote books. His eyes moved over the crowded shelves. 'Have you read all these?' He glanced at her with a certain sharpness.

'Yes.' She wished he hadn't known that. She wanted him to see her as female and physical – all woman. Just for a moment she wanted to forget the cerebral.

She took him into her bedroom and felt horribly calculating as she drew the curtains. They sat on the bed and kissed and he was warm and softly strong and so wonderfully kissable. He was undoing her brooch, proceeding to the stiff silk-covered buttons of her blouse. Each cuff had three buttons. Eventually the blouse came off and he was nibbling at her left nipple, his thick silky hair against her face. Suddenly he wanted all her clothes off and they they were both naked, warm bodies together, somehow perched on the end of the bed.

His hand passed softly between her thighs. He knelt on the floor and pushed her back gently so that her legs hung down over the edge of the bed. 'Just lie back and relax,' he said. His head moved down to rest between her legs.

He's going to lick me, she thought, in panic and confusion. Michael had never done that. She had understood that it would be distasteful to him. It was not hard to understand why. The taste could surely not be very pleasant and her mother had from an early age impressed on her that the genitals were unclean and forbidden territory. She did not especially like that part of her body. Moreover she had no idea how she should respond to this caress.

Desire was swiftly quenched by anxiety. Had she washed properly? Did she smell bad? Would he think her pubic hair too abundant? He couldn't possibly like what he was doing. He was doing it because he thought he should, not because he truly desired to. It was a mere sexual courtesy. This act, if motivated by genuine desire, must surely be the most moving and wonderful tribute the lover could offer the loved one. It was indeed a true act of worship.

Her mind as usual was furiously active.

She knew that this beautiful young man did not cherish any loving or worshipful feelings towards her. He hardly knew her – and she guessed that she was probably not his type anyway. And, in any case, in no way could she handle worship. She would feel awkward and unworthy. She could not believe that anyone would feel for her in that way. She was past her youth now and full of cynicism. She did not laugh easily enough and she alienated people with her solemnity. Who in the world would want to worship her?

She pulled his head up and smiled apologetically. He was clearly disconcerted. She lay beside him and kissed him again and after a while reached down to fondle him. What she felt was warm softness, like a new born kitten.

He was crushed and humiliated, and her ignorance was such that she had no means of helping him. They both gave up instantly, each wanting to terminate the disastrous encounter as soon as decently possible.

'I'm so sorry,' she murmured, knowing that he would never want to see her again, and so much wanting to give him back his male esteem. 'You're a very lovely, desirable man ...'

'I don't know what went wrong. I rather pride myself in this area.' He was clearly baffled. 'I've never been with a woman quite like you,' he added, as though that explained things.

She did not ask for expansion, afraid of what she might hear.

She helped him back into his clothes. 'Service!' he commented, rallying a little.

'I'll be in touch,' he said, kissing her very nicely at the door – but they both knew he had no intention of doing so.

The following weekend she searched in the bookshops and bought everything she could find, fiction and non-fiction, in order to inform herself about up-to-date sex. Should the opportunity for another adventure occur, she would be well prepared.

Her mother returned from Surrey and pronounced herself glad to be home. Helena's lifestyle was a little hectic. So many business colleagues of Philip's to entertain. Helena had been rather short-tempered from time to time. Her mother had to say, though, that she was pleased to see Helena turning out to be such a good wife and hostess.

Elizabeth saw that her mother was old now. She felt a quiet drone of sadness within her when she looked back over the last years of her mother's life and saw how she had been uncoupled from her bright carefree world of spending and entertainment and shunted into a lonely siding of frugal dependency. She saw too what a solemn and dull companion she, Elizabeth, must seem, how her mother longed for cheery chat about fashion and home improvements.

Elizabeth took her out for drives in the car. She tried to leave her alone as little as possible. She tried to be patient when her mother said things like: 'You were late in last night, weren't you dear?' Elizabeth was forty and no longer wanted to explain to her mother where she had been.

She was tolerant about her mother's constant exhortations: 'Why don't you sit in the garden, it's too nice to be up in that study of yours?'

'I'd have thought you'd have liked to get to know that nice young man next door. He's so well-mannered. Divorced and very lonely.'

'There's a programme on TV I think you'd like. We can watch together. It's so nice to have a companion.'

And then there was the maternal offering of advice on Elizabeth's clothes and her hair. That went on right to the end. Elizabeth gently ignored it all.

The house became quirky and disorganised. Her mother still insisted on cleaning and washing and putting things away. Elizabeth discovered wrapped cheese in the sideboard and potatoes in the bread-bin. She once found some stockings in the freezer and a pan of scrambled eggs on the lavatory cistern.

Her mother had a lot of trouble with the digestion of food. The words 'sickly' and 'bilious' were frequently on her lips. She had problems with her bowels too. 'Yesterday I couldn't stop and today I can't go,' she told Elizabeth. 'It's old age.'

Some days she did not trust her digestive system to cope with anything more daring than thin bowls of watery porridge.

She became very dependent on the doctor. She would not go and stay with Helena any more because she feared to be too far from the doctor. Only he understood her particular complaints. When she heard of viruses going about she retired to bed and immediately fell prey to them.

Things on the television upset her and she was restless and couldn't sleep. Her feet hurt and she had bad dreams.

Sometimes she was terribly sad. All her friends were dying. She would speak frankly. 'To come to this,' she would say. 'What is there to live for?' She talked of the awfulness of being old and poor and dependent and burdensome. She talked of how good Elizabeth had been but how terrible it was to depend on the charity of one's children. She hoped Elizabeth would never have that to endure.

She worried greatly about the pain and suffering of dying.

But at the end there was no suffering. It was swift and quiet and painless, just as she would have wished.

Elizabeth clasped Helena tightly at the funeral.

The relatives shook their hands outside the little chapel. 'How you will miss her,' they said, looking sadly at Elizabeth, and she knew that silently they were thinking: 'She was all you had.'

Helena stayed with her for a few days to sort things out. Elizabeth gave her her mother's rings and all the best furniture and any pictures and knick-knacks that she wanted. She felt that, in some way, Helena had had a raw deal as a daughter.

'Time for a new start, Liza,' Helena said as she left.

Elizabeth smiled and kissed her, then walked slowly back into the empty house.

Twenty-Three

Colin was on a fitness drive. He had struggled up from his bed of sloth and pleasure in order to take regular exercise and appreciate the benefits of the open air. Elizabeth even began to suspect that he might be putting in regular appearances at lectures. He had certainly gone so far as to attend one or two of her own tutorials where both of them had behaved with adroit impartiality.

He spent an hour each day fast-walking and a further hour swimming, and even went so far as to make a chart on which he recorded the type of activity undertaken, how far he had been and the time span involved.

As the weather was now getting a little warmer, he would swim in the open air whenever possible, his favourite spot being a stretch of the river about a mile from Elizabeth's house where the water was deep and sparkling clear. Elizabeth would lend him the car or drive him there herself and he would cleave the water with strong firm strokes, his big body thrusting forward like some powered streamlined vessel.

Elizabeth declined to join him, although she was quite a keen and proficient swimmer herself. As far as this project was concerned she preferred to be an observer not a participator.

She liked to sit on the bank and watch the whiteness of his flesh flashing in the water, a whiteness that gradually turned to silver as the daylight drained from the sky. On those clear and sharp May evenings it seemed to Elizabeth as though the pale luminous light and Colin's flesh were inextricably linked in a celebration of the physical; of texture and matter and life itself.

Being Colin he enjoyed, whenever possible, swimming in the nude, which gave Elizabeth the opportunity to observe the robustness of him, the compelling solid reality of his labourer's shoulders and footballer's thighs, the full firm globes of his buttocks. There was nothing fragile or delicate about Colin. He was meaty and substantial and indestructible.

She would sit, watching and waiting, holding a huge folded bathsheet which she wrapped around him as he climbed up the bank. Rubbing him briskly, her hands would touch the firm, cooled skin, and she would be faint with desire for him.

Once, despite the risk of being seen, she allowed him to peel off all her own clothes and they made love on the back seat of the car, parked under the trees. At this stage in their relationship, far from tiring of this frequent and exhausting love-making, she felt that each one of their couplings only served to bind her to him more securely. Desire seemed to feed upon itself and demand ever more in order to be satisfied.

Cramped against the seat back and the door, her bare legs spread out underneath him, she smiled and said, 'This is really rather reckless.'

Colin grinned, highly pleased with his performance. 'A good screw's worth taking a risk for.'

She was silent, stroking him thoughtfully, wondering if he would believe her if she told him that there had been years when she had been totally chaste and solemn and spiritual.

'Don't take things so seriously,' he told her. 'Fucking's supposed to fun.'

'Perhaps there is nothing more grave or weighty or of such fundamental importance than good fucking,' she replied after consideration. She waited for one of Colin's good-natured sighs at the ponderousness of her language, but he just held her very close and still, his heartbeat fusing with hers.

Preparing supper later, she was reflecting on the weight of her belief in what she had said to Colin. She did not expect him to share it, or any of her views for that matter, it was quite enough that he shared his body and his time.

He came up behind her sniffing in appreciation at the summer garden smells of the salad she was assembling. He had recently expressed a desire to eat more healthily – less

butter, less steak, less full-fat cheese. She had been
perfectly happy to oblige. He was on a fitness drive, he was
like a child with a new hobby – it delighted her to indulge
this latest whim.

His arms came around her and she smiled, leaning back
against him.

'I didn't mean to make you do anything you didn't want
to,' he said apologetically, quite unexpectedly.

She did not immediately comprehend. She turned and
raised her eyebrows questioningly.

'Screw ... making love in the car,' he explained. 'I
suppose it *was* reckless.'

'Oh, my dear.' She smiled at him with ripely sweet
benevolence.

He frowned, irritated. 'I didn't think.'

'Think what?'

'Well – it's OK for me ...'

Ah, now she understood. 'But for a woman of my
standing it is really going a bit far to be "screwing" on the
back seat of a car – before it's decently dark at that. At my
age it behoves a woman to behave with a little more
dignity.' There was no trace of sharpness in her voice, but
he clearly felt chastened.

'Don't take the piss, Elizabeth. You were the one who
talked about recklessness ...'

She realised that he was showing some scrupulous
consideration for her feelings. Her heart contracted with
tenderness. 'I wanted it,' she said baldly, 'there was no
question of your prevailing on me.'

He took the vegetable knife from her hand and placed it
deliberately on the table. 'There's this thing about you – as
though there's nothing that will shock you. I've always
taken it for granted.'

He was astonishing her. 'Well?'

She could see the struggle going on in him to find words
to express thoughts that were only partially formed.

She tilted her head and smiled. 'I'm not amoral, my
dear, I do disapprove most strongly of cruelty and wanton
violence and killing. But as for the rest; dignity,
heirarchies, manners, sex – I think of myself in a state of
gentle anarchy.' She was shrugging and smiling as she

spoke, taking a light, almost coquettish tone.

Colin put his hands on her shoulders and gripped her quite roughly. 'Don't! I'm trying to work something out.' His face was filled with earnest and grave striving. 'Something about you. Something that doesn't fit.' He was looking at her with genuine curiosity. It was as though until now he had just been playing. She had been his Action Girl dolly, but now he was after a real live baby, even if it meant more effort.

Elizabeth was truly disconcerted. Here was Colin thinking things out, in pursuit of the cerebral. Was this her big, meaty, hairy boy? Was this the youthful, exuberant puppy who would come battering through the Sunday papers as she read, assailing her with his hot adoring tongue, demanding that she give him her instant attention: 'Hey, put that down, you've had enough of that ...' Was this the Colin who got on with things, watched TV, read a paperback, had a shower, ate a meal, drank a bottle of wine, took her cheerily and thoroughly to bed? Was this the simple, loutish lad who entranced her – who had never once given her cause to think wistfully of an older man with lines on his face and a gentle, resigned weariness to match her own.

'I've been a shit, haven't I?' he said in self-disgust.

She was alarmed at the way things were going. Never before had they talked about 'our relationship'. They had been content simply to please each other. They had been happy just to *be*. She did not want any of that to change. Not before he left her, at any rate. In her mind Colin left whilst they were still in that state of unquestioning *being*.

She could not begin to convey all that. She said, 'You have been truly good for me, Colin. You have given me all manner of things that have enriched me beyond anything I had ever hoped for.' She hoped that came across as genuine, for it was meant to be so.

'I want to talk about the future, Elizabeth,' he said, horrifying her. 'I think I love you.'

He heard her sharp intake of breath and put his arms around her with fierce possessiveness. He held her very close, pressing her face into his shoulder, offering the first caress that was neither sexual nor playful.

Elizabeth experienced a sharp pang of loss, knowing that the original essence of her relationship with Colin had vanished and would never be recaptured. She recognised that after four months, Colin did not say those hackneyed words about love lightly. He meant them, or believed that he meant them. He would never again think of her as the woman with whom he could mess around and get away with murder.

He had put a value on her.

And she was deeply stirred. To be told one is loved has a momentous and a precious solemnity about it. But to Elizabeth that solemnity was awesome and overwhelming. The responsibilities of being loved were grave and weighty. She did not know if she could take them on again.

Elizabeth contrived to obtain a few moments on her own with Miss Baxter. She looked at the girl with fresh interest, wondering why Ken had chosen her as the object of desire in his middle-aged adventuring when Miss Baxter was clearly not in the market for sexual frolics. For one thing, she was a student who had to work hard just to get moderate grades and Elizabeth guessed that she would probably regard going to bed early – and on her own – as important in order to maintain academic standards. Also the neat Miss Baxter had qualities of staunchness and determination that precluded her joining in activities that smacked of fun or naughtiness. Elizabeth was a little reminded of herself as a student. And felt sorry for Miss Baxter.

They had just concluded a discussion on course choices for the next year, and Miss Baxter would have got up to leave if Elizabeth had not indicated that she wished to raise another topic. 'Miss Baxter,' she said gently, 'as your personal tutor I would like to think that if you had any problems you would share them with me rather than the clerical staff.' She made it clear that Miss Baxter was free to speak her mind.

Miss Baxter understood instantly, and predictably went bright pink and was unable to speak at all.

Elizabeth was inclined to leave matters there. She had issued a piece of cautionary advice which Miss Baxter could act on or not as she chose.

Miss Baxter's face registered pinched disapproval. Her small pink mouth was a pretty one, but buttoned up and lacking in generosity. 'Mr Powers is drinking a lot, you know. He's always in the students' bar, every night. People are sick of him.' The nuggets of information just rolled out. 'He came up to my room with some notes I'd done for him. It was after eleven and I was in bed. He couldn't walk straight.'

Elizabeth could well imagine the scene. She sighed. Miss Baxter's staunchness and determination now looked like rigidity and inflexibility. She had it in her to be big trouble as far as Ken was concerned.

'Do you want to make a formal complaint?' Elizabeth asked.

Miss Baxter was taken aback at this offer of real power; to complain about a member of staff, a Head of Department at that, was stepping out of line. Elizabeth saw that Miss Baxter was a rule-keeper, a young person with little ego-strength who needed the protection and reassurance of clearly laid down boundaries. The reasons would all be in her childhood history for anyone who had the will and skill to investigate ...

'No,' said Miss Baxter. 'Nothing happened really.'

Elizabeth spoke to Ken in the Senior Common Room over coffee. 'Ken, I think it would be wise to steer clear of Miss Baxter for a while.'

'Tight-arsed little bitch,' Ken responded, having no intentions of appearing contrite.

'Maybe – and perhaps a trifle dangerous.'

Ken gazed at her, his eyes hard behind the cloud of cigarette smoke. 'You are so careful for my welfare, Elizabeth,' he said maliciously, making her wonder what he knew that she did not.

When she got home that evening Colin was working on an essay at the desk in the sitting-room. He had set the table for supper and topped and tailed some green beans. He

poured her a glass of sherry and asked for her opinion on
an article he had read in the *Journal of Social Psychology*.
He even went so far as to enquire about her day. His hand
rested affectionately on her shoulder and never showed
any inclination to stray lower and search beneath her skirt
to find a suspender.

Twenty-Four

Elizabeth woke in the night to find herself gripped with pain, a generalised, bewildering sensation of intense hurting. As she gained full consciousness the pain localised in the area of her uterus, as though a clamp of iron had been fastened around it.

Colin was instantly awake, alarmed by her groans, concerned, solicitous and reassuring.

She sat doubled up on the edge of the bed, her arms crossed tightly over her belly, rocking herself to and fro, whimpering. Colin, naked and still warm from sleep, wrapped her white cotton robe around her and kissed her hair. He saw that a dark stain of blood was seeping from beneath her thighs, spreading slowly over the sheet. 'Is it your period?' he asked.

She nodded. Her breath trembled soundlessly in her throat. Oh God! This pain was a dark, droning turbulence within her; it was just as she remembered the fierce labour contractions, joining together in relentless continuity as Edward's head lay in the birth canal on the point of being delivered.

'You're soaking,' Colin said gently. He went to the bathroom and found a pad, came back and lifted her shaking body so as to slide the gauze wad underneath her.

Elizabeth turned and clung to him, grateful, needing him – and seized with fear and panic.

'I'm going to call the doctor,' Colin said, quiet and firm.

'No, not yet. No.'

Colin rocked her against him, falling in with her rhythm. 'Ten minutes,' he said, 'and if it's no better I shall be on that phone.'

She felt the calm strength of him and was comforted. The pain was beginning to evoke a response from her;

something long-forgotten but almost automatic. It was what she had been taught to do when giving birth to Edward. Breathing. Relaxation exercises. Steady counting. They had helped her before, made the whole labour and delivery perfectly bearable. She tried to remember.

'What are you doing?' Colin asked, smiling tenderly.

'Deep breathing.' She threw her head back and let her ribs expand. Already she could feel the uniformity of the pain breaking up, could feel beating waves rather than a relentless flood. She became aware of her innards needing to grind something out; that some process of expulsion and rejection was about to occur. Bowels, bladder, uterus; one or all of them demanded that evacuation should take place. She got up in haste needing to sit on the lavatory, almost fainting with the pain when she stood up to walk. Colin would not leave her. A feeble croak of laughter broke from her as she sat there, quietly moaning, seeing the picture; the half-naked woman straddled on the lavatory bowl, the arms of her lover supporting her hips, the absurdity of the scene, and also its genuine, untarnished and total companionableness. 'Oh Colin!' she murmured.

'It's OK. I'm staying with you,' he said in a voice that made her believe him. 'I'll make sure you're all right.'

She could feel the soft wetness draining out; livery lumps sliding warmly away from her – and then something unfamiliar, something of string and gristle, hanging for a moment at the edge of her before it fell away. The red throb of the pain began quite suddenly to dwindle and fade. She sighed out in relief, her body losing its taut vigilance as the threat of continuing and accelerating agony receded. She was aware of a sharp renewal of interest in going on living.

'Better?' Colin said.

'Mmm.' She rested her hands on his shoulders and kissed his face.

Arms wrapped around each other they walked back to the bedroom. 'Do you want a drink?' he asked. 'Tea, coffee – something stronger?'

'Whisky. Bring the bottle,' she instructed.

They sat and drank. The pain had vanished to a far horizon. Soon she felt dizzy with contentment and the alcohol.

'Still OK?' he enquired after a while.

She smiled, absolutely confident now.

'What was all the heavy breathing about?'

She ran a finger around the rim of her glass thinking about secrets. Then slowly, reluctantly at first, she told him about the baby, explaining about the childbirth classes, how she had been taught to have some command over her body.

He looked at her solemnly, a little wounded, reproachful. 'You never told me you had had a child.'

'I never talk about it – him. Never.'

'Why?'

She put her hand up against her throat in a movement of self-protection. She had never told anyone. Anyone! The birth, the baby, the child, her child, just hers, flesh of her flesh, blood of her blood, bone of her bone; the things connected with him had been simply too precious to share. Edward had been her child, he had had nothing much to do with Michael. Michael had had plenty of other flesh and blood connections after all. And Michael had not grown the child in his body and felt it alive within him and felt the grief and emptiness of that body after the birth process was completed. Edward had been hers, her glorious experience of genetics and blood and begetting. She had stroked his flesh and felt in it a reflection of the texture of herself. She had wanted to love him more than anyone in the world. But she had had to share him with with her mother. And of course he had been the ultimate gift she could give her mother. But the gift had been faulty. The genetic strands had become warped and twisted somewhere along the line and produced a creature of sub-standard quality. Elizabeth's son, like her, should never have been born.

Elizabeth reached out and touched Colin's solid, well-fleshed chest. How well she knew this flesh – how thoroughly and intimately. 'He was handicapped,' she told Colin, 'brain-damaged and slow to develop.'

Colin's eyes glowed with sympathy.

'I left him a lot because I was working. But it was a relief really. Part of me wanted nothing to do with him.' She stared in grief at Colin. 'I was a bad mother. I was cold and heartless and wicked.'

He shook his head, in no way believing her, having no

intention of allowing her to punish herself like this. 'You would have been a wonderful mother. You're a natural nurturer – and I should know!'

She shook her head. 'I had all sorts of terrible feelings about him. I was hard and brutal. I wanted him to die.'

Colin looked at her with youthful innocence – and with love. 'Lots of parents with handicapped kids must feel like that. You've just got guts enough to be honest. That's your trouble.'

Elizabeth was shaken by a sigh that came up from the root of her. 'I didn't even mourn him properly. I pretended it was "all for the best" like everyone said.'

Colin reached out his arms and held her whilst she wept, encouraging and helping her to start at last the process of grieving for her lost child.

'Ah, Colin,' she said when she could speak again, 'I have done a lot of weeping with you.' She clasped her hands around his face and gazed up into his eyes. She felt the protectiveness of him, the rough, boyish cheeriness that was tender and sweet and entirely male.

'What about your husband?' he asked curiously. 'Where did he come into all this?'

Elizabeth thought for a moment. 'Michael,' she declared, both mischievous and bitter. 'Fuck him! he spent all my money – and he had no balls!'

Colin was amazed. He knew that she had permitted him to enter the dark secret places of her where no one else had been. He kissed her with the authority of ownership. He looked rakishly intoxicated with love. 'You can't do without me,' he told her. 'Come on – admit it. You won't let me say I love you, but you know I do. And you love me – don't you?'

She lifted her shoulders in a wistful gesture of resignation. 'My dear – has the notion only just crossed your mind?'

The next morning Colin was watchful and advising caution. 'Are you sure you're all right? Should you see the doctor? Why don't you have the day off work …'

He made her smile. She felt strong and renewed. The bleeding was now no more than a normal menstrual loss and the pain had not returned. She kissed him indulgently and brushed aside his protests. She felt an intense, glowing gratefulness for the way he had cared for her, but she knew that dependence was only charming in short doses. 'I'm fine – and I've a lot to do.' The end of the academic year was coming up. There were examination scripts to be marked and references to be prepared and the new timetable to be drafted out.

'I'll drive you,' Colin said. 'I need to be in good time. I've a sociology exam.'

Elizabeth hoped he had done at least some preparation. She looked at him with concern.

'You don't mind, do you?' he asked with raised eyebrows.

'Mind?' she echoed stupidly.

'Us arriving in the car – your car – together?'

Ah! She hadn't thought of that. He was right to be wondering. They had never travelled into college together, never given any indication of the intensity of their affair, or even its existence. It was quite possible that very few people knew. 'No,' she said slowly, 'it is not an issue for me. I shall not be damaged. But you …'

'I would have thought it was the other way round,' he said shortly, removing her keys from their hook and picking up her document case. He was watching her with interested assessment. She knew that soon he could be asking all sorts of questions.

The college was a place of tranquillity even in the midst of end-of-term fervour. Sitting in her room, at the big desk, surrounded by things that were ordered and under her control. Elizabeth reflected once again that, given a certain level of natural ability, one could, at the college, pursue a peaceful existence. Even if one did not always please the various factions warring and whirling around, at least it was possible to retreat to one's tutorial room and please oneself.

Before going into the Senior Common Room for coffee, she looked in at the examination candidates in the great hall. She saw Colin's cropped head bent over the sheets of lined paper. He was writing furiously. Ah well, one could but hope.

The presence of the Principal she missed. He was at the University – at a meeting of the Senate. Ken, too, was absent. It was unusual for him to miss his coffee. She wondered about it.

Colin drove her home, taking the front exit out through the big ornate iron gates. Groups of students sat on the lawns, stripped for summer, relaxing after the day's exams. It was all very public.

'Do you want to go for a swim?' she asked when they got back.

'No, I want to talk.'

She went inside meekly, knowing that she would bow to his wishes. She would actually have preferred to make love, even with the bleeding still going on. Just reflecting on Colin's tenderness the night before, the unconflicted physicalness of it, made her weak with desire.

He poured them both a drink. They sat at the kitchen table. She saw the severity in his expression and felt like a schoolchild about to be taken to task.

'You were having a miscarriage last night, weren't you?' he said.

'It's possible. The symptoms were certainly consistent with an early abortion.'

'Elizabeth, how can you be so calm? Hadn't you guessed you might be pregnant?'

'At my age there's nothing special about periods being irregular. I'm on my way to the menopause most likely.' She felt her heart speed up, warning her.

'Your periods have been as regular as clockwork for the last few months. I've been in a position to notice.'

'All right, Colin. It had crossed my mind – but only fleetingly.'

'You talk as though it doesn't matter. You're talking about a baby – *my* baby!'

She could see how real it was to him. To her it had been no more than a gynaecological hiccup. 'Colin, my darling, there is no question of you and me having a baby.' The whole thing was absurd and unthinkable. She – a mother! Colin – a father! Colin was still a child. Colin was her child. How was it that she had not seen it before, a truth so transparent, so simple? Her heart beat thickly.

'We could try again,' he was saying. 'We could have a child.'

'No!'

He drew back a little, wounded.

'My dearest – I'm past having babies,' she said very

gently. 'I'm old.' And you must leave me soon to pursue a normal existence; get a young and proper mate. Propagate with her if that's what you're wanting. She saw how she had made it his task to be her child and how it was time now for him to grow up – away from her.

'You're not old. And you can still have a baby. You've proved it.' He took her hand in that tender way of his.

'At my age women rarely carry a foetus to full term and when they do the child is damaged or feeble …' She stared at him meaningfully.

'No,' he said confidently. 'Not this time. It'll be fine.'

She guessed that his amiable, kindly young head was full of schemes for bringing her the wonderful gift of a bright wholesome child in her autumn days. He looked so earnest and hopeful and – adult. He almost made her believe. And hope. A wave of anxiety threatened her, causing a sensation of giddiness. 'No,' she whispered. 'No.'

'I care about you so much. I want to take care of you,' he said. 'And the way you care about me, really care … I don't think I can do without that.'

She turned away. Soon, surely, as she went on saying no, he would feel rejected and start to be angry. That would be healthier. This talk of love was not good for either of them. Talk of love was heavy and serious, trailing chains of obligation. Breezy, affectionate indifference had much to recommend it. Love carried approval, and approval tension; one had to work hard to maintain the standards reached, not to lose ground. Sadly she recognised that Colin would never again see her through eyes of cheery indifference.

He said, 'That evening when you came to my flat – I was gob-smacked. To be singled out like that. It was like being chosen by the Queen. And I thought I was a real super-stud. All that mind-blowing sex. But I didn't know anything about you. We'd been fucking our brains out for weeks before I started to really appreciate you.'

She smiled. This was more like the old Colin.

'It isn't just sex, is it?' he asked appealingly so that her heart felt as though it had been squeezed.

Just sex! He did not realise what he was saying. He had taught her that there was nothing in the world better or more worthy. She had never tried to dissociate Colin from the idea of physical pleasure, of pulsing, irresistible, normal lust. She had been starving and famished when she sought him out. He had fed her and still she was not gorged; her appetite was still thriving and demanding more.

'My sweet. It is the very essence of you that is so precious to me,' she told him which, though true, was evading the issue he was attempting to explore. Colin had youthful thoughts of permanence. She in middle-age held to the conviction that things did not last and must be enjoyed for what they were.

He gave her a look as if to say. "That's all right then; that'll do for now". 'You'll see,' he said. 'I'm more than just a good screw.'

She felt her mouth assume a twist of sweet seduction. 'A high level of attainment in that direction has much to recommend it.' She leaned towards him with a parted, welcoming mouth, took his hand and placed it on her breast so he could not resist her. But as they made love she was aware of his smiling at her, smiling knowingly as if to say: Aha! This is more than just sex.

In the evening things had blown over a little. Colin pottered about happily in jeans and nothing else, helping with the drying-up, putting beer in the refrigerator to chill, wondering how litle revision he could get away with for his economics paper the next day. After all, these were not important exams. 'But I'm going to work like a slave next year,' he assured her.

When the doorbell rang he went off whistling to answer it. Immediately Elizabeth was startled to hear Ken's voice and was shot through with alarm.

'Well, well,' said Ken, advancing down the hall and smiling at her. 'How's things?'

He had brought half a dozen cans of beer with him. He was only slightly drunk, but clearly dangerous. Elizabeth knew instantly that he had heard about her arrival at college with Colin and had come to see how the land lay. So conventional, she thought, so parochial; ever on the lookout for a spot of fecklessness to gloat over.

'Hope I'm not interrupting anything,' he said.

She smiled politely, aware of Colin's tautness and disbelief as he stood beside her. 'Come in, I'll get some glasses.'

'What the hell's he after?' Colin hissed, following her to the kitchen.

'Maybe he's just lonely.'

'He's got a nerve coming here half-pissed. Don't you mind?'

She shrugged. Yes, she did mind. But it did not look as though that would make much difference. 'Are you coming?' she asked calmly, gathering up glasses and nuts and ash-trays.

'Not likely. He's a bloody bore. I'll get some work done.' He hesitated, reluctant to desert her, but exasperated and cross.

With Ken, she wondered, or with her for not taking a firmer line? She touched his arm affectionately. 'I can handle it. Don't worry.'

Ken was lounging on the sofa eyeing the surrounding decor. 'Lovely lady, lovely room,' he said.

He was full of trouble; she could tell. She felt the throb of her heart again and steadied herself, breathing deeply and speaking internally: you are strong, you are resilient, you are no longer a driven creature, you can make choices. You are a woman of means and status. All is well.

'I didn't see you today,' she remarked conversationally.

'Couldn't face the hassle in the SCR ...' His eyes were narrowed and challenging.

'Ah ...'

'They're getting rid of me. Didn't you know?'

She opened a can carefully and placed the furled ring top in a small china dish. 'I've heard nothing about it.'

She could tell that he did not believe her. He thought she had access to the Principal's most private deliberations – probably other things too, bearing in mind the way she was carrying on with boys young enough to be her son.

'I've been a regular visitor in the *sanctum*, taking sherry in the best cut-glasses. The Principal has suddenly discovered a deep concern about my career prospects. Flattering, isn't it?'

She smiled. She felt helpless.

'He has this idea that I'd be flavour of the month at

every higher educational institution in the country – except
the one I'm currently employed in.'

'Ah.' Well, that did sound pretty gloomy.

'He was kind enough to set aside time to examine the
direction my academic and personal development might be
moving in. Nice guy – eh?'

'And what direction might that be?' she enquired evenly.

'Downwards as far as I could gather. Sideways at the very
most.'

She was silent. Why protest?

Ken leaned forward, his eyes bulbous and filled with
rancour. 'He wants to clear the centre stage – leave it free
for his favourite lady. You're going to get the plum,
Elizabeth. This new mega department. You're going to be
overall head. It'll be yours for the taking. You won't have to
ask. I can read between the Principal's convoluted lines.'

Elizabeth thought that for once Ken had probably got it
right. She beat back the thrill of selfish excitement that
shivered within her at the prospect Ken had described,
sensitive to his distress, even though she guessed that he
would have had no such scrupulous concern for her if the
situation had been reversed.

'I shall just resign,' he declared. 'To hell with all you
clever buggers. Doreen can support me. She's really into all
this female independence stuff – a job, money, a twenty-
four-year old admirer ...'

Elizabeth saw now that Ken's world was falling down
around him. All the old masculine strongholds crumbling –
and he not even able to get into the stolid Miss Baxter's
knickers.

Ken went over the issues again at some length. 'You must
have known,' he insisted.

'No.'

'No,' Ken agreed, suddenly understanding. 'Our dear
leader – he'd make sure of disposing of the also-ran before
he started openly backing the favourite. All very
gentlemanly and correct.'

The cans of beer were steadily opened and consumed.
Elizabeth prayed that Ken would leave. She could hear
Colin moving restlessly in the kitchen. Ken's voice was loud
and hectoring; clearly audible anywhere in the house.

'Bit of a surprise to see Weston here,' Ken commented. 'Haven't seen him for weeks.'

'Do you want to make something of it?' she asked calmly.

Ken fixed her with a hard, mean stare. 'Has he been to any lectures at all since he's been getting his oats here?'

'That's his affair.'

'He's twenty – a kid. I would have thought it was his tutor's responsibility to ensure that he took advantage of the education the taxpayer is financing.'

Elizabeth felt a piercing shaft of white-hot anger at this pious and hypocritical presumption to pass judgment on her – and on Colin. Would it be satisfying, she wondered, deeply comforting, to hold such clear convictions, to permit oneself to cherish such derision and contempt for others, to know so clearly how their lives might be improved? Would it be marvellously reassuring to be so narrow of mind?

'Has he been cooped up here all this time – just you and him, a cosy couple?' Ken grimaced as though contemplating the unnatural, the unhealthy and the shameful. 'He could get slung out if he hasn't completed the required consignments. Hadn't you thought of that?'

Elizabeth felt a heaviness fall upon her. Ken's conventional and perhaps valid interpretation of her treatment of Colin threw a grey dreariness over the light and delicate joy they had in each other. What seemed like gentle anarchy when she made love with Colin – or talked with Herbert – seemed like licence, indulgence and shabbiness when observed through Ken's eyes.

There is a time for light-heartedness, for delight and playfulness, she thought. A time to hold the world at arm's length and pursue most beautifully and thoroughly that which is there for the having. But Ken would not understand that.

And maybe she *had* been uncaring for Colin's true welfare.

She was not going to attempt to defend herself.

Eventually Ken became bored and left. Going through to the kitchen she found herself confronted by an indignant Colin, who had clearly heard all that had gone on. 'The sod. The sodding bastard!'

She put her arms around her young lover's thick, bullish neck and kissed his face. 'There is no cause for you to be upset. He doesn't touch me and I will on no account allow him to harm you.'

He brushed the last remark aside impatiently. 'How could he *speak* to you like that? Coming here and insulting you in your own house?'

'Colin, my dear. I've got to a stage in my life when there are few things that really upset me – certainly not a man like Ken. Probably not many men at all.'

Colin frowned. 'What do you mean?'

'The simple truth is that it is rare for me to come across a man who is worthy of my notice. Now shall we have a nightcap?' she asked crisply, reaching for the whisky bottle and declaring the subject closed.

The next evening she drove Colin out to his favourite spot for a swim. It was late June and the recent prolonged warm weather had been temporarily nudged aside by some cool cloudy air coming in from the west.

Colin had had a full day of exams. He looked tired and unusually edgy. He complained in the car of a thumping headache.

'Do you think it's wise to swim?' Elizabeth asked, concerned. 'It's really quite cold. If you're not feeling well ...'

'Christ! You sound like my mother.'

She said nothing.

'I can still hear that bastard Powers' voice going on and on,' he said bitterly.

So that was still bothering him. Elizabeth sighed. 'Forget about it, my pet.'

Colin thumped the dashboard. 'Jesus! Why do you let a pillock like him walk all over you! Why didn't you just tell him to fuck off?'

Elizabeth took a sideways glance at him. His face was white and strained. He was exhausted. It was the exams – and all that striving in bed the night before to make sure that he, at least, was worthy of her notice. Ah – Colin. She laid a hand tenderly on his thigh.

'All that ladylike stuff and never raising your voice. You're a bloody saint,' he said.

She saw that he was spoiling for a fight now the introductory hurdles of animosity had been cleared. Well, after all, he had been entirely deprived of acrimony and strife for a very long time.

'But it's a pretty good way of controlling people, isn't it – being so cool and calm? People can't do a damn thing about it!'

'It sounds as though you've been giving those psychology textbooks some attention,' she said drily.

'Perhaps I've been thinking for myself,' he returned menacingly. 'And there you go again; all reasonable and logical and so bloody – nice. Not saying what you really think. Leaving everyone else to put their foot in it.'

'I'm sorry,' she said stiffly.

'Why? What have you got to be sorry for?' he countered perversely. 'You're bloody perfect.'

She was dreadfully hurt.

'And all that crap about people "not being worthy of your notice". That's bullshit. It's sick. People don't say things like that unless they're all screwed up.'

'Stop it, Colin,' she said sharply.

He was stripping his clothes off now as they approached the river. It gleamed in sullen greyness under the clouds.

He swung his legs out of the car, stood up and leaned back in to speak again. He was beautifully, defiantly naked. 'Please yourself for a change, Elizabeth. Stop standing back while everyone else has a turn. Martyrs are a fucking bore. Just bloody please yourself.'

Elizabeth could not bear to stay and watch him. She drove off up the road and found a quiet pub where she ordered a double whisky. Her hands shook as she held the glass. Had Colin just been doing some mindless sounding off – or had he looked, with clear eyes, into the depths of her and seen all kinds of unpalatable things? As a girl she had sought to find what others desired in order to give it to them and be loved. Was she now, in middle-age, a dreary mother-figure who had a need to nurture everyone, maintain a smiling low profile, form a comfortable backdrop to other people's lives so as not to give anyone any trouble? Even in her independent, seemingly assured maturity, was she still pathologically programmed to please? And was there, had there ever been, gain in it for anyone? Bullying from Ken, contempt from Colin; what use was all that?

The whisky shot down into her empty stomach and was soon processed and circulating into her brain. She ordered another. Then she went for a drive. She extracted Colin's raucous, atonal music from the tape deck and slotted in some Bach. She drove very fast and was unable to avoid flattening a small darting rabbit to a bloody pulp in the road. She went in search of one or two garages that were still open and cast an eye over one or two choice vehicles which she might consider indulging herself in when her next royalties cheque came.

Colin would have been swimming for over two hours. That was not unusual, but tonight the sky was already darkening, thick clouds had gathered and the air felt quite cold in contrast with the warmth of the previous few weeks. Her habitual concern and care for another's comfort reasserted itself. She drove swiftly back to the river.

Immediately she saw him, face down on the bank, collapsed and in great need. She flew out with the towel. His face was turned towards her, his eyes open, staring blankly, full of bewilderment and fear. 'Darling, it's all right, it's all right,' she kept saying in panic. His face was white; thickly, grotesquely white, and she noted that his lips were tinged with palest translucent blue. What did that mean? Circulation? Heart?

Oh God!

She ran up the bank and waved violently at passing cars. Minutes were going by. She was weeping with desperation. Eventually someone stopped; a man of around sixty, robust and smiling with a wife to match. 'Now then, love?'

'A man,' she gasped, 'on the bank. I've got to get him to the hospital. I can't lift him.'

There was a moment of hesitation and then both man and wife were totally committed to sharing in the drama. The three of them ran stumbling down to the bank.

'Oh dear, this looks bad,' the man said, observing Colin who looked like some stranded and heaving fish washed up from the river. 'I hope it's safe to move him. Still, if we waited for the ambulance ...'

They managed to lift Colin between them and somehow stuff him into the back of Elizabeth's car. She persuaded the man to drive so she could sit with Colin. The man fumbled about with the strange gears and clutch. He drove terribly carefully. Far too slow. Oh God! Oh God! Oh God!

Elizabeth felt she should do something. Mouth to mouth resuscitation? But Colin seemed to be breathing, if somewhat harshly and unevenly. He was unconscious now, and there was this terrible blueness around his lips. It must be something to do with his heart. She pumped and massaged his chest frantically. At least it couldn't do any harm. All the time she was thinking, this can't be happening.

They drew up at the hospital entrance. 'I'll let 'em know we're here, love.' The man jumped out with admirable nimbleness and disappeared through the glass entrance-doors.

Within seconds there was action. People running. Nurses with white frilled caps, men and women in white coats who looked about seventeeen. They put Colin on a trolley and ran inside with him. Elizabeth heard someone shout, 'Cardiac.'

The towel slipped away from him. They covered him with a blanket. She had to run to keep up, so he did not disappear from her forever. Even as they ran they were attaching him to things overhead, wiring him up and inserting drips.

They took him into a cubicle behind some pleated, flower-patterned curtains. They would not let her follow. They were gentle but firm. A nurse came with a pad and took some basic details: the patient's name and age and address and next-of-kin. Elizabeth could not say anything about his medical history. She knew nothing. She told them to phone his college – but it was late. She doubted if anyone would be there who could gain access to the records.

Behind the curtain there was massive activity; figures shifted and issued commands in tense, low tones. She lost sense of time.

A doctor emerged in due course from the cubicle. His face was grim. He looked straight at her and shook his head. 'He's gone.'

Elizabeth stared at him stricken and disbelieving. 'No.' She got up slowly and walked between the parted curtains. The staff stood respectfully aside. She looked down at Colin's body and then sat on the couch with him and took him in her arms.

The Registrar went off to make his notes. He was tired and touchy after a long spell on duty. He hated to lose a young strong life. After a while he came back and looked between the curtains. For a passing moment he speculated on the relationship between this woman and the dead man. An elderly piece of crumpet maybe? She was certainly quite toothsome, if a little gaunt. Mentally he shrugged. In this job one saw an unending stream of human and social aberrations. In time the honed edge of curiosity became dulled. 'Nurse,' he commanded cursorily to a nubile befrilled young thing, 'do something about that howling. Prise her away from the body and give her a cup of tea. Get an ambulance to take her home if necessary.'

Elizabeth lay in bed, her arms by her side, cold – like a corpse.

Colin had gone. She kept hearing the doctor's voice saying: 'Gone, he's gone.' His body would be enclosed in a plastic bag in a chilled steel drawer. His body would be there in the hospital, unmutilated, with no abrasions or external abnormalities. His body was there just a few miles away from her. She could go there and seek it out and embrace it once more, embrace it through eternity, but *he* would not be there. Where was he? The essence of him; where had that gone? How could it suddenly be nothing? How could a life be so summarily rubbed out? She had seen death close up on many occasions. She had asked the very same questions. There had never been an answer.

She got up and drank a lot of whisky. Neat.

In the night she woke, her arms searching for him, reaching out for his warm soft flesh and the bulky reassurance of him. She sat up and wrapped her arms around her knees and rocked herself to and fro, moaning in pain – just as she had two nights ago when Colin had comforted her with tender patient arms.

Twenty-Five

'He suffered from rheumatic fever when he was two. The heart valves were diseased, although not to a serious degree – at least it was not thought so. He was able to live a perfectly normal life – but there was always a slight risk.' The Principal sighed and spread his hands in a gesture of regret. 'The parents are hoping it won't be necessary to carry out a post-mortem – given the medical background.'

Elizabeth sat listening. She knew that at any moment she could break down into unstoppable weeping. It was not within her control to do anything about it.

The Principal was observing her in his careful, scrutinising manner, no doubt wondering why a tutor, reporting late the previous evening on the death of one of her students, should have been distraught to the point of incoherence.

She began to speak in a flat, restrained voice. 'Colin Weston was living with me. We were having an affair. It was the most wonderful, unrestrained and physically primitive relationship I have ever had – and I have no regrets about it, not on my own account at any rate. As for Colin, well ...' Tears leapt into her throat. She looked at the Principal and felt free to be defiant. 'And I am not saying all of this in order to seek forgiveness.'

'I would not presume to give it,' the Principal answered sharply.

'I thought I had killed him. I analysed it in my usual cool detached way, drawing on my knowledge of psycho-dynamics. Here was an affair that had run its allotted course, had begun to shift away from its original purpose. It was time for it to die, for the two participants to go their separate ways. So the woman, unconsciously colluding with fate, allows a situation to develop in which her lover is

214

unnerved and thrown off balance. She permits an argument to take place. She leaves her lover without resolving the quarrel. She leaves him for just that little bit longer than usual. The elements conspire to the same end and … the affair is neatly terminated by the death of one of the partners.' Elizabeth closed her eyes. She felt as though she might be going crazy.

'You did not kill him, Elizabeth. The risk of a coronary was always with him. The strenuous exercise and the unfamiliar coldness of the water were apparently quite sufficient in themselves to induce a state of shock which made him especially vulnerable.'

Elizabeth gave a sharp, involuntary cry. 'Oh God, Herbert, how little I bothered to know about him. How disgustingly self-centred I was. I shall never forgive myself.'

'Then you will be guilty of the self-centredness of taking the responsibility for the whole of the world and its fate on your shoulders.' The Principal's eyes were hard.

'Yes, I know that too. In my analysis I saw the pathology of a woman locked inside her own claustrophobic self-involvement. I was sickened and revolted.'

'I see only the brave struggling of a person who has been too much alone,' the Principal told her. 'I am learning a good deal about that myself at the moment.'

Elizabeth remembered that he had grief of his own. He was telling her that there was guilt to bear too. Guilt about the way he had been with Hannah. 'He was my love,' she whispered. 'He took the trouble to understand about the needs of my flesh and he allowed me to have access to all the secrets of his. I don't know how I can live without him.' The tears rose up in a painful liquid mound. She could not beat them back. She put her hands over her face and sobbed.

When she had finished the Principal said, 'I would like you to represent the college at the funeral. The parents said they would welcome it very much.' Colin's parents had driven up to Yorkshire that morning. There were all sorts of things to do and forms to sign; the death certificate to be got.

'I don't know,' she said. 'I'm very doubtful of my ability to behave properly. I keep breaking down like this all the time, terrible animal howling. His parents would be frightened and repulsed. They shouldn't be subjected to that.'

He smiled his gentle smile. 'I have every confidence in your ability to behave impeccably.'

She paused at the door. She had no idea how he had judged her. And then it came to her that it was not the judging of her that was concerning him, but rather the loss of a vibrant young life.

Colin's house was entirely consistent with her imaginings. It was cramped and cluttered with furniture and fussy ornaments, it was strident with colour and pattern – and it was intensely comfortable and welcoming.

His parents had insisted on her returning to the house following the funeral service and the burial. Standing beside the grave she had felt no inclination to weep again. She had watched the coffin bump jerkily down into the ground and land with a thud – Colin's body was no light-weight – and had been taken over by a greedy desire to have the whole sense of that body again. Standing shoulder-to-shoulder with those who had known Colin most intimately, even at the moment of most intense sharing in the severity and solemnity of their grief, she was aware of the wayward insurgency of her own body, putting up a tremendous fight at the prospect of being consigned to celibacy again, demanding not to be left to rot in sexual disuse and neglect. A picture of Ken came unbidden into her head; Ken loud and raucous and rancorous; Ken, a pathetic gatecrasher at the wrong party, needy of comfort; Ken, by no means physically undesirable – quite acceptable to go to bed with if only he could be temporarily struck dumb. Ken, without a doubt, available ...

Her heart began to beat lumpily. All this would pass. It would all pass she told herself, terrified at the process of fragmentation which seemed to be taking place within her.

'We're so pleased you came,' Colin's mother said. 'We just wanted the family and one or two special friends today. There are plans for a memorial service at the college for the students and staff. The Principal told us that. It's a lovely thought.'

'Yes, I believe so.' Elizabeth could hardly bear to look into those clear, calm blue eyes that were so full of maternal grief. She knew that inside, Mrs Weston would be silently shrieking and clamouring for her lost son.

Mr Weston joined them. He offered Elizabeth some wine. 'Colin wouldn't have liked a sober occasion,' he said with brave humour.

'No, he loved life,' Mrs Weston observed.

All three were temporarily choked up. They swallowed the wine.

'He seemed so strong and healthy,' Elizabeth offered politely.

Mr Weston nodded. 'He was. This heart thing never bothered him.'

Mrs Weston smiled fondly. 'We had to coddle him a bit when he was little – after the rheumatic fever. But you couldn't spoil him, not really. He had such a lovely nature. Always cheerful. Happy-go-lucky.'

'I tried to get him to give up smoking,' Mr Weston reflected, 'but I can't say I was a shining example myself. Filthy habit. I wish I had a stronger will.'

'He was getting worried about his weight though. He wouldn't eat any fried things when he was home last time,' said Mrs Weston. 'It's all the rage with the young, isn't it – healthy eating and keeping fit?' She faltered just for a second. They all drew a sharp breath. 'I think he'd got a girl, that's what it was all about. Vanity!' Tears rushed to her eyes and gushed out. 'I'm sorry. Please excuse me.' She got up and dashed from the room.

Mr Weston sighed and sniffed heavily. 'He spoke about you, Mrs Lashley. He admired you very much. Said you were the best teacher in the college.'

'That makes me very proud,' Elizabeth told him softly.

Colin's elder brother came up to speak to her, releasing his father to circulate amongst the other visitors. How like Colin he was; Colin in early middle-age, a cheerful lad with money and a paunch. Elizabeth wanted to embrace him. It struck her how Colin would now remain forever young, their much-loved, eternal boy.

She stayed on for far longer than she had planned. She felt quite at ease with this family. She liked them very much. And strangely she felt no burden of deception weighing on her. One day perhaps …

She went to stay overnight with Helena.

'We thought you must have lost your way in the dark,'
Helena said, placing fillets of fish in white wine marinade
in the microwave. On the table an avocado dip and crisp
French bread were waiting.

'That phrase may have far more significance than you
think,' Elizabeth remarked in expressionless tones, leaning
up against the fitted oak units, utterly exhausted, longing
for a few goblets of good wine to send her into oblivion.

'Oh Gawd!' said Helena in the mock Cockney accent
which charmed Philip. 'Don't start …' She took the
trouble, then, to take a thorough look at her sister. 'You're
a bit glam for a funeral, aren't you?' she quipped, wanting
to keep things light – at least until the meal was over and
Philip mellowed with some claret.

Elizabeth touched the collar of her suit, the black suit
Colin had loved to peel from her piece by piece as she lay
on the bed in whatever position he had chosen to place
her. She stared at Helena in stricken appeal.

Helena laughed. 'It's just that glitzy brooch that gives
the game away …'

'Dad gave it to me. I often wear it. It's one of those
things from the past that are precious,' Elizabeth felt
herself stirred into defensiveness. She traced round the
edge of the enamel and diamanté sunflower with cautious
delicacy as though it might shatter.

'You sentimental softie!' Helena was keeping very busy
serving up the splendid supper she had prepared. She was
holding Elizabeth at a distance with her friskiness and
banter. She was holding Elizabeth off because she, Helena,
was so used to not being confided in – not in regard to the
serious and important things anyway. Elizabeth had it
revealed to her in a swift flash how Helena had been
gently written off, relegated to second place and excluded
– by her, Elizabeth, and her mother. *Their* mother. Except
that Elizabeth had claimed her mother greedily all for
herself. She had used to think that Helena had escaped
from the maternal bonds. That she had been lucky.
Things suddenly looked different. Yes, maybe she had

escaped, but the price had been a form of banishment. And Helena, just as much as Elizabeth, had had to bear all the burden of primary rejection. No one had rejoiced much at her birth either, and she too had had the unenviable task of trying to replace the dead Margaretha, and in addition, the impossible assignment of living up to the shining example of the good and saintly Elizabeth.

'Helena,' she said in a low voice so that her sister turned round immediately, giving full attention. 'This funeral I've been to. It was not just a mission of common courtesy – representing the college and so on. I was having an affair with the student who died, a glorious, passionate, carnal affair. And now – just at the moment, I wish that I were dead too.'

Philip, walking in, made a commendable effort to conceal his scandalised feelings at this confession, but could not help glancing furtively around and closing the door swiftly in case young ears might hear and be corrupted.

'Oh, love!' Helena exclaimed, moving rapidly across the room to wrap her arms around Elizabeth. 'Love, love, love.'

Her house, when she returned, had an alien feel to it. It mocked and taunted her with its order and silence – and all its teasing memorabilia of Colin.

She had foolishly and sentimentally bought a joint of lamb. The white fat around it made her retch when she unwrapped it from the paper. She thrust it to the back of the refrigerator.

She felt tired and empty and in despair. Life taught one nothing, she thought, except the inevitableness of misery – and one's unfailing and infinite capacity to get things wrong. She wanted to sleep but she knew she would not achieve it. She thought of the Mogadon and Valium and Librium she had thrown out from her mother's bedside chest. She took six Paracetemol, enough to knock her into temporary unconsciousness, not enough to cause her liver to fail. She sat by the window, looking out into the dark grey-green of the July evening, waiting for the tablets to work and thinking about the waste of things.

Term had ended now. The students had gone home.

Elizabeth had posted Colin's exam results to his parents. Three scraped passes and two marginal fails. It could have been worse.

Her stomach felt uneasy still, swollen and delicate as it had when she was pregnant. She knew she should eat but she just wanted to sleep, to be in oblivion all the time. She went into the kitchen and put milk on to heat. She made thin, smooth porridge and carried it through to the sitting-room where the television flickered. She sat down and spread a napkin on her knee.

Through the day she had been considering the issues of fate and circumstances as opposed to the inadequacy and feebleness of will. Now, exactly a week after Colin's death, she was filled with self-dislike as well as grief. Yet still she could not submit finally to a philosophy that decreed that she should be judged as deficient and second-rate.

She lowered the spoon into the porridge but she could not eat. She put both plate and spoon on one side and sat in lonely reflection.

After a time she got up and went into the kitchen where she flushed the cold slippery porridge down the sink. She took the lamb from the refrigerator and garnished it with rosemary and garlic.

It had occurred to her to nail her colours to the mast of fate and circumstances once and for all. And in that framework she would advise herself that much of what had happened to her had been perfectly ordinary and normal. She had been unluckier than some but much luckier than most. It was true that much of what she had *experienced* had been unnaturally intense, and that had been her misfortune – but not her tragedy. Life had imposed certain constraints but it had never seriously denied her opportunity. She was sound in mind and body: she did not have cancer, or brain damage – or diseased heart valves.

As her fingers punched the telephone's little white squares she was reflecting that she was free; free to make decisions, free to initiate events. She may have made some bad mistakes. Terrible things had happened and she might have some responsibility to bear. She may, unwittingly, have initiated tragedy. But she was still alive. She had a right to claim some future joy.

At the other end of the line the voice was beautifully modulated, impeccably controlled and unmistakably bleak. 'Hello?'

'Herbert, this is Elizabeth. I'm preparing a meal. I have a disinclination for eating on my own.' She paused. 'I would so much like to share it with you ...'

He arrived bringing two bottles of wine. He was a generous man. He laid his arm with tenderness around Elizabeth's shoulders. 'Elizabeth,' he said. 'My dear.'